MW00479888

TRAPPED INSIDE THE MAELSTROM

Tales of Horror and Madness

By Tarphy W. Horn

Cover art by Vibrant Designs

ISBN: 978-1-7373698-4-4

The following stories contain content which may be disturbing to some readers:

"Sharing": sexual harassment
"Ring of Doors": descriptions of torture

Visit the author at www.tarphywhorn.com

For James, Jarod, and Jordan; Jim and Donna; and the teachers who encouraged me to keep writing.

CONTENTS

THE TRANSITION

Alaina's murder was flawlessly carried out.

Initially, she had no idea who wanted her dead, or why. Maybe she'd acquired a psychotic online stalker who didn't like her urban gardening blog. Or maybe it was the creepy guy she met at the bar who said redheads were the spawn of Satan and should be wiped from the Earth. There was recently an angry young man at the library who threw a book at her when she charged him with what he claimed was a preposterous late fee. One time she ran over a teenager's soccer ball when it rolled onto the street, and the teenager threw a rock at her back window. Maybe one of her neighbors didn't like her singing.

The possibilities were endless, she supposed. She could speculate forever. It wouldn't change the outcome.

On the morning of her last day on Earth, Alaina smiled at the warm sunlight pouring into her kitchen through the sliding glass doors. She planned to meet up with a friend for a three-mile jog, and the weather would be perfect.

She decided she had time to care for her plants and add a recipe for tomato soup to her blog before she left. She breathed in the aroma of freshly ground coffee beans filling the air. All in all, it should've been a pleasant Saturday.

And it was pleasant. Until she was murdered.

After drinking her coffee and eating a cinnamon roll, she walked onto the balcony. Eleven containers of herbs sat in a neat row. Purple, pink, and white petunias spread out in every direction from pots that could barely contain them. Her three tomato plants had grown taller than the railing, and she had more cherry tomatoes than she knew what to do with.

She cared for the plants with an almost neurotic obsession. After watering each pot, she sat among the flowers and plucked off the dead blooms. When that was finished, she stood up to collect the latest round of tomatoes.

She didn't hear the murderer sneaking up behind her. He could've appeared out of thin air. She couldn't have fought him off, even if she had seen him coming. He was far too powerful. He shoved her in the middle of her back, just below the shoulder blades, with enough force to send her toppling off the balcony. As she flipped over the railing, her fingers instinctively grabbed the iron bars. She held on ar found herself dangling more than 100 feet from ground.

Alaina looked up at her killer and screa The individual wore a black trench coat and the realistic mask she'd ever seen. Its teeth were r and gray with rot. Yellow eyes bulged from that barely contained them. Its face was a putrid green, and the ears were pointed, like elf ears. Its stench was familiar, but in her state of terror she couldn't quite place it.

The murderer waved goodbye to her. It wore gloves with long, multi-jointed fingers ending in claws. Impossibly, the bars of the railing she clung to disappeared. With her hands still reaching up, she succumbed to gravity. Unidentifiable blurs of color passed through the air as she fell. Angry wind stung her face. She heard a few screams from the apartment building as she dropped past balconies and windows. She waited for her life to flash before her eyes. It didn't, and she was disappointed. She had just enough time to hope her sister would take care of her plants before her fall came to an abrupt halt.

During her final, surreal seconds on Earth, her skull shattered as her head smacked against the concrete parking lot. A gray sedan had to swerve to keep from driving over her. She felt no pain; her nervous system was destroyed on impact. Shadows crept across her waning consciousness.

She tried to focus on the blurry face watching from her balcony. The murderer raised two of her flowerpots with its too-long fingers and tossed them over. She doubted she'd be able to catch them.

The glimpse of the jagged bones jutting through her skin should've shocked her more than it did. She marveled that her bones were ivory colored, not pure white like she'd always assumed. Dark red stains splashed across her broken, twisted limbs. She knew those splotches were important, but she couldn't remember why.

Her existence in the land of the living ended. Alaina was thrust into darkness so dense it was tangible. As she tried to grab onto the not-exactly-there space surrounding her, she realized her body had been made whole again. She also realized she was naked. A brush of gentle breeze propelled her onward, although no frame of reference existed to tell her what direction she was heading.

She'd never believed in an afterlife. She didn't know how to feel about actually having one.

A pinprick of light in the distance penetrated the void. The shapes of winged Angels formed from the light as it expanded. These great shining beacons, with protrusions shaped vaguely like arms, reached out for her. Beautiful voices reverberated through every molecule of her being. Waves of peace and exultation came alive inside her soul.

The darkness melted away completely, leaving only the beings of light. Vivid colors vibrated through her consciousness. The answers to every question ever asked by humanity etched themselves into her mind. (Aliens really were recovered and taken to Area 51. She *knew* it.)

One Angel wrapped a silk and pearl robe around her shoulders, and a comfortable warmth settled inside her. Another Angel filled her soul with unspeakable love.

You are now worthy to stand before the Pearly Gates of Heaven, said one of the Angels.

As the great gates slowly swung open, Alaina saw every member of her family from every generation dating back to the beginning of the beginning.

Now this is a cool welcome party!

An Angel appeared before her and spoke. "You must now say all that was left unsaid. You cannot enter the afterlife until your soul speaks from your heart and cleanses your mind."

She didn't hesitate. Words poured out of her. She couldn't seem to stop her mouth.

Aunt Sissy, guess what? I finally finished college! I prayed to you on my graduation day, did you hear me?

Andrew, it wasn't your fault. The other driver ran a red light. Swerving into the other lane was your only choice.

Grandma! I missed you so much! I'm so sorry I pawned your wedding ring, but I needed money to pay my rent.

Aunt Deb, I'll admit it. I'm the one who poisoned your dog. It chewed up my favorite shoes. They were expensive.

Uncle Eli, I know I should have helped you and not let you drown in our pool. I worked as a lifeguard, after all. It would've been easy to save you. But you made those annoying noises when you chewed your food, and I didn't want to have to listen to that anymore. Cousin Tina, I know I shouldn't have started your house on fire. How was I supposed to know your boyfriend was asleep on the couch? I knew you'd already gone to work and wouldn't get hurt. That should count for something. Besides, I'd never seen a building burn down, and I was curious.

Bro. It was wrong of me to shove your girlfriend in front of a car. But she called me a bitch, and I don't tolerate that kind of disrespect.

Andrew, I suppose I should tell you, the other driver was me. Oops, ha ha. I shouldn't have fled the scene, but how was I to know they'd send you to prison for vehicular manslaughter?

A sharp claw snagged her leg, and she cried out in pain. She looked down and saw the thing that pushed her off the balcony.

"What? What is this?"

"Time is up!" growled its raspy voice.

Now she recognized the smell. It was sulfur.

"No! There's been a mistake!" she wailed.

The Pearly Gates swung shut, with her family on the other side of them.

They needed to hear her confession, said the Angel as it released its hold on her soul. Devoid of emotion, it tore away the robe. She froze, colder than an icicle, once again naked in the void.

Her family may now find peace in their eternal rest. Take her away.

"Why do *they* get to go to heaven?" Alaina whined. "I want to come to! I can't go to Hell. I apologized to them!"

The Angels vanished, and with them went the light. Alaina's body slowly deteriorated back to the state it was in at her death. Jagged bones jutted through skin. Punctured lungs left her gasping for breath. Torn flesh itched as streams of sticky blood dried on it. A large piece of her scalp flopped against the side of her face.

There was one difference, however: her nervous system remained intact. She felt everything.

Flames rose to surround her. Scalding lava dripped from the blood red clouds floating across the black sky. A heavy, steaming metal chain wound itself around her, crushing her broken arms against her sides.

A chorus of demons, reeking of sulfur, gathered to encircle her.

"I'm telling you," Alaina squealed, "there's been a mistake! You've got the wrong person! I have a twin! It's her you want, not me! Take her!"

The petunia pots from the balcony flew into her face and crushed her jaw. The pots had landed on her body after she died. Dead black petunias and shards of blackened pottery dropped into the bottomless maelstrom beneath her.

"There has been no mistake," said the murdering demon. "It is time for your initiation."

INNOVATIVE SOLUTIONS

Cara keyed in the code on her desktop computer to join the online managers' meeting. Calling it a 'meeting' was a bit of a stretch, she supposed. It would start out cordially enough, but peaceful exchanges would only last for ten minutes or so. After that, the affair would degenerate into a session of people hurling insults at each other and vying for the title of Biggest Asshole in the Company.

Cara, after spending two years unsuccessfully petitioning the Chief Financial Officer to upgrade their payroll software, had finally taken matters into her own hands. She created a spreadsheet program that would streamline the entire payroll process. But the accounting department wanted nothing to do with her new way of doing things.

Kind of ironic, in a cutting-edge software company; Innovative Solutions, Inc. developed data protection and recovery software.

Cara's biggest obstacle was Madelaine, who she secretly referred to as "Mad the Pain." The old hag complained they'd been "doing it this way for years," and they weren't about to "start doing something different now" because "the old way works just fine."

The 'old way' required Madelaine to work forty hours a week, and two part time employees to each work thirty. Madelaine had a master's degree and an astronomical salary that she didn't earn. If Cara could get rid of her, she could hire one person to take the place of all three of them. The accounting department's payroll expenses would be cut by more than half.

Just as she expected, when she pointed this out to the other managers, they stood by Madelaine. Loyalty was nice and all, but so were profits and bonus checks.

"You can't just fire people to meet your bottom-line goals," Delaine snapped.

Delaine was the Human Capital Manager. She'd refused the title of 'Human Resource Manager' when she was hired. She said it was too cold and made her sound unapproachable.

Cara thought Delaine was a drama queen and an idiot.

"If you don't agree with how we do things at this company, maybe you should go back to Phoenix," she continued.

Cara was from Philadelphia. Delaine, as the Human *Capital* Manager, was well aware of this. Cara awarded Delaine one point in the Asshole competition.

"I'm not trying to usurp your management style. I have nothing against Madelaine, personally," Cara lied. "I'm talking about efficiency."

"Do you want to get us sued for age discrimination?" demanded Shaunte, their Legal Consultant. "Cause that's what you're going to bring down on this company. A lawsuit."

It won't matter if we're already bankrupt thanks to decision making based on feelings instead of common sense, Cara thought. Maybe she should try diplomacy. Even getting these hard-headed people to compromise would be a win at this point.

"How about this? We implement my upgrades. When she refuses to cooperate, we fire her. Refusal to do her job would be legal grounds for immediate termination."

"You are one cold-hearted bitch," Delaine said, shaking her head.

"Tell me something I don't know. The problem isn't me. The problem is your incompetence as a Human Resources Manager."

"You mean, of course, 'Human Capital Manager,'" the woman snapped. "And I am hardly incompetent."

Cara wanted to laugh. The angry look on Delaine's face was very satisfying. Quite frankly, Cara enjoyed pissing her off. It was so *easy*.

"What I mean is if you're too emotional to take the actions needed—"

Ron, the IT manager, decided to throw his hat in the opinion ring. “It’s not about emotions, Cara.”

Cara struggled to keep her biting retort to herself. She thought he was the one person whose support was a given. He definitely earned a point in today’s Asshole competition.

“That’s right,” Delaine said.

God she’s a self-righteous prick. If Cara could’ve reached through her computer screen and slapped her, she would have.

“You can’t run a successful business if you treat your employees like crap. And, as you may have noticed, we are running a successful business.” Delaine crossed her arms.

“A business is only successful until it becomes unsustainable,” Cara responded calmly. *Duh,* she added to herself. “Your business practices are allowing costs to skyrocket.”

“You haven’t been here long enough to understand our business model.”

Great. Now Janine was butting in.

“We make decisions based on our past experience. If you take care of your employees, they take care of you.”

“Really. Perhaps I missed the memo. How, exactly, are they taking care of us?” She couldn’t keep the sarcasm out of her voice anymore. “With their efficient use of time? Their innovation and willingness to learn? Are they buying our tech? I assume they’re adding to our revenue stream in some way. Cause they're definitely not helping our bottom line."

On Cara's screen, two rows and five columns of people were muttering and rolling their eyes. Ron looked at her nervously. She would be speaking to him later. *Damned turncoat.*

"Employees are expensive. Period. Especially when they're unproductive and unwilling to change. A "successful business", as you put it, always tries to improve its bottom line."

And so it went. The meeting continued for another twenty minutes, before Delaine finally said, "I need to sign off." Looking directly at Cara, she added, "I have an interview to conduct. We're hiring an additional employee in the shipping department."

Cara looked at her with a bored expression. If Delaine wanted to get a rise out of her, she'd have to do better than that.

"Please look for someone who will benefit the company, not weigh it down."

Delaine pursed her lips. One by one, the other faces disappeared from Cara's screen, but Delaine simply frowned at her keyboard. Maybe she wanted to argue privately. That suited Cara just fine.

Cara waited for Delaine to say something. Even after the other managers logged off, the woman continued to clack at her keyboard. Cara started to say something wildly inappropriate that would be cause for awarding *herself* an Asshole competition point.

But Delaine looked up at the screen in that instant and scoffed. “What are you looking at?”

“You, still on my screen.”

“The sarcasm gets old, Cara. What do you want?”

“What do *I* want? You’re the one that ended the meeting for your *appointment.* Yet here you sit. I assumed you wanted to discuss my proposals in private.”

“Why the hell would I want to discuss anything with you? You’re the most hard-headed person I’ve ever met.”

Cara raised an eyebrow. “Resorting to personal attacks, are we?”

She looked back down at her keyboard. “My computer won’t let me close it down. I mean, it’s always slow, but this is ridiculous.”

It’s slow because it’s bogged down with ancient software. You reap what you sow, dumbass.

“Hm. Enjoy.” Cara got up and walked toward the break room, since her assistant couldn’t even manage to put two teaspoons of sugar in a cup of coffee.

Ron accosted her in the hallway.

“Look, Cara,” he said as she glared at him coldly. “I wanted to push for your idea. What you said – you’re absolutely right. But Delaine, she, uh, she has something on me.”

This piqued her interest. She stopped walking, and he leaned in close.

Keeping his voice at a whisper, he said, "She walked in on Cole and me in the supply room. And you know what a homophobic bitch she is."

Unbelievable.

"You know better than to pursue relationships at work! Why would you do something so stupid?"

"We were only kissing. And you know why. We love each other, and we have very few opportunities to even *talk* privately. If Delaine were to say something to my wife—"

"She'd take you to court and make sure you never saw your kids again." Cara sighed. She could hardly blame the man for having priorities. "Honestly. Delaine and your wife would get along very well."

Ron snorted. "They'd hate each other."

Cara smiled and put her hand on his shoulder. "I'll see if I can think of a way to get her off your back."

"This is why I love you, Cara. But it's not your problem. We'll come up with something."

She squeezed his shoulder and went on to get her coffee.

When she returned to her desk, Delaine's frantic-looking face was still on her screen.

"For God's sake," Cara mumbled. "Just press the power button."

"Do you think I haven't tried that?" she snapped. "It's frozen."

"Then unplug it," said Cara slowly, like she was giving directions to a toddler. She shook her head and sipped her coffee. *How stupid is this woman?*

"I, uh." She cleared her throat. "I can't find the cord."

"I don't have time for this."

Cara reached for her mouse when Delaine said, "I think I'm… inside my computer."

Cara stared. "Yeah, wasn't that the plot of an 80's movie? Honestly, Delaine. I've always known you were a little off, but I didn't know you were full-on delusional."

"God damnit, Cara! Look! I mean, *really look*, at the screen. What do you see?"

Cara focused her attention fully on Delaine. A grayish haze surrounded the woman as she looked around in every direction.

"I see that you're using a filter. Or you've got some mad Photoshop skills."

"I don't know how to use Photoshop," she growled. She moved back from the screen, like she was sliding backward in her desk chair. She stopped suddenly, as if she'd hit a wall. The blood drained completely from her face.

Delaine wasn't talented enough to fake *that* scene.

"I'm trapped! What do I have to do to make you understand? God, of all the people in the meeting, I can't believe I got stuck with you."

Cara's phone rang.

"I have a call. Then I'm coming to your office and we're going to talk. I'm closing this window now."

"No! Cara—"

Cara clicked her mouse, then answered the phone. She opened another program and helped her coworker with some computations. She forgot about Delaine.

After finishing the rest of her workday (which meant spending four hours running around like she was herding cats and two hours doing her own work) she remembered she'd planned to visit Delaine's office to get to the bottom of her nonsense.

She walked to the elevator but found herself unable to push the button. She hurried back to her office and stared at her computer screen. The conference call screen was minimized, but still running. She sat in her chair, scrolled across the screen, and clicked the mouse.

Delaine's face filled the entire screen. Cara gasped in surprise and rolled back from her desk.

"Where have you been?" Delaine shrieked. Her words sounded tinny. "Your call couldn't have lasted all day. Are you planning on leaving me in here? Even you can't be that much of a psychotic bitch."

Cara rolled her eyes. For a Human Resources Manager, or whatever she called herself, she certainly swore a lot. "You're not exactly giving me reasons to help you. Quit yelling at me. Or I'll mute you."

"Screw you. Look. I can't reach anyone else. They all logged out before you did. I can see you through my screen, but there's nothing in here. I'm surrounded by a gray cloud."

Cara had never felt so unsettled by a workplace situation. While she didn't entirely believe Delaine's stuck-in-my-computer theory, she couldn't deny something strange was happening.

"Have you called the I.T. department for me yet?" Delaine demanded.

Cara scoffed. "And tell them what? That you got sucked into your computer? They're busy helping Research and Development with testing. They don't have time to stop and investigate pranks."

Cara admired the I.T. department. Ron understood the concept of management. His department was the picture of efficiency. She wasn't ready to bother them with…with whatever this was.

"*Pranks!?* You evil bi—"

"Besides, do you really think Ron cares about helping someone who's threatening to destroy his family?"

Delaine recoiled. "*Get me out of here!*" she screamed. She pounded her fists against the inside of the screen, and it shook on Cara's desk.

"What the hell was that!?" Cara shouted as she jumped up to steady her screen.

"What the hell do you think it was?" Delaine shouted. *"Do you believe me now?"*

The weird gray cloud in the background now had blueish white sparking lines running horizontally across the background. Delaine looked behind herself. She turned and put her hands against the inside of the screen. "Cara! Help me!" Strands of the woman's hair were flowing behind her, as if attracted by static electricity.

"I – I don't know what to do," Cara admitted. She didn't think she'd ever uttered those words out loud before. Delaine was actually in there. Where could 'there' even be?

"Call somebody!"

"I want to try something." Out of sheer morbid curiosity, she clicked on "Save As."

"What are you doing?" Delaine squeaked, as the Save As screen blocked her view.

"An experiment," Cara responded.

"A what?"

Delaine seemed to be getting a bit hysterical, Cara thought. She decided to name the file "Test."

The cloud surrounding Delaine shimmered.

What the hell? Cara wondered.

"Tell me what you just did!" Delaine demanded.

"I saved your file. Now I'm going to close it."

"You can't do that!" she cried. "Cara, don't you dare—"

Cara closed the file. The screen went dark, and she saw Delaine's handprints covering the inside of her screen. She sighed. Cara liked her screen immaculate. There was no way she'd be able to wipe them off.

Who should I call? she wondered. *Ron? The CEO? The police? The FBI? Area 51?*

She opened the test file back up. Delaine popped up on her screen, surrounded by the gray cloud.

"You really are in there, huh?"

"Oh my god, you stupid cow!" Delaine's eyes widened as she looked at Cara. "Sorry. I'm a little stressed. Yes. I'm *really* in here."

"How on earth did you manage to get inside your computer?"

"I don't know!"

"All right, all right. Hold on a second."

Cara picked up the phone and called Ron. "I need you in my office immediately. There's something you've got to see."

* * *

Delaine's face was plastered against the other side of the screen, looking around Cara's office. Cara was sitting at her desk tapping her fingers impatiently when Ron arrived.

"What's going on?" he asked Cara.

"Delaine's stuck in the computer."

"She's what?" Ron looked at the screen, and Cara swore she caught a glimpse of a smile.

"She's really in there. And you seem… weirdly calm and… not in shock."

Without speaking, Ron pulled out his phone and started texting.

"Ron?" Delaine looked at Cara with tears spilling from her eyes. "Somebody tell me what's going on." Her voice had risen at least an octave.

Cara cleared her throat. This absurd situation was growing stranger by the second, and it was clearly beyond her control. She needed answers. Now. To get Ron's attention, she explained to him how she'd saved and reopened the "file".

"Hm. Smart," he commented.

That… was not the reaction she inspected.

"Could you hurry it up?" Delaine barked. "I'm going insane in here! And it's very cold."

Ron slid his phone into his pocket. "Cara, if she's really been captured in a file, we may have the ideal solution to both our problems."

"Tell me what you mean by that!" Delaine demanded.

"What kind of solution?" Cara asked, trying valiantly to ignore the terrified face behind her screen.

"Ronald Nickerson!" Delaine shrieked. "What do you mean by ideal solution?"

"Let me use your mouse, Cara."

Cara and Ron traded places.

"I don't know what you think you're doing, Ron. You know what will happen if you cross me. Get me out, and do it now."

"Give the man a chance to think," Cara snapped.

"I'm done thinking. I know exactly what to do." He grabbed a pen from Cara's desk. He scribbled three words on a piece of paper and held it up for Cara to see.

"Will that work?" she asked.

"Based on my research and what you've just learned, yes. It will."

"Then do it already!" Delaine yelled.

"Of course, ma'am." He winked at her. Before she could react, he closed the file.

"You know how this happened," Cara accused.

He smiled. His eyes had a coldness she'd never seen in them before.

"Research and Development is working on a technology that will allow technicians to diagnose network problems virtually. They have found a way to look inside cyberspace, from *inside cyberspace*. I can't say anything else because I'm beta testing the—" He looked at the screen. "The process." He smirked.

A smile slowly slid across Cara's face as she realized what he was saying. "Ronald. Did you test some kind of prototype on Delaine's computer?"

He ran a finger across his lips like he was zipping them shut.

"Impressive! I didn't think you had it in you."

"People do crazy things for love."

"Hm. I wouldn't know."

A few more mouse clicks, and the two of them stared at the file name on the screen. “Shall we confirm it? Can you live with it?” Ron asked quietly.

Cara said, “Very happily, thank you very much. But won’t someone know what you did?”

“No. We covered our tracks. It was tricky, but our software helped with that, too.”

“Wait, did you say ‘we?’”

He chuckled. “You don’t really think you have the monopoly on hating Delaine, do you? She’s been blackmailing half my team for various reasons for months. We’ve been planning this for a long time.”

Cara’s eyes lit up. “Let’s tell her what we’re doing. I want to see her face.”

Ron’s eyebrows shot up. “Jesus. You’re a bigger sociopath that I realized. No. We’re not going to tell her. Let’s just get it over with.”

Cara reached over him and grabbed the mouse.

“Damn it, Cara!”

Delaine’s face filled the screen as the file opened. Cara had never seen an expression of such pure hatred and fury. “You did this,” she said in a low, calm voice as she glared at Ron. “You have no intention of getting me out of here.”

“As much as I want to test our retrieval process, no. Cyberspace is as good of a place for you as any.”

She turned to Cara. “And you. You helped.”

"Sadly, I had nothing to do with it," Cara said. "I'd tell you I'll miss you, but I won't. Goodbye, Delaine."

"Wait!"

With a couple clicks, Ron confirmed that yes, they were sure they wanted to delete the file permanently.

THE RING OF DOORS

Taj's alarm woke him after a few short hours of restless sleep. Staring at the dull, grey, bloodshot eyes reflected in his bathroom mirror, he cursed himself for drinking so much whiskey. He splashed cold water over his face before going to the kitchen to make the strongest coffee he possibly could. His first shift as Executioner began in two hours.

He'd received the assignment after the previous Executioner was officially declared insane and relieved from duty. While he was grateful to finally have a job, he wished he'd been appointed to a position that involved less torturing.

Ironically, an 'Executioner' didn't *kill* anyone. He presided over the ritual of sending convicted criminals through the Ring of Doors and into the correct subdivision of Hell.

An unseen entity, known only as the Punisher, manifested the Ring. Dozens of doors lined the inside of the horizontally rotating wheel. Each door marked the entrance to a different Hellscape, where a criminal's greatest fears played out in the environment best suited to intensify their eternal suffering. The Punisher arranged the details of their personal punishment, then paused the spinning Ring long enough for each convict to pass through the correct door.

Huddling in his heavy coat, Taj walked the two miles to his new worksite. He'd hoped the sunshine and cold, fresh air would help ease his nervousness. He would be the seventh person in eighteen months to serve in this capacity. Prior to that time period, appointees lasted for ten years or more before they were retired.

Over the last year and a half, however, the Punisher had developed a disturbing affinity for creativity. While he had never been exactly humane, his prior punishments at least had logic and rationality. The unending cycles of pointless cruelty he now forced on offenders were so gruesome and terrifying, Executioners couldn't bring themselves to send even the most heinous criminals to their fates.

Taj supposed the responsibility of punishing so many murderers had finally unraveled the strange entity's sanity, too.

After arriving at the End-of-Life Processing Station, Taj climbed the two dozen uneven stairs to the entrance. He wasn't surprised to see a Guard standing at attention in the doorway leading into the mountain location. The Guard stepped over and blocked the door when he saw Taj. Taj handed the man his identification card and duty appointment letter. The Guard scrutinized them, then looked at Taj with suspicion as he returned his credentials.

"Key," the man said tonelessly.

"Oh, yeah. Almost forgot," Taj mumbled. He dug the tiny square device from his uniform pocket. The Guard grabbed it from Taj's fingers and held it over the barcode scanner he wore on a band around his wrist. The key beeped three times. The Guard nodded and returned it.

Taj started forward, expecting to be admitted to the building. Instead, the Guard said, "Strip."

Taj stared at him. "Did you just say *strip*? As in, take my clothes off? Right *here?*"

The Guard looked back at him impassively, appearing bored.

Taj wasn't embarrassed of his body. Although he was beginning to develop a bit of a beer belly, he worked out enough to have well-defined arm and thigh muscles. Still, this had to be some sort of joke, maybe an initiation ritual they put the newbies through. They were at a high enough altitude that being naked outside, even in sunlight, would be cold, if not dangerous.

"Look, man, it's my first day on the job. I just want to get moving."

The Guard blinked, still wearing the same unmoved expression. "Strip," he repeated.

He's serious, Taj thought. *He wants me to shed my clothes right here in front of the door.* Taj scoffed and shook his head.

The Guard put his hand on the weapon strapped to his belt, never breaking eye contact.

"Okay, okay!"

Scowling, Taj slid out of his coat, then unzipped his jumpsuit and let it fall to the ground. He pulled his t-shirt over his head.

"Are you happy now?"

As he stood there, wearing nothing but his boxers and boots, with his coat and clothes laying at his feet, the Guard said, "Strip."

"I just did! You want me to take off my underwear? You gonna give me a rectal exam? Should I take off my boots, too, so you can see if there's lint between my toes?"

The Guard stared at him and said nothing.

"Unbelievable," Taj muttered as he bent to untie his boots.

"Perhaps you'd prefer an appointment to the mines," the Guard said casually.

"My god, you *can* form entire sentences. I'm doing it, alright?" Taj removed his boots and socks, then dropped his boxers.

"Turn around."

Crossing his arms and shivering, Taj turned his back on the Guard. "Listen, you better not try sticking anything in my—"

"Clear," the Guard announced. Taj heard the locks on the other side of the cedar door click.

After dressing in record time, Taj walked into the building. Another Guard met him inside and, without speaking, shoved him back against the door.

"Now what?" Taj demanded. "Trust me, that guy out there? He was incredibly thorough."

On his right, a third Guard appeared from behind a door labeled 'SECURITY OFFICE.' She carried a thickly padded dark blue vest. A grid of something resembling veins wound through it, bulging under the material. The Guard held it up with both hands.

"Put your arms through here," she said by way of greeting.

Taj raised his eyebrows. The other Guard backed away to give him room.

"Okay, you uh, want me to put it on backwards?"

The woman stood silently, holding up the odd garment. Shrugging, Taj tossed his coat to the other Guard, who let it drop to the floor. Taj rolled his eyes.

"Nice," he mumbled, and slipped his arms into the vest. The coat-dropping Guard pulled it tight around his back and began to fasten the metal buttons.

"Is this for protection from radiation or something?" Taj asked.

The Guard behind him yanked the vest tighter as he continued to fasten buttons.

"Hey, easy, man! I need to breathe!"

The Guard from the office looked at him with the same dead stare as the guy outside. Taj wondered if the ability to bore holes in a person with one's eyes was a job requirement.

"You don't need protection from radiation," she said, with barely a hint of intonation.

Taj tensed. "Then what is this thing for?" Turning his head to the Guard behind him, he said, "Hey, seriously! You didn't ask for my safe word! Loosen this thing up!"

The Guard finished buttoning it and stepped back. "Clear."

The third Guard walked back toward the Security Office. "Follow me."

Taj threw up his arms. "Let me ask *again.* What the hell is this thing for?"

"Incentive."

Taj tugged down on the vest, which didn't move at all. Scowling, he followed the Guard into her office. The small room was bland and unremarkable, with grey walls and a stone floor. Six screens, each focused on a different area inside the mountain, hung on the far wall. A desk and chair were the only furniture in the room. Only two things sat on the desk: an open laptop and a headset.

"Nice place you've got here," Taj commented, managing to keep most of the sarcasm out of his voice.

The Guard didn't answer him. She leaned over and tapped some numbers on the laptop's keyboard before turning to Taj.

"Try removing the vest."

"Uh—"

"Remove the vest."

Taj gritted his teeth and closed his eyes. He hated mind games.

"Remove the vest."

"I'm doing it!"

Reaching behind himself, he slid his fingers under the center of the vest to find the bottom button. He didn't understand the point of this nonsense. This entire ritual *had* to be part of some twisted mess-with-the-new-guy joke.

As he touched the metal button, an electric shock tore through his hand. He swore vehemently. "What the hell is *wrong* with you people?" he shrieked. He shook his hand out and rubbed his palm with his left thumb. "Why did you do that?"

"To make sure the vest is in proper working order, and to ensure you understand that you cannot remove it."

Taj stared down at the woman with his mouth gaping. She stared back. When the State appointed him to this job, they failed to mention strip searches and electrified vests.

"We've had issues in the past with Executioners refusing to carry out their duties," the Guard explained. "The Governors believe the threat of electrocution is a strong motivator."

"Electrocution," Taj repeated numbly.

"The wires embedded in that vest can deliver a small jolt, like the one you just experienced. They can also produce enough electric current to power this entire facility for thirty, maybe forty seconds."

Taj stepped back toward the doorway. Trying to keep his voice steady, he asked, "How many people have you fried?" He had never questioned the morality of the System, but he did question the morality of the Governors cooking their employees. Maybe he *should've* asked for an appointment to the mines. Maybe he should request a transfer.

The Guard ignored his question. "When you arrive at the Executioner's platform, you'll find a headset. Put it on. You'll use it to hear and speak to the Deck Guard, the prisoner, and me. The Ring will communicate with you through a screen, and you'll read out loud what it says to the rest of us.

"Go straight through that door. Get moving. And son?" The Guard put her hand over the keypad. Taj flinched. "Don't lose your nerve."

It took all his self-control to keep from fleeing the room. The door she directed him to led to a brightly lit, white-walled passage. Before long, it became an uneven stone tunnel that burrowed a quarter mile into the mountain. At the end, an elevator waited to take him eight hundred feet underground.

Taj hated elevators. Heights and confined spaces were two of his least favorite things. This contraption didn't look sturdy enough to hold a mouse, let alone a person. On the bright side, the terror of potentially freefalling eighty stories momentarily distracted him from the fear of being electrocuted.

He took a deep breath as the elevator doors slid shut behind him. Listening to the creaks and groans as it descended, he pictured all sorts of horrible outcomes. The supporting cables could break, and he could plummet to his death. The elevator could start on fire and burn him alive. It could just stop working halfway down the shaft, and he'd be trapped in a box inside a bed of rock.

None of those things happened, although the elevator landed with a mysterious and disturbing *clank.* Taj pushed the doors open and stepped out into his new workplace. If not for its grim purpose, the view would've been spectacular. Dozens of sapphire blue bulbs dangled from a cable that had been strung over the vast, cylindrical cavern. Their ethereal light bathed every surface. Stalagmites and stalactites on either side of him grew toward each other like monstrous teeth. Streaks of phosphorescent green, blue, and purple minerals flowed across the stone walls. Spotlights from the ground lit both the Executioner's platform and the Punishment Deck.

A narrow bridge of wooden planks led across the cavern's jagged rocky surface to the Executioner's platform. After reaching his station, he stood awkwardly in front of its podium. He lightly touched the black screen on its surface. To the right of the screen sat the Button; dormant, silent, waiting to perform its solemn duty.

Hovering near the opposite wall of the cave was the massive, spinning Ring of Doors. It surrounded the Punishment Deck. Looking at it directly hurt his eyes, the way staring at a mirage for too long or trying on someone else's glasses would. A kaleidoscope of colors continuously swirled across the surface of each door, like something out of a psychedelic science fiction movie.

"Executioner is in position," the Deck Guard called out.

The Punisher's eye-for-an-eye method of dispensing justice had, for the most part, kept society out of chaos and anarchy for more than ninety years. The threat of being forced to relive one's own nightmares in a continual loop until the end of time was a highly effective crime deterrent. Unfortunately, there were still criminals who believed the potential payout of breaking the law was worth the risk of suffering this fate.

Taj put on the headphones and adjusted the microphone. Pausing to look down at the wired vest, he wondered how many other employers threatened to murder their employees if they failed to do their job.

"Executioner is in position," the Deck Guard repeated testily.

Taj cleared his throat and read the information scrolling down his screen.

"The criminals responsible for the bombing of the Peoples' Hospital's Department of Experimental Genetics, who have been tried and convicted before a competent, licensed judge, will today be justly sent to their Hellscapes, where they will spend the remainder of Time in repeating loops of punishment for the heinous acts they have committed."

"Executioner," the Deck Guard said, "begin the proceedings."

Here we go, I guess, Taj thought. He felt a mixture of guilt and dread as he looked at his screen. "Jones Morris," he read.

"Louder!" the Guard from the office commanded, her piercing voice in the headphones making him recoil.

"Jones—"

"*Louder!*"

"*JONES MORRIS!*" Taj yelled. He breathed heavily. Despite the cool temperature, sweat dripped from his forehead. He wiped it off with the back of his hand. Looking down at the screen, he continued reading. "You've been convicted of detonating a bomb within the Peoples' Hospital's Department of Experimental Genetics.

"Your actions resulted in the deaths of four patients and three employees, grievous injuries sustained by an additional thirty-five employees, and destruction of property with an estimated damage of $22.76 million. Do you have any final words to offer before punishment is carried out?"

"Those monsters deserved everything they got!" yelled the baby-faced Jones Morris. "They're experimenting on children. *Children!* Did you know that? They tell the parents of newborns their babies are dead, then they haul them off to their labs. They poison them. Mutate their DNA. Make them into monsters. Sometimes they do worse. Don't you get it?"

Taj froze. He had no idea how to respond, or if he should respond at all. *What if this kid's telling the truth?* he thought. *It doesn't justify his actions, but—*

"Do your job," the Deck Guard demanded. In a lower voice, he added, "Remember, you are here to aid in the administration of justice, not sympathize with his crime."

"I will now announce the Punisher's judgment," Taj read loudly. "Guard, present the prisoner to the Ring of Doors."

The man grabbed Morris' shoulders and forced him to face the inside rim of the spinning Ring. After several excruciatingly tense minutes, the Ring slowed to a stop. A shimmering blue door came to rest in front of the Deck.

Information appeared on Taj's screen. "Your punishment will begin on a ship on the ocean," Taj read. "You'll stand, watching the sunrise spread its light over the water. You'll spend three days enjoying everything the luxury cruise liner has to offer: your favorite foods, casinos, live shows, and a well-stocked bar."

Taj looked at the screen. That – wasn't what he expected.

Jones Morris pumped his fist. “Ha! See? The Punisher knows we had a higher purpose! He’s rewarding me!”

“Keep reading!” snapped the Deck Guard.

“At the end of the third day, as the sun dips below the horizon, a sea creature will emerge from the deep. It will pull you from the boat and – and tear you apart, limb by limb. Your helpless torso will be dragged to the bottom of the sea, where you will rot for seven years, one year for each person you murdered. Squid, crabs, eels, and octopuses will attack you, dig holes in what’s left of your body, eat your eyes, chew on your tongue…” Taj felt nauseous. His voice broke. “But you will not die. At the end of seven years, you will find yourself, whole, on the deck of the luxury liner, watching the brilliant sunrise. You will enjoy three days on the ship. And just when you start to believe it was all a bad dream, the sea creature will appear, and the cycle will begin again. You will remain in this loop for all of eternity.”

Jones Morris, slack jawed, stared at the Deck Guard and fell to his knees. “But I—”

“Press the button and open the door,” the Office Guard commanded. “It is time.”

“No! Please! Don’t make me go! There has to be a mistake!” Morris turned his head frantically back and forth from the Deck Guard to Taj.

“At this point, they always beg,” commented the Office Guard. Taj jumped. “Right up until the end, they think they'll get away with breaking the law."

"Executioner, please," he pleaded. "I have six kids. They've already lost their mother."

Taj winced. *Jesus.*

"Perhaps you didn't hear me, Executioner. Open the door!"

Taj stared at Morris. It wasn't as if he thought he'd be sending people to an eternity of reading dictionaries or herding an infinite number of cats. But he didn't realize the punishments would be this unsettling.

"When I do, his punishment starts?" Taj hesitated. "And continues, over and over, literally forever?"

"That's the idea. Open it."

Taj took a breath and looked at the Button. The little green, glowing circle looked so harmless.

Press the button. He's a killer. Press the button. He's a killer. He's a killer. A killer. Taj hadn't expected to feel so much reluctance. All he had to do was *open a door*. He held his trembling finger over the button, cursing himself for being so weak.

The hair on his arms stood up. The vest emitted a quiet hum, then crackled. Blinding yellow arcs spiked across his chest. Taj cried out and fell to his knees. His hands reached for the freshly scorched skin, but the vest kept him from touching the injury. The smell of burnt flesh turned his stomach, and he gagged.

The Office Guard reprimanded him. "Like it or not, you are the Executioner. That was a warning. Don't make me turn the power up to level two."

Taj, still on his knees, reached up to the podium and found the button.

"No!!" squealed Morris.

"I'm sorry," Taj answered quietly.

The Ring's door slid open, revealing the deck of a cruise ship. The sun peeking over the horizon spread its light across the water.

"I suggest you walk through on your own," said the Deck Guard. "At least go with dignity."

"I can't do this," whispered Jones Morris. "Don't make me do this."

A wrinkled green hand burst from the sea on the opposite side of the ship and reached through the doorway. It wrapped its bony fingers around Jones Morris' body and plucked him from the Punishment Deck as he wailed and cried for mercy. The door slammed shut, leaving Morris to his fate.

"Well, that was easy," the Deck Guard commented. He disappeared back through the entryway and returned with another criminal while Taj dragged himself up and looked at the screen. A name was already waiting.

"Don't we get a break between people?" he asked.

The Office Guard snorted. "Read the name."

He nodded. The excruciating pain from the burns was, as the Office Guard had promised, a powerful incentive to do the job. The embarrassment he felt at being punished like a child was also an effective motivator.

"Havrik Tarlin," he shouted. The Ring of Doors resumed spinning. It reminded Taj of a roulette wheel, except the wager was sanity instead of money, and every bet was a loser.

"You were an accomplice to the detonation of a bomb within the Peoples' Hospital's Department of Experimental Genetics.

"Your actions contributed to the deaths of four patients and three employees, grievous injuries sustained by an additional thirty-five employees, and destruction of property with an estimated damage of $22.76 million. Do you have any final words to offer before punishment is carried out?"

"I don't deserve this."

The Deck Guard and Office Guard laughed.

I work with crazy people, Taj thought. He cleared his throat and continued reading. "I will now announce the Punisher's judgment," he read. "Guard, present the prisoner to the Ring of Doors."

The Ring spun, and Taj's eyes followed the swirling colors on the wildly spinning doors. The visual sensory overload, the pain of the electrical burns, and the emotional shock of watching a monster snatch someone *literally out of reality* caused his stomach to gurgle. He lunged to the edge of the platform and vomited, spraying the half-digested remains of a stale donut and ultra-strong coffee onto the rocks.

He braced himself for the chastising and laughter that were sure to come from his new coworkers, but they said nothing. As the Ring wound to a stop, more words began crossing the computer screen. Making a heroic effort to keep his voice steady, Taj read, “You will spend eternity buried in an iron coffin. You will be dug up and released for a period of free time when your turn comes around. After free time, you’ll be returned to your coffin until it’s your turn to be released for free time again.”

“Iron coffin?” Tarlin squeaked. “What does it mean by ‘free time’?” His voice rose with every question. “What is this, daycare?”

Taj, unwilling to risk the Office Guard’s wrath, wasted no time pushing the button. “Let’s see what’s behind door number two,” he mumbled. The Office Guard chuckled in approval, causing Taj’s stomach to turn again.

“I won’t go,” Tarlin whispered as his eternal destiny appeared before him. “I’m not going in there.”

“This is one of the Punisher’s favorites lately,” the Office Guard observed.

Endless rows of tombstones stood in the black dirt, stretching as far as the eye could see. No names identified the graves; instead, the tombstones displayed the prisoner’s crimes. Squinting, Taj could make out the engravings for the newest burials. Bile rose in his throat as he read “destruction of property”, “negligence resulting in non-lethal injury”, and “theft of alcoholic beverage”. Crimes, yes, but not crimes that deserved eternal torture.

“Why are the courts sending people here who don’t deserve this kind of punishment?” Taj whispered. He knew questioning procedure was not in his best interest, but this was unfathomable.

“We have no choice,” the Office Guard said softly. “The Punisher is, shall we say, insistent.”

Dumbfounded, Taj looked at the Ring of Doors. Where had this Punisher come from? And why was he here?

“Don’t ask questions,” the Office Guard said, as if she had read his mind.

He dragged his eyes back to the Hellscape.

A figure in a black robe dragged a coffin to the front of the doorway. Although the nightmare creature wore a hood over its head, Taj could clearly see a set of four curved red horns where its face should be.

“What is *that*?” Taj blurted.

“The Punisher creates creatures from the nightmares of the criminal. It’s from dear Mr. Tarlin’s mind,” the Deck Guard responded. Laughing, he added, “Glad I’m not in *his* head.”

Taj’s eyes grew large as a sudden, terrifying thought occurred to him. “How does the Punisher know what we dream about?”

The wisecracking Guard sobered immediately. "We don't know."

The horn-faced figure gestured at Tarlin, then at the box.

"Oh, no. I'm not getting in there. No way. No *way*! You can't make me go in there!"

The Deck Guard grabbed him by his ponytail and yanked his head back. "Oh, but we can," he whispered in the prisoner's ear.

"I have human rights!" he protested, trying to get away but held immobile by the Guard's grip on his hair.

The Deck Guard laughed. "You're no longer *human*. See your tombstone? Doesn't even have a name. You don't even get to keep your *name* in this Hellscape."

Taj's eyes dropped to the screen, and he resumed reading. "Each of the 139,500 criminals buried here is periodically granted one hour of freedom. When it's your turn, you'll be dug up, and you can spend the time doing anything you want."

"A whole hour?" Tarlin squealed. "My turn? When is that? Once a week? Once a *month*?" His voice betrayed his hysteria and absolute terror.

Taj read the words on his screen twice before clearing his throat and relaying them. "Free time is granted to one prisoner at a time. With the current population, each prisoner is granted their hour once every 15.9… years. You will remain in this loop for all of eternity."

Tarlin, still held by his hair, began crying. "Please, please, I'll do anything. I don't deserve to spend the rest of time in a box. We did a service for mankind! I used to work in those labs! You can't imagine what they're doing to people in there!"

Getting nowhere with the sneering Deck Guard, he turned to Taj. "Please, mister! I mean Executioner. *Sir.* Don't let them do this to me! We did what was right! We took out a few to save many!"

Taj watched in horror as the Deck Guard shoved Tarlin through the door, impaling him on the monster's four horns. Angrily, it shook him back and forth until he flew to the ground, howling and crying. Taj had never heard a human being make such an unnatural sound of pain and hopelessness. Growing blotches of blood soaked the front of Tarlin's prison jumpsuit as the Thing lifted him from the ground and dropped him into the coffin. The iron lid slammed shut, cutting off his screams. The hooded, horn-faced figure padlocked the coffin, carried it to the open grave, and dropped it in. The door closed, and Tarlin was lost.

"He'll bleed out!" Taj exclaimed.

"Possibly," said the calm voice from the Office. "But he won't die."

Taj closed his eyes and put a hand over his mouth. He unwillingly imagined spending eternity alone in the dark, unable to move, staring at an iron lid a few inches from his face. He'd spend almost sixteen *years* waiting to get out, then face being thrown back in after just minutes.

Remember what he did, Taj told himself. *Remember the lives he destroyed. He deserves this. He deserves every minute of it.*

It was a lie. No one deserved what this Punisher dreamt up.

"I can't," Taj mumbled. "I can't do this anymore."

The sudden pain from the electric shocks was completely debilitating. Taj lay on the floor, drooling, and tried to pull the vest away from his skin as his body convulsed. His hands melded to the vest as the current ran through them and up his arms. He knew he was screaming, although the sound seemed unimportant and far away. The punishment ended, but his body continued shaking.

"*Now* can you do it?" the Office Guard asked.

Taj knew he should reply, but he couldn't think of the right words. He bit his tongue hard enough for blood to trickle from his mouth.

"Aaaagghh aaraar." He spit.

"I need your answer, Executioner."

The burns on his skin rubbed against the inside of the vest. He'd not felt such constant, intense pain in a long time. He'd not felt such hatred. Forcing his mouth to form words, he whispered, "I'll do it."

"Good decision," the Deck Guard said mockingly.

"The next level of current will cause permanent damage to your brain," the Office Guard added.

Taj managed to pull himself up to stand in front of the podium. He sniffled and wiped tears from his eyes with throbbing fingers. The next name popped up on his screen as the Guard brought out another prisoner. Taj wondered how many more prisoners he'd have to send to their horrifying fates today.

The Office Guard spoke gently through the headphones, as if she hadn't just tried to barbecue him. "You've got to stop thinking of them as people."

"How am I supposed to do that?" he whispered, still not able to speak normally.

"Don't look at their faces. It helps. You get used to it. Believe it or not, you're doing better than most do on their first day."

The next person up was Syran Beck, who built the bomb they'd used on the Hospital. His last words were, "Our actions were justified! That place is torturing and killing innocent people! We're fighting a corrupt system! They aren't listening to us! We had to do something to get their attention!"

Taj felt sick to his stomach. He wondered what he would have done if he knew dozens, maybe hundreds or more babies were being experimented on while their devastated parents mourned their pretend deaths. What if it happened to his child? Or sibling? Would he risk torture himself?

He decided the answer was irrelevant. “As your punishment for building the bomb,” Taj read in a flat voice, “you’ll begin your day on the first floor of a ten-story parking garage, tied to a chair. In front of you, on a table, will be a timer, counting down from a hundred. When the timer reaches zero, a bomb will detonate, and you’ll fall. The building will collapse on top of you. You’ll be trapped in the rubble for a certain length of time, unable to escape, feeling the pain of a burned, crushed, and broken body. Then you will be rescued and healed, and it will start over. You will relive the detonation and aftermath over and over, until time ends. However, each time will be a little different. You won’t know if you’re being rescued within hours, days, weeks, or months. You’ll lay there in a claustrophobic nightmare of pain and uncertainty, like those who survived the bomb you built. You will remain in this loop for all of eternity.”

Taj tried to see a monster instead of a human being. Maybe it was a skill he’d learn over time.

He wondered what kind of monster *he* would become, doing this day after day.

After this shift, I’m going home, putting aloe on these burns, drinking whiskey till they stop hurting, and renting porn.

Taj pressed the button, opening the door to Beck’s eternal nightmare.

Don’t think of them by name. Think of them as ‘Prisoner.’

He could do this. His eyes ran steadily with tears from the pain. Pain that was getting worse instead of better. Pain that he couldn't endure for much longer.

The fourth convicted criminal was a woman named Ella Worthington.

"I wasn't involved!" she cried when given the chance to offer her last words. "I'm innocent! I wasn't even there!"

Prisoner. Her name is Prisoner, not Ella.

Taj thought of the tombstones for those who'd committed minor offenses.

The Punisher's announcement surprised him. "Indeed, you are innocent of the crimes committed by the others. You will be allowed to spend eternity in an environment of your choice."

"Oh my god, thank you. Thank you." She fell to her knees as Taj pushed the button. The Ring of Doors slid to a stop. The environment of her choice was a crystal-clear lake, with a background of mountains and sunshine.

Taj's screen blipped again. "However. You knew the plan and failed to try to prevent it. Your punishment for that crime is having to face those whose bodies were mutilated as a result of your silence. When you wake in the morning, one of the dead or injured will be waiting by your bed." Taj reluctantly continued. "They will follow you throughout the day. You cannot speak to them. They will stand over your bed at night. When you wake from sleep, another of your victims will be there. You will remain in this loop for all of eternity."

"What?" she cried. "You can't do that to me!"

"They all say that," smirked the Guard.

"It's not fair!"

"They all say that, too."

The Deck Guard pushed her through the door. Once she crossed the threshold, her body shimmered and then disappeared.

No new names appeared on the screen.

"Looks like we're done," called the Deck Guard. "You survived your first day. Congratulations."

"Get this thing off me," Taj said, looking at nothing.

"Indeed," smiled the Guard. "Go on upstairs and Dani will unbutton you. Taj is your name, right? You learn to do this job without hesitation, Taj, and they won't make you wear that thing anymore.

"So." He clasped his hands. "See you again tomorrow. We're gonna have a kid who went insane and killed her family. Want in on the pool to see what Hellscape she's given?"

"Pool?"

"Yeah. Twenty dollar buy-in. Rod thinks she'll be trapped in her own house with the ghosts of her family. Leah thinks the Punisher will lock her in a mental hospital. Dani thinks it'll be some kind of monster dystopia thing. I'm with Leah—I'm going with the kid being stuck in a straitjacket for the rest of her afterlife in a padded room. What do you say?"

"I say that is some stone-cold, morbid shit. I'm getting out of here." He turned and headed down the walkway toward the elevator, needing the drink and porn more than ever now.

"You better develop a sense of humor, pal," the Guard yelled after him. "You won't survive this place if you don't."

* * *

In spite of the almost unspeakable pain he felt, Taj walked out of his way to stop at the liquor store. He splurged on some expensive whiskey and a couple slices of cold pizza. The Deck Guard was right. He had to toughen up. At the end of the day, it was just another job. If he didn't do it, someone else would.

Once inside his apartment, he traded the uniform for comfortable jeans and a fresh t-shirt. After putting some soothing gel on his burns and eating the soggy pizza, he poured a little soda into a tall glass of whiskey. His liver would hate him, but he deserved to be drunk. He set an alarm, grabbed the remote, sat down in his recliner, and drank till he was unconscious.

Taj's alarm woke him after a few short hours of restless sleep. Staring at the dull, grey, bloodshot eyes reflected in his bathroom mirror, he cursed himself for drinking so much whiskey. He splashed cold water over his face before going to the kitchen to make the strongest coffee he possibly could. His first shift as Executioner began in two hours.

TRAPPED INSIDE THE MAELSTROM

Pinecones soared from the majestic tree and accumulated in random piles for her entertainment. The Girl deigned to watch. A wasp crawled over her bare foot, trying and failing to elicit a twitch from her toes. She absently mocked its failure.

She knows she's not sane.

She doesn't want to be.

Her mind wandered through the museum of Earth. She absorbed the complexity and interconnectedness of all that lived, even the rocks and the caves and the dirt. If only she could collect the patterns of nature and keep them safe. Time caused everything to rot.

Memories of dreams leaked from her subconscious and drained like water through a sieve before she could collect them. She distractedly mourned their loss as they faded away.

The desperate ache of unrealized expectations surrounded her soul and filled the void left by the dreams. The dreams were traitors.

Voices whispered to her from the Deep Edges as she sprawled out across the golden wasteland. She plucked the skeletons of weeds from their earthly graveyard. The roots clung to the dirt that had sustained them, reluctant to let go. She looked up at the sky of blue, and her depression deepened. She changed the sky to red.

She knows nothing is real. She doesn't care.

They all envied her exalted existence. Their ordinariness made her feel safe. She used the false audience's admiration to help relight and refuel her extinguished metaphorical candle. Her replenished power allowed her to heroically drop the rope and rescue the stragglers dangling over the abyss. This ability was her birthright.

The wasp stung her toe. Fury replaced the indifference with which she'd disregarded it. She didn't mind the discomfort, but she did mind the interruption from experiencing her fascinating misery. Visualizing the physical pain and encapsulating it in a bubble, she pushed it from her mind to make room for her dark musings.

She knows no one understands her thoughts.

She grieves for the ignorant.

Trying to find solace in the old familiar places, she let her mind dive into memories she made as a child. Old photos were her only proof that those places ever existed in everyone else's reality, as she herself once did. She wished she had words to describe the disappointment that wrapped its fingers around her when she returned to those places and found them inaccessible. Changed. Destroyed.

Removed. Time had sealed them away. Time had destroyed them. People had destroyed them.

If only she could've sealed those Moments in time bubbles and kept them safe. Memories faded. Knowledge was lost. She no longer belonged in the places she'd once considered home. Violent waves of anger and hurt threatened to smother her as she fought to free herself from the box.

Suddenly, her mind overflowed with secret knowledge. She was fantastically lucky and blessed, and she understood this with amazing clarity. The Universe revealed its darkest secrets. It showed her planets blazing with rubies and carnelian and surrounded by moons of emeralds and sapphires. It spiraled her through gold and silver flakes of cosmic dust. Opal and diamond stars twirled like ballet dancers on the theatrical stage of Infinity. She sat front row center.

Frantically she groped through the Veil to find the words to describe what she saw. The correct vocabulary eluded her. She scribbled furiously in The Notebook. Panicked, she poured the blessed knowledge onto page after page, preserving the Truths of reality to share with mankind. The Experts would bow to her brilliance.

Upon rereading her writings, she was horrified to discover gibberish. The whispers from the Deep Edges had tricked her.

Ah, well, she thought, this line of thinking required too much technical knowledge to produce a believable story anyway.

She knows something separates her from everyone else.

She knows she is trapped inside the maelstrom.

The ability to engage her alter egos slipped away. Time was wasting, rushing away from her, and she was failing to fulfill her existence on the Plane Which She Controlled! The anger building up interfered and slammed the doors.

The nurse came into the room where the Girl sat. He administered the usual assortment of drugs used in the treatment of schizophrenia, anxiety, and delirium. After a moment of confusion, she fell into a black sleep, a sea of nothingness, a temporary death with no light beckoning to her from the end of a tunnel. Tomorrow she would reset and repeat.

THE INEVITABLE

The trio of researchers knew the knowledge they'd stumbled upon wasn't meant for humanity. I pleaded with them to stop their experiments before they caused irreversible damage to space and time. I pleaded with them to stop playing God. In the dark recesses of their minds, they had to know their arrogance would have consequences.

Certain constants in the Universe aren't meant to be trifled with. The Universe protects itself. It punishes those who meddle. It annihilates those who knowingly destroy vital components of Reality.

I warned them.

When the invasion began, all three scientists pretended they were shocked. They spent their remaining days loudly and publicly blaming everyone but themselves. They flung accusations around like black confetti at a despised uncle's funeral. Even at the end, they refused to admit they'd doomed the human race to an incomprehensibly devastating fate. They refused to admit they'd forced the Universe to ensure another version of mankind would never emerge and recreate their mistakes.

By my calculations, six million years of evolution will be completely reversed in seventeen days.

At least the Apocalypse wasn't caused by zombies. I'm not sure why that comforts me.

The overwhelming majority of humankind, including my friends and relatives, fled when the noises began. Some people sought refuge in mountain caves; others bribed their way into underground bunkers. Members of fringe religions organized mass suicides. Governments discussed the pros and cons of attacking with nuclear weapons.

Deep down, they know nothing they do matters. Deep down, they know we're all damned.

You reap what you sew, as the saying goes. It only took three people to disrupt the quantum structure of the Universe. But the other eight billion of us failed to stop them.

Hours pass. I've chosen to spend my remaining days alone, sprawled across my plush, burgundy couch. My wine cellar is stocked; I made sure I wouldn't be sober while I suffered through the inevitable. I'm streaming horror movies for as long as the Internet continues to exist.

I grab my third bottle of sweet pink Moscato and yank out the cork with an echoing *pop*. I try not to think about the infinite vault of knowledge and human experience that's being lost, piece by piece, as the entire population of Earth is… diminished.

The noises grow louder as they approach my house. They're much closer than they've ever been, and much louder than I've ever heard them. For the first time, I hear heavy claws drag along the sidewalk outside, like steel nails on a cement chalkboard. Turning the television's volume up does little to drown out the sound.

For a fleeting second, I wish I'd tried to hide.

Shards of kitchen window glass clink and clatter as they fall into the sink or fly across the room and pierce the drywall. Bright, lime green light pours through the entire house. Alien growls and screeches fill the air as my house is breeched by the Universe's Guardians.

For the first time, I wonder what I'll become. How will it feel when my DNA reverts to something primal?

I sigh and stare at the movie credits rolling down my TV screen. Guess I won't get to see the sequel.

SHARING

Zoe glanced at the time and realized her guest would be arriving in just a few minutes. She still couldn't believe she'd let Lena convince her to perform Criminal Magic.

The two women worked for a moderately successful advertising firm called Nelson, Menendez, and Matthews. Lena, a graphic designer, had an office one floor above the customer service department where Zoe worked.

Lena had been in a relationship with the customer service manager, Justin, for almost a year. Zoe despised the man from the moment she'd met him. She had enough self-awareness to know her own feelings for Lena influenced her immediate dislike of the man, but others shared her opinion that he was scum. He had an arrogant, know-it-all attitude, and his womanizing escapades were legendary.

Zoe kept her opinions to herself, since Lena seemed happy with their relationship. But when Justin made the mistake of propositioning Zoe, she realized she could no longer turn the other cheek.

Calling Lena for that conversation was one of the most nerve-wracking things she'd ever done. As predicted, Lean was furious. What she hadn't predicted was Lena directing that fury at her instead of Justin.

At first, she'd refused to even believe her. Zoe dreaded giving her the details, but she reluctantly described the unnecessary touching, suggestive comments, and ridiculous amount of attention he'd been lavishing on her. Lena's voice raised an octave as she accused Zoe of trying to steal him. Before she could remind Lena that she wasn't interested in men, Lena dropped the call.

When she'd arrived at work the next morning, she found Lena waiting at her desk. Her eye makeup was smeared below her red puffy eyes, and half of her auburn hair had already fallen loose from the bun on top her head. She looked like she'd spent the night crying.

"I've been so stupid," she confessed in a whisper.

Zoe secretly agreed, but she didn't say so.

"I'm sorry for how I reacted, Zoe," she said. She grabbed a tissue off Zoe's desk and wiped her nose. "I've known for a while now he's been cheating. He comes home late at night, if he comes home at all. He's angry all the time." She gulped back a sob. "I thought he would change. I guess I wasn't enough for him."

Zoe noticed one of her coworkers watching them from around the wall of his cubicle. She held up her middle finger, and he shrugged and went back to work.

She put her arms lightly around her friend. "He's an ass. You'll be better off without him, I promise."

Lena rested her chin on Zoe's shoulder and clung to her.

"I know. I just don't know how to get away from him." She pulled away and met Zoe's eyes. "I've got to find my own apartment, so I have some place to go, and you know how impossible that is in this city. Most of all, I'm afraid if I leave, he'll retaliate somehow. What if he spreads a bunch of lies about me and I lose my job?" She put her hand over her eye and winced.

Zoe looked around to make sure they had privacy. "You've got another headache?" she asked in a low voice.

Lena frowned. "I'm under just a *little* bit of stress right now."

Zoe sighed. She suspected the headaches were more than stress. The woman downed over-the-counter pain medicine like it was chocolate candy. "You've got to get solid proof that he's cheating," she advised. "Then, before you confront him, talk to his boss and let her know what you're afraid of. She'll listen, and she'll be discreet. If he tries accusing you of something at work, she'll know there's a motive behind what he's doing."

Lena took a deep breath. "You're right. So, you'll help me?"

Zoe blinked. She wondered what she'd said to give her that idea. She wanted nothing to do with Lena's love life, unless she became a part of it.

"Of course," she heard her traitorous mouth say. "But I'm not sure what I can do."

"The next time he hits on you, record it on your phone."

That… wasn't what she expected.

"Look, I find excuses to get *away* from him when he does that, okay? He freaks me out. I'm not going to just let him paw me so I can record it. Gross."

When she saw the look on Lena's face, she added, "Sorry. No offense."

"I know guys aren't your scene. I'm not asking you to let him touch you!"

Zoe sighed. "Look. He's *your* boyfriend. You work one floor up from his office. Can't you lure him up there? Doesn't he stop in for a quickie sometimes?" *I would*, she thought, and immediately felt guilty for thinking such a thing about her unsuspecting friend. "Maybe he'll call out someone else's name when you have sex. Or mention one of his other girlfriends. Or compare you with—"

"Stop, alright? You can't honestly think he'd confess something to me!" She searched Zoe's face. "You can't be serious."

"Lena, I want to help you. If there's some other way I can help, I will. But I've been avoiding him like the plague. I can't – I can't play along."

Lena dropped her eyes and backed away. After a second, she shook her head and smiled bitterly. "And I shouldn't have asked you to. Shit. I wasn't thinking." With a deep breath, she said, "I better get back to work." She turned to walk away.

"Lena?" Zoe put a hand on her arm, and she froze. "I'm sorry."

"You've done nothing wrong," she replied without looking back.

* * *

That afternoon, a commotion by the office's community printer drew Zoe's attention. To her complete lack of surprise, Justin was standing much too close to a woman (Darcy from the order room, she thought). Zoe watched her wrestle her arm away from his touch. She grabbed some papers off the printer's tray and stormed out of the office with a look of disgust on her face. Justin stood behind her, smirking as he watched her go.

"That's what I thought," he called after her.

For just a second, Zoe considered asking Darcy to help Lena get proof of the asshole's infidelity. She quickly nixed that idea. Darcy didn't even wait for her print job to finish. She obviously wanted to stay as far away from the man as Zoe did. And it wasn't fair to ask her to do something Zoe herself refused to do.

The shrill ring of the phone made her turn her attention back to customer complaints.

A few minutes after six o'clock, Zoe stood and stretched. She barely had a chance to turn around before Lena walked over to her. She leaned into Zoe, put one hand on her waist and the other on her cheek, and whispered in her ear.

"You're a Level Four, right?"

Zoe swallowed. This was so unfair. It was exactly how her Lena-traps-me-in-my-cubicle-and-ravishes-me fantasy began. Except in her fantasy, Lena wasn't asking about her magic capabilities.

"Yes," Zoe said quietly when she recovered her wits. "Why do you ask?

"Then you can perform a Consciousness Swap."

Zoe pulled back to face her fully, not bothering to hide the horror on her face. "No, I most certainly cannot!" she hissed. "Are you crazy?"

"No one would ever know!"

"If something went wrong, they'd know!" Zoe pulled Lena fully into her cubicle. "You have no idea what you're asking!" She lowered her voice. "Consciousness Swaps are Criminal Magic. If another witch found out, I'd be given a magical lobotomy!"

Lena's eyes widened. "You mean, that's an actual thing?"

"Yes! It's an actual—" Zoe realized she was shouting. Several people were looking on with interest. “Yes,” she whispered. “That’s an actual thing. It’s a fate worse than death.”

Lena closed her eyes. “I know what I’m asking of you crosses a line, but it would only be for one day.” She lowered her voice to the throaty pitch that could successfully order Zoe to dance naked on a flaming bed of nails. “Please Zoe, I need your help. We’ve been friends for so long. We know each other well enough to pull this off. I’ll call in sick. And I could answer your phone and handle customers.”

Zoe raised her eyebrow. “Re-a-lly?” She pronounced the word with three slow syllables. “You can’t stand dealing with people.”

“I can sweet talk some crabby business owners for a day. Look, I’ll owe you.” She took Zoe’s hand and softly ran her thumb across her palm. She briefly squeezed shut the eye affected by her headache.

Zoe shook her head. It wasn’t like Lena to try to manipulate her like this. And it wasn’t like Zoe to let herself be manipulated.

“I’ll clean your house every week for a month,” Lena offered.

Zoe squeezed her eyes shut. Swapping bodies was unnatural, and several pairs of witches who had tried it in the past were unable to return to their own bodies. In at least one instance, the two people involved went insane.

“Two months?” Lena pressed.

Zoe groaned. At this point, she admitted three things to herself. One, she wanted to see Justin fired before he did something more harmful than flirting, if he hadn't already. Two, she was genuinely afraid he may hurt Lena, and three, getting out of housework for a while would be really nice. She hated cleaning.

That didn't mean she couldn't milk it for all it was worth.

"Six months. And I want you to wear a French maid's uniform while you're doing it."

"Oh my god, Zoe, you can't be serious!" She looked at Zoe with an unfathomable expression.

Zoe crossed her arms and raised an eyebrow. Lena sighed.

"Fine. Fine, I'll do it. Weirdo."

Grinning, she said, "You can start a week from Saturday."

"Are you really gonna make me wear that stupid costume?"

The look Zoe gave her must have been convincing, because Lena shook her head and slumped her shoulders. "Weirdo," she muttered again.

"Uh, okay," Zoe said. She cleared her throat and tried to focus. "Well, give me a little time to make arrangements," she told her. "I have to contact someone." Under her breath, she murmured, "Hopefully, she's in a good mood."

Lena kissed her cheek. "Thanks, Zoe. You're the best." She winked.

* * *

Fortunately, or unfortunately depending on one's perspective, Zoe's contact *had* been in a good mood. Wing, a short, serious woman who owned a small metaphysical supply store, had connections to people with more 'creative' interests than most of those who practiced magic. She had the supplies Zoe needed stored in her back room. Wing also instructed her on the precise wording and inflection to use to invoke the magic.

"This part is *incredibly* important," she'd told her, swiping a handful of purple hair from her eyes. "You cannot deviate from the wording of this spell. At all. Don't try to customize it or add to it. This is blood magic, operating on both the physical and spiritual plains.

"There's a reason using this spell is Criminal Magic." Wing's face became devoid of emotion. "As you must be aware, the consequences of failure are dire. I know of your work. You are quite gifted in your craft, and your skills extend far beyond Level Four classification. I believe you're capable of pulling this off. I wouldn't help you otherwise. But once you leave my home, you're on your own. Do not contact me about this again."

* * *

Zoe sat cross-legged on the wooden floor and rehearsed the words in her head one last time. Common sense (or maybe her conscience) demanded she suppress thoughts of Lena crawling up on her bed to dust her wooden headboard. On the low table in front of her, the altar was arranged to Wing's exact specifications. When she heard her front door open, she clicked her lighter and touched it to the candle wicks.

Lena joined her in the attic. She had her palm pressed against her eye. "Will you be stuck with my headache when we switch?"

Zoe raised an eyebrow. "I don't know." Lena's severe headaches seemed to be happening more and more frequently. One more reason to help her get away from Justin. The stress of their relationship was obviously detrimental to her health.

Lena frowned. "Guess we'll find out."

"We can postpone this if you want to."

"No!" Lena shouted, then winced and shut her eyes. "Please. I found a pair of red heels under our bed. Zoe… he brought someone *into our bed.* When I confronted him, he said he owned the furniture, and he could do whatever he wanted on it!"

"Wow. That's the lamest excuse to justify cheating I've ever heard." Zoe shook her head. "Let's get on with this before I come to my senses and change my mind."

She'd never understand how anyone could seek out other girlfriends when they had someone like Lena waiting at home. If only Lena wasn't straight.

Now was not the time to think about it. She gestured to the other side of the table. Lena sat down and stared at her expectantly.

"First I'll cast the Circle. I'll speak the first part of the incantation." She looked at Lena. It had never bothered her before to ask someone for the right to make a tiny cut in their hand, or to cut a lock of their hair for a spell. But she was suddenly hesitant. To make these requests of Lena seemed invasive.

She's going to exist inside your body, and you're worried about being invasive? her inner voice chided.

Lena didn't bat an eye at the requests, to her relief. "Then you'll do the same thing to me, in exactly the same way. I'll make the offering, then add our hair and blood. When the incantation is finished, our consciousnesses will meet on the spiritual plane. We must acknowledge each other and offer mutual consent in that realm. The spell will then rehouse our consciousnesses in each other's body. Do you have any questions?"

"Why do you need my hair and blood?"

"It's an offering to the powers of the Earth that signifies our intentions are true. It also proves physical consent, and it acts as a guide to send our consciousnesses into the correct bodies."

Zoe opened a red leather-bound book.

"Wow, this is some rare stuff," Lena commented, touching the crushed blue leaves on the altar. "Where did you say you got it?"

"I didn't."

Lena gaped at her. “Holy shit. You went to a fringe witch?”

“I can’t exactly walk into the Coven’s monthly gathering and ask for help with this! It’s illegal. We’re doing this completely off the record.”

Lena covered her eye with the palm of her hand and winced. “Please don’t yell. Look, as long as you trust your source, that’s all that matters to me.”

Zoe looked at her with concern. “Are you sure you’re up for this?”

“Just get on with it.”

“You must be sure you’re ready. Once I close the Circle and start the incantation, it has to proceed without interruption. Our consciousnesses could both be lost on the spiritual plane otherwise. Needless to say, that would be unpleasant.”

Lena waved her on, still holding one eye closed.

Zoe began the ritual. She took each step slowly, sighing with relief as she felt each component fall into place. She picked up her athame and held her hand out for Lena’s palm.

Lena reached toward her, squeezing both eyes shut then blinking rapidly. “This is a bad one, Zoe,” she murmured. “I can’t see out of my eye. It’s nothing but black.”

“Then we need to hurry. I told you, this can’t be stopped. Our consciousnesses are being released from their earthly confines as we speak. Concentrate on my voice. I’ll guide you off the physical plane.”

Zoe sounded much calmer than she felt. When Lena's headaches became this severe, they took her out of work for several days at a time. Spending the next 24 hours immobilized by pain wouldn't help them at all, and she didn't have enough supplies to do the spell again. She should've insisted they wait.

Turning the page of her spell book, she uttered the carefully written words Wing had given her. She spoke slowly, concentrating, making sure she had the perfect inflection in her voice and intent behind her words.

Zoe felt herself rise from her body. She'd reached the spiritual plane twice before, and it was as beautiful and exotic as she remembered it. Misty waves of different shades of blue coursed through the infinite space surrounding her. Incorporeal energies, each a burst of colors as individual as its owner's personality, floated near her. But there was no time to linger and enjoy herself. She needed to find Lena and get on with it.

A burst of greens, gold, purple, and ebony floated nearby, and Zoe recognized her friend. She'd never seen such a dark color in someone's consciousness. Perhaps it was a side effect of her intense pain. She wished again that she'd have refused to perform the ritual. She made her way to Lena and touched her consciousness with an increasing sense of dread.

"If you will grant consent for me to occupy your physical body, do so now."

Zoe worried Lena wouldn't be able to convey her answer, but the "yes" reverberated strongly from her consciousness. Communication could be difficult for newcomers; Zoe was impressed.

"If you will grant consent to become one while we transfer from body to body, do so now."

Measuring time passing on the physical world while on this plane was nearly impossible. She watched the swirling colors of Lena's consciousness. They seemed calm. Serene. The ebony faded to a charcoal gray.

Good. Time to finish this up.

"I grant consent for you, Lena, to occupy my body. I—"

Before she could finish, Zoe snapped back into her own body like a rubber band. She opened her eyes. In the dim light, she saw the form of Lena's limp and empty body slumped on the ground.

Gods above! she thought, terrified. She'd done everything correctly. She was sure of it. Lena could not still be on the spiritual plane.

On the other hand, she had to be somewhere, and she certainly wasn't in her own body. Zoe began poking through the ingredients in her altar. She had to get back to the spiritual plane to look for her.

Then, with indescribable horror, she realized she didn't.

"*I made it. I'm in your body!*" Lena said excitedly. "*Wait. Zoe, something's wrong. I can't move! Why can't I move? Oh god, I don't hear my voice! I'm sure I'm talking out loud, why can't I hear myself? Am I deaf?"*

Zoe closed her eyes and focused on Lena's consciousness. It was attached to the edges of her own. They must've begun to switch bodies when something interrupted the ritual.

"Zoe? Help me! Can you hear me? What's happening!?"

Zoe felt numb. She crawled to the other side of the table to Lena's body.

"Lena?" Zoe knelt beside her and felt her neck for a pulse. There was none. Lena's unblinking eyes were wide open. One had a fully dilated pupil. A bit of blood ran from her nose and had already dried.

"Is that my body? What's wrong with my body?"

"I think…" Zoe closed her eyes. This couldn't be happening. "I think your body is dead."

There was a pause. *"Doing this – it killed me?"*

"No." Zoe sat down on the ground with a thud. With a sigh, she added, "I think doing this saved you."

Another pause. *"What are you talking about?"*

"Your consciousness must've left your body in the exact instant you died," she murmured. "I gave you consent to occupy my body, and since you didn't have a body to go back to, your consciousness did the only thing it could while still bound to this plane. It entered *my* body. I, on the other hand, had no body to switch with, so I also came back into mine."

"I can't be dead!"

Zoe's hand shook as her fingers gently closed Lena's eyes.

"What are you doing? If I go back to my body, I can reanimate it, right?"

"Neither the laws of Nature nor the Tenets of Magic will allow that." Zoe felt as if a tsunami hit her body.

"How can you be so calm about this?" Lena demanded.

"Calm is not how I'd describe my feelings right now," Zoe said hollowly. She laid back and stared at the ceiling. "We'll find a way to fix this," she said gently. "It's just gonna be a bit weird till we figure out how."

"A bit weird? I don't have a body! What am I going to do without a body?"

You might want to worry about what we're going to do if someone finds out this happened, Zoe thought. Now she felt a chill bouncing around inside of her.

"Zoe, are you--you're not gonna--I mean are you going to eject my consciousness?"

"What? No. Of course not. I wouldn't even know how. I'll think of something. For now, though..." Zoe sat back up. She put a hand on Lena's forehead, then gently stroked her hair. "I have to destroy all evidence of having done this spell. I have to, um. I'm gonna have to…" If she couldn't make herself say it, how could she possibly make herself do it? "I have to get rid of the corpse."

"Get rid of my body? No! You can't! There still may be a way to reanimate it! You just haven't found it! Maybe we could ask your fringe witch—"

"Absolutely not. Wing and I aren't close. If she finds out this went wrong, she'll report it, and I'll be lobotomized."

Zoe realized she had no way to move the body, and no place to put it if she did. After a few days it would start to smell, and the neighbors—

"Quit thinking about my body like it's garbage!" Lena demanded.

Shit. How can I have a private thought with someone in my head? thought Zoe.

"That's what you're worried about? I'm stuck in your body! I can't move! Oh GOD! When you have sex, I'll have to watch! I'll probably feel it!"

Zoe snorted. "That's what *you're* worried about?"

Lena stayed silent. Zoe remembered she had a tarp in her basement. If she could roll Lena's body onto it, she could slide it down the stairs. For now, she could haul it into the garage and put it in the trunk of her car.

"Zoe?"

"Yes?"

"How do you think I died? My headaches have been worse lately. Do you think it was a tumor?"

"I don't know. Didn't your mom die from an aneurysm? Could've been that."

"I guess it doesn't really matter, does it?"

Zoe had no answer.

She found the thick, gray tarp folded up on a shelf. She suppressed a shudder at the thought of wrapping an actual corpse in it. After taking it back to the attic, she spread it on the floor. Feeling inexplicably embarrassed, she bent and slid her arms under Lena's. With considerable effort, she dragged her onto the tarp. After covering her up, she took the bungie cords she'd brought along and wrapped them around the body.

I always wanted to tie her up, she thought. *How ironic.*

"Why would you want to tie me up?" Lena demanded.

Oh. Oh god.

"Wait a minute. The way you touched my hair... Oh my god. Oh my god *you have sex fantasies about me? How long have you thought about me like that? We're friends!"*

"Lena, look, it's not like I want to be attracted to a straight woman! I can't help who I—"

"That's why you wanted me to wear a French Maid costume. I thought you just wanted to humiliate me in hopes of talking me out of doing this. But it's

actually some twisted fantasy of yours, isn't it? Oh god. I feel sick."

"No, you don't," Zoe said coldly. "You can't feel sick without a body."

Hiding the hurt she felt from Lena's harsh reaction was difficult, but it helped that Lena was distracted by the horror of her words.

Zoe finally managed to maneuver Lena's body into the trunk of her car. She opened the padlock on her tiny shed and grabbed a shovel. She carefully laid it next to the tarped bundle.

The shock of Lena's death, not to mention her not-death, hadn't fully hit her yet. Grieving her would be weird, since she wasn't exactly dead. It was no wonder this kind of magic was forbidden by their laws.

"Would you prefer that my consciousness would've died, too?" There was no malice from her now, only fear.

"Of course not. This is just a little awkward and embarrassing. Not to mention disturbing."

"Awkward? Disturbing? I just watched you drag my body through your house and dump it in your car like it's a sack of laundry! And the tying me up thing—"

"Gods above!" Zoe shouted. Losing control of herself wasn't in her nature, but at the moment she didn't care if every neighbor on the block heard her yelling. "I'm sorry! What do you want me to do? Sign up for conversion therapy?"

"Stop it! You know that's not what I mean. I have a right to be freaked out right now! Stop trying to make this about you!"

Zoe slid down against the side of the car until she hit the ground. "I'm sorry. I wasn't trying to be disrespectful. But like it or not, this is about me, too. I may have gotten the better end of this situation, but my body has been *invaded.* And now I feel humiliated because of something I can't help. And I'm angry with myself for letting you talk me into doing this in the first place! And I'm angry at you for not going to the damn doctor for your headaches! And I might, in fact, actually be upset that you're dead!"

Tears of anger and frustration fell down Zoe's face, which made her feel even worse. As hard as she tried to stop, the tears kept flowing. She suspected Lena's feelings might be mixing with hers and contributing to her emotional meltdown. She wrapped her arms around her legs and buried her face against them. She gave up trying to stop crying and sobbed.

Finally, reality began sinking in and she stopped suddenly. With a deep breath, she whispered, "Um, look, you should think about where you want to be, um, buried. We gotta do that tomorrow night."

Lena didn't answer.

Zoe didn't expect her to.

* * *

The next morning, Zoe used a different door than usual to enter the office building. She wanted to avoid as many coworkers as possible, both hers and

Lena's. She had no idea who in this office could use magic and who could not. If someone sensed something was off, they'd turn her in for sure. Maybe she was being paranoid, but she felt like her body was screaming, *"Look at me! I got screwed over by Criminal Magic!"* Fortunately, although a few unfamiliar faces stared at her, no one spoke to her.

The first thing she did when she got to her desk was call Lena's supervisor.

"I'm afraid Lena won't be in to work today," she said. "She's very sick."

"That's one way of putting it," Lena said.

Zoe marveled that anyone could sound so bitter without making a literal sound.

Lena's boss asked what was wrong with her, and she wanted to know why Lena wasn't calling for herself. Zoe replied, "Oh. She can't get away from the toilet. She has *explosive* diarrhea. She was afraid you'd overhear it in the background."

"I hate you."

"I can live with that."

"I'm sorry, Miss Tillson, what did you say?" Lena's boss asked.

"Uh, pardon me. I was talking to… a coworker."

"I see. I will let her team know she won't be in today. Thank you for calling."

Zoe ended the call. She took a sip of coffee.

"I hate coffee," Lena muttered.

"You can taste it?"

"Yes. And I hate what you're wearing. It's too tight. How can you stand having your arms so constricted? Your shirt is entirely too small."

Zoe sighed. This sharing-a-body thing was going to be complicated. She had to figure out how to reverse this magic, and quickly.

Her phone rang, and she took her first phone call of the day.

Lena kept silent for most of the morning, except for her occasional comment about how nervous, terrified, or bored she was. Zoe was about to sign out and go to lunch when her phone rang.

"Let's just go eat! I'm hungry!" Lena exclaimed. *"I mean,* you're *hungry."*

"I have to take it," Zoe mumbled. "Nelson, Menendez and Matthews, how can I help you?"

"What the fuck is wrong with you people?" demanded an angry voice.

"I'm afraid you'll need to be more specific, sir."

"Don't get smart with me, lady. You idiots shipped me 4,000 promo books. I asked for 14,000!"

"What a dick! As if it's your fault?"

Zoe mentally shushed Lena. "Who's your sales representative?" she asked the irate customer.

"What does it matter? You're all a bunch of dumbasses!"

"You've got to be kidding me. You deal with this shit on a daily basis?"

Zoe took a deep breath. "Sir, if I know who placed your order, I can find out how to rectify the problem."

"Rectum? *Rectum?* Did you just call me an asshole?"

"Is this dickbag for real?"

"Lena! Stop!" Zoe thought. *"I can't think!"*

Returning her attention to the phone, she said, "Not at all, sir. I suggested you tell me who you were working with so we can rectify, meaning *fix*, the problem and get the additional promo books to you as quickly as possible."

"Oh, so now you think I'm stupid and don't know what 'rectify' means. Do you think you're better than me? Is that what's going on here? Cause you're the one who's stupid."

Zoe took a deep breath. She knew when she was wasting her time. Some people were more interested in picking fights than in getting their problems resolved.

"I'm going to put you through to my manager, so he can help—"

"Oh, so now you're passing me off to your manager? You think you're too good to help me? You got better things to do?"

Zoe reached for her phone's transfer button, but she lost control of her finger. She could hear words leaving her mouth, but they weren't hers.

"You listen here, asshole," Lena said through Zoe's mouth, in Zoe's voice. "And yes, this time I am, without a doubt, calling you an *asshole*. She – *I* – didn't mess up your order. *I* am trying to help you fix it. I have been extraordinarily patient, while you've insulted me, called me names, and put words in my mouth. If you're interested in having your problem solved, then you will tell me, now, who you worked with. I will connect you to that person so they can get you the rest of your books. Or, if you continue to harass me, I will contact our legal department. Every call is recorded, so they will know I've done nothing but try to help you and you've done nothing but harass me and make yourself look like an idiot. They will have our contractual obligation with you terminated, and you'll still be short 10,000 promo books. So think very, very carefully before you speak your next words."

A crowd had gathered around her cubicle. A couple guys gaped at her, and one woman smirked. Another woman laughed uncontrollably. Other onlookers were trying to figure out what was happening.

Lena stopped talking and relinquished control of Zoe's body.

"I'm working with Jaquil Bronson. I hope you've enjoyed having a job, little miss. Cause I'm gonna make sure you are fired by the end of the day. No one speaks to me like that!"

"I'll put you through," Zoe said, "and have a good day." She transferred the call and stared at the phone like it might bite her.

The small group of onlookers applauded.

"What the hell was that?" she demanded, voice squeaking.

"I couldn't let you just sit there and take that abuse! The guy was a complete bag of dicks!"

"What that *was* was inspired," said one of the guys by her desk.

"Hell, that was legendary!" said the laughing woman.

"You do know we don't have an actual legal department, right?" A woman in the rapidly assembling crowd pointed out. "And your claims have no legal merit."

Duh, Melody, Lena thought.

"We need to talk," Zoe hissed at Lena.

"What'd you say?" asked Melody.

"I'm well aware we don't have a legal department," Zoe responded. The woman moved her hands to her hips. "That guy isn't, though."

A few scattered snickers and laughs followed. Melody shrugged and walked toward the elevator.

"Wonder what she's doing up here?" Lena mused. *"She works in advertising."*

Zoe stood up. "Excuse me, I need to run an errand."

Her impromptu fan club returned to their own desks. Zoe marched to the closest restroom. She went in a stall and slammed the door.

"Don't *ever* do that again!"

"I'm sorry. I didn't even know I could take control. I just got so mad when he talked to you that way! Do customers normally treat you like that?"

"Don't change the subject! How dare you use my body without my permission!"

"Whose body am I supposed to use? Look, I said I'm sorry."

Zoe closed her eyes. God. Even in her head, Lena sounded mortified, and Zoe felt ashamed for snapping at her.

"I don't exactly have a lot of experience existing without a body," she added. *"I'd think you could give me a little leeway here."*

"I know you're dealing with a lot. But you can't just talk to people that way when you work in customer service! When that guy complains, and he will, I'll get fired for sure!"

"Did you say you know I'm 'dealing with a lot'? I died, *in case you've forgotten."*

"How could I forget? You're using my body!"

Zoe jumped when she heard a toilet flush. She'd been so distracted she hadn't realized she wasn't alone in the restroom. She sat perfectly still, listening to the *splurt* of the automatic soap dispenser, the splash of water in the sink, and the drawn-out *whoosh* of the automatic dryer. Zoe held her breath when the restroom's other occupant stopped outside the door of her stall.

"Don't let him use your body, honey. Have some self-respect."

Zoe didn't answer. The woman walked out, heels clacking dully against the linoleum floor. Zoe heard the door swish shut.

"Look, I'm still processing all this. I – we, whatever – need to grab some lunch and get back to work. Just in case I somehow still have a job."

Zoe went to the office's kitchen and pulled out the remains of her leftovers from the day before. She waited in line to use the microwave, then went back to her desk to eat. Her anger with Lena's impulsive reaction lessened a bit. After all, she'd done it because she didn't like how Zoe was being treated.

"I wasn't trying to be insensitive," she said softly before taking a bite of noodles and rice.

Lena didn't answer.

"Look, we'll get through this. I've decided to go back to Wing, okay? Hopefully she's heard of a situation like ours. I'll explain why we did it and hope she understands and doesn't report us."

"And if she doesn't understand, you'll get your brain blended up. And where does that leave me?"

Zoe choked on her noodles. "Gee, thanks for caring," she muttered.

She looked up to see Justin standing over her. He purposely blocked her exit from the cubicle. Cripes, she hadn't heard him over the background noise of the office.

"A rather strange conversation to be having with your noodles, don't you think?" he mused.

"Maybe stop talking out loud, before you get us committed. Can we take care of what we originally planned? Just in case I get a body back and it somehow matters?"

"Yes," Zoe answered silently.

"I'd like you to come with me, Miss Tillson," Justin said.

"I'll bet you would," Lena thought, irritated.

"I'm eating," Zoe responded.

"You can eat later. Come with me, please." He grabbed her upper arm and she jerked it away. He scowled at her.

"I can get up by myself, thanks," she snapped.

"You'll do what I tell you, and you'll do it immediately. You're in a heap of trouble." He smiled, showing a great many teeth. Zoe shivered.

"Be careful."

"I will."

"That's much better," Justin said.

"I wasn't talking to—"

Justin raised his eyebrows, still grinning like a malicious monkey.

"Let's just get this over with before my food gets cold."

Zoe stood up and squeezed around him. He put his hand on her lower back, guiding her to his office. She walked faster, trying to get away from his touch, but he followed her movements and kept his hand pressed against her.

"You weren't joking, were you? About him finding excuses to touch you?"

Zoe didn't answer. He led her into his office. While he turned to close the door, she slid the phone from her pocket and started the voice recorder.

"Please, have a seat."

"I'll stand, thanks."

"Suit yourself. Now," he said as he sat on the edge of his desk, "first things first. I got a complaint from a junior executive that you threatened a customer. A *big* customer, as it turns out."

Shit. Here it comes. Zoe bit down on her tongue.

"OW!" cried Lena in her mind.

"And what I mean by *big* customer," he continued, "is that he's far more important to the company than you are. And we have to be able to tell him we punished you for your disrespect, or we could lose the account."

"What a bunch of bullshit!"

She knew this was coming, but that made it no less infuriating.

"You need to listen to the recording." Zoe balled her hands into fists. "I had everything under control until—" Until Lena took over. She couldn't exactly say that. "I kept my cool. He's the one who escalated the situation."

"You called him an asshole!"

"He *is* an asshole!" Zoe exclaimed.

"He's a *rich* asshole. Johnson had to eat a lot of crow, and now he has to give him the extra promo books for free just to keep the account. It's costing him thousands of dollars. It's going to decrease his bonus. He's rather unhappy. I'd go so far as to say he's furious."

"Coddling rich assholes is his job," Zoe asserted.

Justin got off the desk and walked over to her. He stood close enough that she could smell his coffee breath, but she refused to give him the satisfaction of knowing he intimidated her. She didn't move.

"Coddling junior executives is yours, if you want to keep your job." He pressed his thumb to her chin. "If you know what I mean. Johnson is expecting you."

"Bite him!" Lena encouraged.

"I'm not going to *coddle* Johnson, or anyone else. Christ, he can't even sexually harass me himself? He had to make you do it for him?"

"You need to watch what you say," Justin said. He grabbed her chin, squeezing her jaw hard enough to bruise. His eyes narrowed as he growled, "It's not sexual harassment. It's *restitution*."

"Wooh! Now you've pushed his buttons!" Lena cheered.

Zoe pushed him backward by the shoulders and slipped out of his reach. "I've done nothing wrong. You can tell Johnson I think he's disgusting."

"Hm. Disappointing. Would've been fun to watch. In that case, I'm afraid I'll have to fire you."

"You're a miserable pig."

"Shit! Zoe, I'm sorry."

"Screw you, Lena," Zoe thought.

"You will clean out your desk and vacate the premises. Unless, of course, you can convince me to let you stay." He smiled in a way that was probably supposed to be sexy, but in reality made him look like a badly carved jack-o-lantern.

Zoe gaped at him. "Are you being serious right now? Get it through your thick skull. I'm not having sex with anyone to keep this job."

He approached her, backing her against the wall. A look of fury flashed through his eyes.

"Oh my god, Zoe. Get out of here before the miserable bastard tries to hurt you."

"Good plan," Zoe replied.

Zoe shoved Justin in the chest, but he caught her wrists.

"Is that so? We'll see. I like a challenge." He reached up and pulled the clip from her hair before she could pull away. Her hair fell around her shoulders.

"There. That's better."

"What a bastard," Lena commented with disgust. "*I should've known what an absolute dick he was. You knew. Why didn't you say something sooner?"*

"I'm leaving," she asserted, ignoring Lena. "And if you try to stop me, I'll scream."

He laughed. "Scream all you like. This office is soundproof."

"Oh, that's it! I'm sorry Zoe, but I'm handling this."

"You've got more experience dealing with him than I do. This time, you may use my body with my blessing."

Lena stomped on his foot with Zoe's boot, then stepped back and kicked him between the legs. He stumbled back a couple steps, but quickly regained his balance.

"Oh, you'll regret that, sweetheart."

He lunged at her. She curled her hand into a tight fist. Her fingernails broke skin as they dug into her palms. She took a swing, and the punch connected with his eye. This time when he stumbled, he fell to the ground.

Zoe took back control and ran. She stopped at her desk long enough to grab her keys and wallet. She felt her pocket where the phone was still recording. The elevator could take several minutes to arrive, so she fled down the stairs.

* * *

Once they reached the bus stop, Zoe inspected her sore knuckles.

"That was one hell of a punch," she commented.

"Thank you."

"Do you think he'll come after us?" From the corner of her eye, she watched a man walk toward the bus stop.

"I don't know. Just keep a lookout."

The man approached her and asked, "Hey, can you spare a dollar?"

"Where'd you learn to fight like that?" she asked Lena.

"I grew up in Chicago."

The man looked bewildered. "I'm not violent, ma'am, just hungry. Anything helps."

She barely noticed as he checked out her bruised knuckles and disheveled hair. Distractedly she opened her wallet and dug around for some bills. She didn't ever carry much cash, but she thought she'd stuffed a few folded-up dollars in one of the wallet's pockets a while back. "Where do you want to be buried?" Zoe asked softly.

The man took a couple steps back. "Ah, geez, you ain't got a phone. Who the hell you talkin' to?"

"I don't know. I – someplace nice, I guess. I just – I wish you weren't so anxious to get rid of my body."

"I can't drive around with your body in my car!"

The man backed up a few feet. "I was just asking for a dollar, no need to be like that. Sorry!"

Zoe finally located a couple of ones and held them out, but the man put his hands up in front of him.

"I'm, uh, I'm good. But thanks." He walked away from the bus stop, looking over his shoulder every few steps.

Zoe realized she'd been talking out loud and swore. Remembering to communicate with thoughts instead of spoken words was surprisingly difficult.

"Your body is dead, Lena. Rigor mortis will have already set in. Your heart doesn't beat anymore. Your lungs don't breathe. Don't you understand?"

"Understand. Understand? *Here's what I* understand. *I understand I just watched my boyfriend hit on you. I understand that I attacked him. I understand that I'm going to spend the rest of my life trapped in a body that I have no control over. I understand that I was supposed to die, but I didn't."*

Zoe was speechless. The bus pulled up and she got on.

* * *

"The forest. I want to be surrounded by trees," Lena said after a couple hours of silence.

Zoe flipped her grilled cheese sandwich in the pan, then opened the fridge and grabbed a bottle of water. "We'll just drive till we find a place."

Lena didn't appear to have heard her. *"Or you could just dump me in a river, I guess."*

"Lena—"

"No, wait, don't do that. I'll float to shore, and they'll do an autopsy to see why I died. I don't want to be cut up."

"Lena—"

"I want my body to be returned to nature. Plant a tree over me or something. Just bury me as deep as you can so nobody finds me and moves me."

"*Lena!* I'll put you someplace nice! Don't worry, okay?"

Zoe felt her incredulity as if it were her own.

She was going to need help if Lena wanted to be buried deeply in a forest. Digging a hole in ground that was full of tree roots would take a long time. If someone discovered her, she'd have a difficult time explaining what she was doing. Her first impulse was to call the one person she trusted enough to share something like this with. Unfortunately, that person wouldn't be answering their phone ever again.

Zoe's heart started pounding in response to Lena's sudden anxiety attack.

"I can't do this. I died. I'm dead, *Zoe. Dead. I have no future. No job. I can't make my own decisions. I've lost my privacy and free will. And I'm gonna have to* watch you bury me. *My sanity won't survive this, Zoe. Watching you dump me in your trunk was bad enough."*

"There's a way for us to separate. There has to be. We'll find it."

"And then what? I have no place to go! I knew you'd try to ditch me!"

Zoe groaned. "You know that's not what I mean! For now, you need to be able to protect your mind. Isolate it. So you can feel – I don't know – like an individual person."

An awful thought occurred to her. Could Lena still exist as an individual person? Was it just her consciousness in Zoe's body, or also her soul? Exactly how much of her had survived her own death?

She put her grilled cheese sandwich on a plate, downed the rest of her water, and went into the dining room. She eyed the two half-full bottles of cheap wine sitting in the center of the table. She grabbed the Moscato. This was a drink-straight-from-the-bottle kind of night.

As she unscrewed the lid, Lena said, *"You can't drink yet."*

"Pretty sure I can. I wonder if you'll get drunk, too?"

"No. I just remembered. Molly and Sponge. I have to get home."

Zoe sat the bottle down and swore. "Oh my god. I didn't even think about your cats."

"We need to bring them here."

"Uh, no we don't," Zoe said. "You know I hate cats!"

"You're a witch! How can you hate cats?"

"Are you serious? Not every witch loves cats! Should I wear a long black dress, too? Carry a magic wand?" She took a bite of her grilled cheese. Over a mouthful of sandwich, she asked, "Would you like to see my broom? Oh! Oh! Better yet! My pointy black hat?"

When Lena didn't answer, Zoe sighed and put her food down. "When I'm done eating, we'll go feed your cats."

* * *

Zoe searched for the correct key as rain fell on her. By the time she unlocked the door to Lena's house, her hair was soaked.

Molly, a gray and black tabby, stood at the door hissing. Sponge, a white cat with black splotches, padded cautiously across the hardwood floor to see what was happening.

"They know," Lena said.

Sponge growled, low and throaty, keeping her distance. Meanwhile, Molly wove in and out of Zoe's legs as she walked to the cupboard.

"Don't worry, sweet baby girls," Lena thought.

"Give me a break," mumbled Zoe.

"Put a can of the turkey flavor in the blue bowl for Sponge, and a chicken-flavored one in the pink bowl with a white stripe around it for Molly. Then take some of the dry food, crumble it up, and sprinkle it on top. Sponge likes to eat by the window, so—"

"Are you serious?" Zoe interrupted. Great stars, she hated cats Especially *spoiled* ones.

"I can't do it myself."

Zoe sighed and followed Lena's instructions, grumbling the entire time. Molly kept weaving in and out of Zoe's feet, until she stumbled and practically fell.

"Damned cat!"

After the cats were fed, Lena said, "*Okay, now you need to clean their litter boxes.*"

Zoe laughed. "Um, no. I draw the line at litter boxes. They have food. They have water. They'll be fine."

"They'll crap on the floor. You have to do it."

"Forget it. We're getting out of here."

"Zoe?"

She took a breath. "Yes?"

"I want you to bring the cats. Please. I need someone there for me when it happens."

"Uh, I'm gonna be there."

"I know. But you're going to be burying me. This is kind of personal, okay?"

"Personal," Zoe repeated in a flat voice. "Personal, unlike having to bury someone I care for? Having to bury a friend who isn't actually dead?"

Lena didn't answer.

Zoe gathered up the cats (gritting her teeth when Sponge bit her) and placed the protesting animals on the back seat of her car.

"They better not crap back there," she said.

She drove through the rain for almost two hours. She had no preplanned destination. She decided she'd know a good place when she saw one. When they came upon an isolated country road, Zoe turned off the highway.

"Where are you going?"

"Hopefully someplace extremely secluded."

"What if you forget where you left my body?"

"It doesn't matter! Don't you get it!?"

The black and white cat, Sponge, hopped up to the front and rubbed his cold, wet nose against her arm.

"Gross!" Zoe wiped the spot with her hand as she slowed down the car. "I see a little bridge up there. Looks like that road will take us to that grove of trees. See it?"

Lena didn't answer.

Zoe sighed. "Well, I think that's our spot."

Once she crossed the bridge, she left the gravel road and turned into the trees. Twigs scraped the doors, and mud splattered against the windshield. She couldn't risk going too far and getting stuck or blowing a tire, but the deeper she drove into the woods, the safer Lena's grave would be. When she felt she couldn't safely go on, she stopped and turned off the engine. At least the rain had died down.

Zoe wasn't physically strong, so dragging the body wouldn't be easy. As dark as it was with the moon shrouded by clouds, getting lost was a danger if she strayed too far from her car. She decided to pick out a spot and dig the hole before she got the body out of her trunk.

"How can you be so calm about this? Do you bury people often?"

When Zoe didn't respond, Lena asked, *"What if something happens and I get kicked out of you and end up in my dead body? What if I wake up buried in the dirt? In a body I can't move?"*

"I told you before. You won't."

"But how do you know?"

"Think about it! I couldn't go into your body after you died. And you didn't go back, you came into *my* body."

"What if I never have a place to go? What if you're stuck with me? What if your only choice to get rid of me is to kill me?"

"Look," she answered, irritated. "If we're forced to live like this, then we'll figure out how to make it work, together. How many times are you gonna ask? Let's take one thing at a time. Let's get this the hell over with."

Zoe took her shovel out of the trunk. She found a site that had trees on three sides and punched a hole into the wet earth. The tree roots were deeper than she expected, so digging wasn't as difficult as it could've been. After digging for what seemed like hours, she had a hole deep enough and long enough to hold the body.

"Thank god you're so grossly skinny," she mumbled.

"Didn't seem to bother you when you were having fantasies about me," she pointed out.

"I imagined you were fat."

"Unbelievable. I had no idea you were such a jerk!"

"It's a recent personality development."

Zoe plodded back to the car. A shiver ran through her as she stared at the wrapped-up lump that was Lena's body. She was alone in the dark, in the middle of nowhere, with the dead body of her friend.

She felt like someone was watching her. Anyone could be out wandering around. She didn't know whose land she was on, and they could've seen the headlights or heard the tires bouncing over the grated metal bridge and come to investigate. Zoe looked over her shoulder, certain something moved behind her.

"Who's there?" she called out.

"You're being paranoid," Lena said.

"Maybe."

She wrestled Lena's body from the trunk and dragged it to the near end of the open grave. The tarp loosened, and some of Lana's hair slid out.

"Zoe! Put it back!"

Through gritted teeth Zoe answered, "It's just hair."

"FIX IT!"

Zoe found it amazing that a voice in her head could be so *loud*. She lowered the body to the ground. Kneeling by the head, she tucked the hair back inside the tarp. She shook her hand in revulsion before she could stop herself. She should've thought to bring gloves. And something to cover her nose, since the tarp didn't contain the smell of rot and decay emanating from the corpse.

Zoe decided to pull the body around to the left side of the grave and roll it into the hole. She took a couple deep breaths of cool, humid air through her mouth. She stood from her squatting position and lifted the end of the stiff body. She took a deep breath and rested its head over her shoulder. Her hands slid underneath, and she pushed the body upright as she straightened her knees and stood.

A twig snapped in front of her. Zoe swore as she stood up on her tiptoes to see if she was being watched by a person or an animal. Her right foot slid in the mud, and she lost her balance. Her left ankle twisted and gave out. Instinctively reaching for something to hold onto, her arms wrapped around the top of Lena's body. As she fell backwards, the tarped corpse fell with her. It landed directly on top of her, pinning her to the dirt in the bottom of the grave.

Zoe lay frozen in shock for a few seconds. Lena's hair slid from the tarp again and fell into Zoe's mouth. She gagged and spit as she turned her head. Her heart thumped wildly against her ribcage as she struggled to move under the unyielding bundle.

Inside her head, Lena laughed.

"Seriously!? Exactly what about this situation is funny?"

"I'm just thinking the tables have turned. It's not much fun to be trapped, is it?"

"You do realize, don't you, that if I'm trapped down here, so are you?"

Lena didn't answer.

Zoe's arms were still wrapped around Lena's body. Trying to hide her revulsion, she slid one hand down to the floor of the grave. With all her strength, she tried to push herself onto her side. But Lena's tarp-wrapped legs lay between Zoe's bent ones, and she couldn't free herself below the waist.

"Guess you didn't make the grave long enough," Lena commented.

Zoe wondered how she could've ever had feelings for this woman.

In the suffocating darkness of the forest, the clouds opened up. Water began to pour from the sky.

"We're going to drown!" Lena's shout echoed inside her head as if she'd screamed out loud.

"No, we're not," Zoe snapped.

Lena took control of Zoe's voice. "HEELLP!" she screamed. "Oh god, someone please help us!"

Zoe wrestled back control. "Will you stop it!? We are in the middle of nowhere! No one can hear you except wild animals! Do you want wolves finding us?"

The cold rain came down harder, battering Zoe's face and making it difficult to think. She refused to drown in a muddy grave under a damn corpse. She had to find a way to get out.

She bent her right arm and slid her hand in next to Lena's shoulder. After practically dislocating her wrist, she got her fingers beneath it. She bent her right leg back as far as she could and pushed her toes under Lena's legs, just above her knees.

Zoe felt tears running down her face as Lena sobbed.

"Stop feeling sorry for yourself!" she shouted. She pushed as hard as she could and managed to get partway out from beneath the body. With more room to move, not to mention an arm and a leg free, wiggling herself completely free went quickly. Zoe put her hands at the top of the grave, about four or five feet up. She lifted her knee straight up and used the other to try and hop out. She could only get waist high. She looked down at Lena's body.

"Oh don't you dare. DON'T YOU DARE!"

Taking a breath, she stepped onto Lena's corpse's back. It gave her enough height to lean forward out of the hole. She placed her palms on the ground, pushed herself up, and climbed out of the grave. After what seemed like an eternity, she was free.

Lena moved Zoe's eyes to look down at the body. Zoe couldn't stop her. Her heart beat furiously with Lena's panic.

"You can't leave me like that! I can't stay down there!"

Zoe felt Lena try to take control of her legs. With shaking hands, she started pushing mud into the grave.

"You at least need to cover me with something!"

"You're already in a tarp! Those are expensive, by the way."

"You should've brought a sheet!"

"I'm so sorry," Zoe said sarcastically. "It's my first time burying a body, and I haven't developed a good technique yet!"

After a moment, Lena said, "*We need to take my cats to my sister's house. You can ask her to keep them for a few days. Tell her I'm too sick to care for them.*"

"You and your damned cats," Zoe muttered. She was currently more concerned with the obvious depression the filled-in grave left in the ground. How likely was it that someone would wander back here and notice?

Zoe looked up and saw headlights coming down the road.

"Uh, Zoe?"

"I see it! Shut up!"

"You're the one making noise. I'm in your head."

Zoe held her breath as the truck passed by. It was driving too fast to have seen her parked car, and the rain and darkness disguised them further.

She gathered some brush from nearby and covered the grave until it blended in with the rest of the groundcover.

"You're not going to mark my grave, are you?"

"You know why I can't."

"Fine. Let's get out of here before I—"

"Before you what?"

"Before I take over this body and dig myself back up!"

Zoe rolled her eyes as she grabbed her shovel and tossed it in the trunk. As soon as she sat down in the driver's seat, Molly crawled into her lap.

"Sweet baby girl," said Lena.

Zoe grabbed the cat and tossed it onto the passenger seat.

"Did you just throw my cat?" Lena cried.

"I had to move her! What if she hopped down by the pedals? Do you want to die in a car accident because there's a cat under my feet and I can't use the brakes?"

Lena remained silent, and Zoe realized what she'd just said. With a sigh, she drove back to the highway.

* * *

Lena gave her directions to her sister's house. Neither of them spoke until they arrived. As she pulled the car into Theresa's driveway, Zoe sensed Lena's feelings toward her brother-in-law.

"Oh my god," Zoe said, shuddering. "You have romantic feelings for your own brother-in-law?"

"Shut up! It's none of your business!"

"Oh my *god*!" she exclaimed as her eyes grew wide. "You've *slept with him*?"

"Not since before Justin! And how could you possibly know that?"

"I don't know! Maybe because you're thinking about it? In vivid color. Gross. I can never unsee that."

"Can we please just get this over with?"

Zoe got out of the car and awkwardly knocked on the door. She had scooped up one cat in each hand, and they were each trying desperately to escape. Lena's brother-in-law answered. His eyebrow shot up when he saw the cats.

"Hi, I'm Lena's… neighbor. She asked me to bring her cats to you."

"Is she okay?" he asked.

"Yes. No. She will be." She handed off the cats, which he reluctantly took and immediately dropped on the floor.

"You ass!" Lena exclaimed in Zoe's head.

"She's sick right now," Zoe told him. "She's too sick to take care of them."

"Is she in the hospital?" Theresa asked, joining her husband at the door.

"Uh, no. She' s not *that* sick. She just needs someone to take care of them for a little while. That's why she asked me to bring them."

The brother-in-law crossed his arms. "Why don't you take them?"

"Because I hate cats!" Zoe blurted.

"Is she too sick to answer the phone? I haven't been able to reach her for a couple days, and that's not normal."

Normal is a concept that no longer belongs to this Universe, lady, Zoe thought, but managed not to say. Instead, she said, "She was probably sleeping. Or maybe she lost her phone?"

Theresa put her hands on her hips. "Then how did she get a hold of you?"

"Give it a rest," thought Lena.

"Maybe the battery went dead after she called me." Zoe was getting nervous. Why were they giving her the third degree?

"Maybe because you're a muddy, wet disaster?"

"Look, uh, I'm taking care of her. I'll have her call you from my phone, okay?"

Lena's brother-in-law stared at her. Zoe was sure he could see right through them.

"She knows how I feel about cats." Disappointment radiated from Theresa, and she obviously expected a reply.

Zoe caught sight of a dog asleep on the couch. "She said to tell you she'll repay the favor by dog-sitting."

"Ugh, you have no idea what you're offering!"

"Does it matter right now?" Zoe mumbled under her breath.

"Sorry, I missed that," said the brother-in-law.

"Oh, uh, nothing." She smiled.

"Eventually they're going to report me missing, and someone is gonna figure out that the last place I went before I died was your place."

"Helpful," mumbled Lena.

"I guess we can take care of them until she feels better," said the brother-in-law, giving Zoe's body a predatory look that made her extremely uneasy.

"Thank you. She has been very worried about her—"

"Say 'sweet baby girls!'" Lena insisted.

"—her sweet baby girls."

Lena's sister rolled her eyes. "She has an unnatural attachment to those cats."

"You can say that again," Zoe agreed.

"Shut up!"

"You shut up," she mumbled.

The couple looked at her like she'd grown a second head.

"What did you say your name was?" Lena's brother-in-law asked.

"Uh, Justine."

"Right. Well, thank you… Justine." Theresa tilted her head and studied her.

"You're welcome." Zoe turned and hurried back to her car.

"So now what?" Lena asked as they pulled onto the road.

"We go back to Wing," she said.

"Are you sure you want to do that? If you do, we need a weapon."

"Are you insane?" Zoe asked. "We're not using a weapon on Wing! Listen. We're going to have to disappear after this if she can't or won't help us. Maybe even if she *can* help us."

"What does that mean? Disappear?"

Zoe didn't answer, but she could tell Lena got the message.

* * *

The next morning, having cleaned up and packed some necessities, they drove to Wing's place. Zoe knocked on her door and called, "Wing! Wing! Are you home?"

After a very long couple of minutes, she opened the door. As she stared at Zoe, her expression changed from mildly annoyed to possibly homicidal. She obviously knew Zoe was not alone in her body.

"You idiot!" she snapped. "You're both *idiots*!"

"How does she know?" Lena asked.

"Look, we had a good reason for what we did!" Zoe told her.

"Everyone says that to defend their crimes!" Wing responded.

She felt like she'd been slapped in the face.

"I told you I washed my hands of you!" Wing growled. "Do you have any idea what you've done?"

"Yes, we're pretty sure we get it! Please. You're the only one I know who can help us."

Wing snorted. “Help you? What do you expect me to do? I’m assuming her body died while you were switching, and that’s how you found yourselves in this predicament?”

“Yes. How did you know?”

She put her hands on her hips and shook her head. “Oh, you are *so* screwed.”

“What’s going to happen to me?” Lena demanded with Zoe’s voice.

Wing blinked and looked at them. “Zoe? Was that you?” she asked.

“No, that was Lena,” she answered. She was growing more impatient and frightened by the minute.

“Did you allow her to use your voice, Zoe? Did you specifically give her permission?”

Zoe was startled to realize she hadn’t. “No, why?”

“Has she taken control of you before?”

“I don’t know.”

“Have you?” Zoe asked, but Lena didn’t answer.

Wing sighed. “Damn you both,” she muttered. She glared at Zoe. “When your body dies, your spirit will move on to the afterlife. Lena’s, however, will not. Her consciousness will be trapped.” Wing shook her head. “You interfered with a natural process. She was fated to die. No part of her should still be here, in any form.”

"Can you help us?" Zoe asked. She kept her voice soft, but she'd been irritated to begin with, and she really didn't feel like being lectured.

Lena took control of her vocal cords. "If we could send Zoe to the spiritual plane instead of me, would I be able to exist alone in her body?"

"What?" Zoe exclaimed.

Wing tilted her head. "It could probably be done," she acknowledged. "But that would be another violation of nature." She rubbed her chin with one finger and squinted at the collection of crystals on her table.

"Wait a minute. You can't actually be considering it!?" Zoe exclaimed.

"You are the one who performed the magic," Wing pointed out. "It's not actually Lena's fault that it failed."

"But it was her idea to do the magic in the first place!"

"You should have been responsible and refused!" Wing exclaimed. "You are, technically, the one who is at fault."

"It's not my *fault* she died!"

"Are you sure?"

Zoe drew in a sharp breath.

"Whether it's your fault or not, you interfered with nature's plan. You knowingly cast Criminal magic, despite your sacred vows to do no harm. Despite your vows to honor nature. The punishment for such willful disobedience is severe."

"*You* knew I was planning it. You didn't try to stop me. In fact, you sold me the supplies," Zoe accused. "You're an accomplice. You didn't 'refuse' to take my money!"

"This isn't helping!" Lena said, taking control once again. "Let's get on with it. You need a bit of blood to send her to the spiritual plane, right?"

"You're not stealing my body!" Zoe shouted furiously. "After all that begging me not to get rid of your consciousness, now you're trying to do the same thing to me?"

"Survival of the fittest." She shrugged Zoe's shoulders.

"You didn't survive!"

Lena fought her and turned to Wing. She wrenched Zoe's hand out toward her. "Take the blood, but make it a small cut. This body has enough scars already."

Zoe turned to the door and ran, but when she got to the door, Wing body slammed her against it. "Our choices here," she said in Zoe's ear, "are having you lobotomized, in which case Lena is punished for something that isn't her fault. Or we send you to the spiritual plane and allow Lena to live out your – her – natural life, but in your body."

"You hypocrite! How does *that* not violate the laws of nature? You cannot be my judge and jury," Zoe shrieked as she struggled to free herself.

"Unfortunately, you were right. I helped facilitate your little spell. I, too, would be punished for your failure."

"*I* will never tell anyone," Lena broke through to say. "I wouldn't even know who to tell. I will leave here and disappear forever."

"Lena, do you think you can hold her here for several moments while I get ready?"

"No, but I think I could hold her long enough for you to restrain her."

"You definitely cannot," hissed Zoe.

"Alright. I have duct tape around here somewhere." Wing left the room.

Zoe fought, but Lena managed to move Zoe's legs enough to maneuver her to a kitchen chair. Zoe felt like she was a zombie, alive but not.

She realized, almost as an afterthought, that Lena was still focused on controlling her legs. An idea took form in her mind, although it wasn't a pleasant one. Before Lena could notice what was happening, Zoe regained control of her arms. Gathering her nerve, she told herself she'd be doing this to Lena, not herself. Squeezing her eyes shut, she pounded her fist into the front of her neck with all her strength.

Lena, stunned by both the loss of control and the pain, fell to the floor. She coughed and drew deep breaths but couldn't get any air. For a moment Zoe thought she crushed her own airway. Lena pushed herself up, gasping and wheezing. She grabbed Zoe's throat. Zoe struggled to catch her breath, but she was dizzy.

Wing came back and put her supplies on the table.

"I didn't have duct tape, but I found some rope." She turned, swearing when she saw Lena on the ground. "You'll have to do better than that," she said with disgust. "Sit down and put her arms behind the chair."

Lena pushed Zoe's consciousness away like she was a speck of dust in the wind. She was learning quickly how to gain control. Zoe wondered if she'd been hiding the strength of her ability to take over, waiting for an opportunity to take over her body permanently.

As furious as she was, the thought hurt.

"Lena?" Wing asked.

"Hurry up! I don't know how long I can hold her."

Zoe scrambled to her feet, struggling to control her body. She looked like the toy of a drunk puppeteer. As she stood up straight, she nearly lost her balance from lingering dizziness. She turned toward the door and walked straight into Wing, who held up the rope and smiled. She wrestled Zoe to the ground. Although Wing was smaller, Zoe couldn't fight her and Lena at the same time. Wing grabbed her hair and smacked her forehead on the kitchen's ceramic tile floor. Zoe, stunned, lay motionless as Wing tied her wrists behind her back.

Zoe was barely aware of Wing making a cut on her palm. Something with a smooth, cool edge pressed against her hand (*a ceramic spoon, probably,* she thought). Wing was probably collecting the drops of her blood.

"Gross!"

Lena turned their head and watched Wing drip the blood into the puddle of liquid accumulating around the candle wick.

"First, I'll try to put a barrier between your two consciousnesses."

Wing opened a large, black book with gold gilded letters. Zoe couldn't read the title.

"I thought you said we couldn't be separated," Zoe said, using her fury to take control.

"I can sense where one of you ends and the other begins. You're very different." She scowled at them. "This is not a quick and easy spell. Lena, you must take control and keep it. I will surround your consciousness with light and energy that will tether it to this body. You must be inside that bubble when I close it. Energy outside of it will be sent to the spiritual plane."

They can't do it without my consent, Zoe thought. *And they can't force me to consent.*

Zoe braced herself as Wing performed the beginning of her spell. Zoe couldn't move. She watched her own body grow smaller as she floated above and away from it.

The last thing Zoe heard on the earthly plane was Lena's euphoric whoop and Wing's sigh of relief.

* * *

The familiar blue that made up the spiritual plane wrapped around her. From every direction, she heard, *"If you grant consent for this consciousness to occupy your body, do so now."*

"I consent," someone said.

"What!? That wasn't me!" Zoe screamed. *"And I do NOT consent! She's an imposter!"* Blue waves closed in, squeezing her, hurting her, enveloping her, and then there was nothing.

* * *

When Zoe opened her eyes, she found herself looking at an incorporeal being made up of every imaginable shade of green. The colors within it fluctuated. It glowed with an inner light. Other than the vague shape in front of her, she was surrounded by pure blackness.

She'd been returned to her own body… and she was alone inside of it.

"Where am I?"

"Someplace a human should never, ever be." The being had no face, or mouth, and Zoe realized she was receiving its communication telepathically.

"Then why am I here?"

The entity shrunk itself and hovered in front of Zoe. "Lena tried to steal your body and occupy it.

This cannot be allowed. It is abhorrent to nature. Her crime is unforgivable."

"Lena's gone. I don't feel her." Zoe realized she was floating too.

"No."

"What's happened to her?"

"She has been returned to her own body."

"But her body is dead and buried!"

"Yes. It should've been impossible for her consciousness to go into your body after her own body died. It should've moved on to the spiritual plane."

"Then why doesn't she go there now? Will her consciousness ever be released from her corpse?" Panic rose inside of her. Despite everything, Lena didn't deserve such a fate.

"No. There is nowhere for her to go. Her consciousness should've been released from this plane at the time of her death. Instead, it became tethered to you. It no longer has a place in the natural order. It must be contained, away from the living world, and the only container that exists is her body. Because she has no magic, there are no other options."

"What about Wing?" she asked. Her throat was so dry, she thought it might crack open.

"Wing will be judged and punished by her Coven as they see fit."

"What does that mean?"

"Don't worry about her. Worry about yourself. You have committed Criminal Magic."

Zoe felt numb. "Yes. I admit it. And you cannot imagine how sorry I am. But I never intended for anyone to be harmed. I was trying to help someone avoid a potentially dangerous situation."

"Nature knows your intentions were pure. Your compassion is noted. But you cannot be permitted to perform such an action again."

"I won't! I swear!"

"Good intentions are quickly forgotten."

Zoe felt a presence inside her head, like when Lena occupied it, but a billion times stronger. She felt like water was trickling down the inside of her skull. She wondered absurdly if her brain was melting. She watched a steady flow of light blue beams rushing from her chest.

"I feel empty. Why does my mind feel empty? What have you done to me?" she whispered.

"The only thing we can to ensure you don't commit this crime again. You refer to the procedure as a 'magical lobotomy.'"

DAY TERRORS

Warm sunlight spilled through the curtains onto my face. My chest heaved as I sat up, gasping for breath. Sweat poured down my forehead. Opening my eyes, I looked around at the safe, familiar haven of my bedroom. Aside from my ragged breathing, the room was quiet and still.

I reached toward the little mahogany nightstand on my side of the bed. My eyes were still sleep-blurred, and my half-drank glass of water crashed to the carpet before my fingers found my phone. The screen showed 8:21 a.m. I begged my body to get up and put a towel down on the wet carpet, but the soft pillows were simply too inviting to ignore. Lying down on my side, I closed my eyes and tried to shed the lingering memories of my ghastly nightmare.

The shadowy, faceless people wandering around in my subconscious mind goaded me into running for President. My great leadership bid was intended to be a prank, but to my horror (and their giddy excitement), I rapidly became the most popular candidate. I panicked. Presidents got shot. Presidents got assassinated.

I yawned as a pair of large, warm feet entwined with mine at the end of the bed. The person-shaped mound of warm blankets and pillows snuggled up behind me made no other movement.

From the kitchen down the hall came the voice of our son, Austin. “Get down the plates,” he ordered.

I heard a cupboard door slam shut. “I got ‘em,” came the enthusiastic reply from our daughter, Lily.

I smiled with one corner of my mouth. They were finally old enough to fix their own breakfast. It was one thing they managed to do together willingly, without violence, and without dragging Kevin and I out of bed.

My half-asleep husband lifted the blanket over me and pressed his body against my back. I pulled one foot away from our tangled limbs and ran my big toe playfully along his leg. He quickly recaptured my foot; even half asleep he was outrageously ticklish. I was too tired for a full-on tickle war, since the damned night terrors sapped my energy. Wiggling my foot back into a comfortable position, I nestled deeper into the soft cotton sheets and closed my eyes.

My smile faded when images from the nightmare flashed in front of me.

I was preparing to campaign for my unwanted presidency – in France, because dreams aren’t logical. I stood in a room in a conference center, facing a wall that was covered with mirrors. The room's other three walls were white. A tiny white table stood in front of me. On it sat a glass bowl filled with shiny red apples.

My campaign assistants were splotches of wavering air on either side of me. They advised me to throw the apples at my enemies. In the mirrored wall in front of me, I saw the reflection of thousands of apples pouring into the room through the doorway.

My own reflection was absent from the mirror.

"You see?" said a cheerful voice. "You're protected."

I didn't feel protected. I felt like lightning was about to strike, and I had nowhere to take shelter. The hair on my arms stood up as I looked for the silent, invisible enemies I knew were hiding in the room.

"You must eat the apples," instructed a deep, male voice, in a tone that left no room for argument.

A whispered "shhh" brought me back to reality. My heart *thump – thump – thumped* in my chest as adrenaline coursed through me. My taut muscles were like rocks under my skin.

In the kitchen the refrigerator door slammed shut hard enough to rattle its contents. I jumped.

"I don't want milk! I want juice!" cried my daughter.

"Then get it yourself," Austin snapped. "I was trying to be nice."

I took a deep breath and sighed. At least they'd gotten along for a little while. Soon we'd have to get up and face the day, but I wanted to put off adulting for a little while longer. Apparently, Kevin did, too. Normally he got out of bed long before I did.

My conscious mind continued to process the dream.

Apples continued to flow into the room. A woman emerged from beneath a five-foot-high pile of fruit. She looked like a time lapse video of a plant growing. Her olive-green tank top and black jeans contrasted surreally with the apples and the white walls. She had no face, but I could feel her nonexistent eyes boring into me.

Dozens of apples rolled toward my feet. They grew larger as they got closer.
Several people wearing camouflage uniforms and carrying rifles barged through double doors on the other side of the room. Their rifles fired apples

instead of bullets. None of the vigilantes spoke. Their leader had long, fire-red hair swirling around her shoulders. She chewed gum with a nasty smacking sound as she positioned her weapon against her shoulder and aimed at me. The woman standing in the ever-growing mountain of apples laughed.

Another "shhh" brushed my ear. The warm, whispered breath made my skin tingle. I wiggled away, scrunching up my shoulder. I was glad for Kevin's solid presence, but the irrational terror from the dream still held me in its grip.

"Morning, Kev," I said, forcing myself to sound cheery. "Are you feeling okay? You never sleep this late."

"Hmm." His fingers gently moved the long hair off my shoulder. Warm lips brushed against my neck, teeth gently grazing the skin. His arm wrapped back around my waist like an iron band.

So *that's* why he'd stayed in bed.

The sweet smell of pancakes and bacon drifted through the doorway. My stomach rolled. Between hunger and tension, I felt nauseous.

I scrunched up my shoulder and moved away. "Baby, I can't right now. There's too much on my mind, and I'm starving. Rain check?"

Maybe the last vestiges of my nightmare would disappear once I got up and started going about my day. I really needed to get out of bed. He backed off but said nothing. As I moved to sit up, I felt legs tighten around my ankles. He pulled the heavy comforter over the top of both our heads, blocking out the sunlight from the window. His arms once again pulled me tight against his body. Still, he said nothing. After a moment, he began snoring, and his hold on me loosened. Maybe he just wanted us to get a little more rest.

Pancakes could wait a few minutes, I supposed. Hopefully, the kids wouldn't eat them all before we got up.

From down the hall, I heard my daughter ask, "Could you please pass the apples?" A plate clanked as it was picked up off the table and passed to my daughter. “Thanks, Daddy!”

“You’re welcome,” replied my husband.

THE PRESENTATION

Sidney Wallace, through no fault of his own, arrived at the office late for the second time in five days. He told his boss, Wilshire, about the gruesome accident on the freeway that stalled his commute for forty-five minutes.

"I don't want to hear your excuses!" the furious man shouted. "I don't care if Einstein came back from the dead, stood in the middle of the Interstate, and handed out IQ points! If your sorry excuse for an ass is late one more time, you're fired!"

After stalking to his desk, Sidney dropped heavily into his uncomfortable chair. A long, demanding day loomed ahead of him. The blood-red numbers on his digital clock already showed 8:47 A.M. He had only six hours until he made his presentation to the Board of Directors.

Unwittingly, he flashed back to the twisted mess of metal and blood splattered across I-35. He'd narrowly avoided adding to the multiple-car pileup. When the tiny red Corvette ahead of him slammed on the brakes, he'd swerved out of the way. The driver of the black Ferrari he cut off laid on his horn as he veered into the next lane and blew past Sidney. The tiny red Corvette slid under a flatbed trailer.

Sidney sighed. He needed to put the horrible accident out of his mind and focus on work. If he couldn't dazzle the Board and prove his worth to the company, Wilshire was likely to fire him. He'd already warned Sidney several times about his "substandard productivity and lack of motivation."

Wilshire was a jerk.

Sidney pulled the flash drive containing his presentation out of his pocket and plugged it into the computer. As he reached for the keyboard so he could log on, his large, overly clumsy hand knocked over a nearby Styrofoam cup. The remains of yesterday's coffee flowed across the desk, soaking papers, pens, his mouse, his keys, and the only printed draft of his presentation. The cold, brown liquid finally rushed into his lap and soaked the crotch of his pants.

Yelping in surprise, he jerked his legs back. In the process, he banged his knee on the side of his desk. The cup couldn't possibly have held the volume of coffee that poured out of it. Frantically, he shoved his papers out of the way, but it was too late. He dried off his desk, then threw the ruined pages and soggy tissues toward the garbage. The already-overflowing can's precarious tower of slimy banana peels, half-empty cans of soda, wadded-up piles of paper, and other detritus toppled to the carpet.

"You've got to be kidding me," he snarled. "I can't do this right now!" He reached down to pick up the trash and stuff it back into the can. As he leaned down, the seam at the back of his pants gave way with a loud *RRRRIIIPPPPPP*.

Great. Now what was he supposed to do? He couldn't deliver his presentation to the Directors with a giant hole in the seat of his pants.

Don't panic, he told himself. He opened the top drawer of his desk and reached inside. Maybe he could find something he could use to fix the torn fabric. As he rummaged through his supplies, his fingers plunged into a large, sticky wad of gum. What in the world was gum doing there? He never chewed gum. *Gross*.

He wiped the offensive glob against the edge of his desk with a shudder. With a sudden, frantic spark of inspiration, he grabbed his stapler, bent over at the waist, reached around himself, and awkwardly stapled the torn fabric of his pants back together. It was a pathetic but effective solution.

Now, finally, he could stop wasting time and get to work. He needed to go over his presentation, so he didn't look like a blithering idiot in front of the Directors. Thanks to the coffee debacle, he had to print out another copy.

At the login prompt, he typed "1GudGolfer". An error message beeped loudly on the screen, announcing that his password was invalid. He entered it again, slowly. A computerized voice angrily shouted that it was still invalid.

Sidney marveled that a computer could sound angry, then decided he was imagining things. Witnessing that accident must've stressed him out more than he realized.

Grinding his teeth, he dialed the Information Technology department. A sweet, automated female voice thanked him for his patience. She informed him that all technicians were busy, but if he would please leave his name, extension, department, supervisor's name, supervisor's extension, zodiac sign, date of birth, height, weight, the last four digits of his social security number, and a brief description of the problem, someone would get back to him as soon as possible.

Fuming, Sidney closed his eyes and said, "This is Sid Wallace. My extension is 437. My password isn't working. It's giving me an invalid password error message. Call me ASAP. This is urgent."

The automated voice instructed him to begin recording his message at the tone.

Biting his lip hard enough to draw blood, he repeated the message and hung up. Looking at his computer screen, he muttered, "I don't even know my zodiac sign."

The phone rang. Scowling, he answered.

"Wallace."

"Hey, Waldorf. This is Ted from I.T. I understand you're having some trouble figuring out how to use your password," he said in a bored, condescending voice. "Have you tried retyping your password?"

Was this idiot kidding? Sidney bit down on his tongue to keep from calling Ted a variety of colorful, unflattering names. He needed his help and doling out insults wouldn't help.

A warm trickle of blood on his tongue and a rapidly swelling lip did nothing to improve his mood.

"Yes. I've retyped it."

"Retype it again."

Marveling at his own patience, he tried again. "Okay, Ted. I retyped it. Again. I'm not misspelling it. Something else is the problem."

Ted droned on, with complete seriousness, "Is your computer turned on?"

"Of course, my computer's turned on! How else would I know my password doesn't work?" Beads of sweat began forming on Sidney's face.

"Is the screen turned on?"

"Are you even listening to me?" Sidney asked tightly.

"Of course, Waldinger. I'm here to help. Try retyping your password."

Sidney slammed the phone down in frustration. He planned to find the I.T. department later and pay "Ted" a little visit. He'd knock the teeth from his snide little mouth. First, though, he needed to get access to his computer.

As a last, desperate resort, he typed his password again. His home screen finally popped up.

However, instead of displaying the usual picture of three bikini-clad women on a beach, the background now featured an erupting volcano.

Very funny, Ted. We'll talk later.

Shaking his head in exasperation, he clicked on the program to bring up the presentation.

Amazing, he thought. *The way this day's going, I'm surprised the file is even here.*

A message appeared on the screen: *File opening... 10%... 15%... 25%... 26%...* Sidney pulled the handkerchief out of his pocket and wiped off his forehead. He started tapping his foot. The metallic taste of blood lingered in his mouth.

While he waited for his file to open, he leaned around the cubicle's partition to ask his coworker if she was having problems with her computer. The petite redhead was wearing a headset and clicking through data on a spreadsheet. Although she was wearing wool pants and a heavy jacket, she reached down and turned up her space heater.

Are you kidding me?

"Psst. Melissa?" he whispered loudly.

She turned to him, eyes bugging out, and gestured at her phone.

"I know! I know you're on a call. Could you just turn your heater down a bit?"

She rolled her eyes and shook her head. She returned her attention to her computer, which was obviously working just fine.

Unbelievable, he thought. He pressed the switch to turn his desk fan on full blast. Nothing happened. Looking under his desk, he saw the cord laying on the ground. Groaning, he leaned down and plugged the fan back in. From behind, he heard *RRRIIIPPPPPPP*.

Sidney swore viciously. He reached back and discovered the hole in the back of his pants had doubled in size. He'd need to get more staples from the office supply room.

The screen showed his file was 33% loaded.

He squeezed his eyes shut and counted to ten. Taking a deep breath, he pressed the switch on his oscillating fan. Once again, nothing happened. Looking at the ground, he saw the cord was not plugged into the wall.

He must've snagged it with his foot and pulled it loose. With a grunt, he jammed the plug back into the outlet and turned the fan on. Blessed, sweet air blew immediately onto his sweaty face.

Sighing, he noticed the computer screen. *File opening... 98%.* Maybe this day could be salvaged after all.

The screen went dark.

Judging by the sudden outbreak of swearing in Spanish, English, and Hindi in the nearby cubicles, Sidney concluded a circuit breaker must have blown. He picked up the phone, squeezing the receiver in a failed attempt to control his frustration. A guy named

Chuck answered his call to the building's maintenance department.

"Good morning, Chuck," Sidney said tightly. "It looks like we've tripped a breaker here on the 26th floor. I'm on the south side of the building."

"You're outta luck, pal. The guy who flips the breakers is out sick today," said Chuck in a heavy Brooklyn accent.

Sidney closed his eyes before replying. "So, have someone else do it," he said between clenched teeth.

"Sorry, pal. Union rules. Can't do another man's job." Chuck hung up the phone.

Dropping the phone on his desk, Sidney slid back in his chair. He wiped some more sweat from his forehead, then got up to go to the electrical control room. He'd flip the damned breaker himself.

The guy who flips the breakers, he thought incredulously. *Does that lazy prick expect me to believe there's only one guy here who is capable of flipping breakers?*

It took around fifteen minutes to find the electrical control room, locate the breaker panel, and reset the switch that had tripped. When he got back to his desk, he realized he'd forgotten to stop at the supply room for staples.

Whatever. One of his drawers held a roll of duct tape. He'd make it work.

Sidney turned his computer back on and reinitiated the slow process of opening his slide presentation. After securing the back of his pants with carefully placed strips of grey tape, he decided to get some water.

He walked quickly toward the break room, glancing at his diamond-studded watch. The face of the watch read 8:55.

"Great. The battery died," he muttered. As he walked, his pants pulled at the awkwardly repaired and re-repaired seam. He slowed to a shuffle, keeping his legs close together.

He looked up just in time to see the very wide eyes of Alisha, one of the interns from the accounting department, as she collided with him. Folders and papers went flying, and her coffee doused the front of his shirt.

"Watch *out*!" he shrieked as he lost his footing and tackled her to the ground. Several nearby coworkers rushed to her aid.

"Watch where you're going, you giant oaf!" huffed one of the suits as he helped Alisha to her feet.

"Girl, you need to SUE his ass," said a pale brunette he'd never seen before.

What?

"Misogynistic punk, thinkin' he can just walk wherever he wants to. Like you don't have a right to be here." A woman with braids hanging to her lower back leaned over Sidney. She pointed a finger at his face. "I got my eye on you, honey. Watch yourself."

Mutters and stifled laughter met his ears as he clambered to his feet and hurried around the corner.

"Did you see the back of his pants?" a woman's voice drifted after him.

"Yeah. The cheapskate can't even buy new clothes when he needs 'em."

Every muscle in his body was tense as Sidney entered the break room and headed straight for the sink. He grabbed some paper towels and dabbed at his soiled shirt.

Sighing in defeat at the pointless endeavor, he picked up a Styrofoam cup and filled it with water from the water cooler. As he lifted the cup to his lips, the Styrofoam cracked from his overly intense grip, and cold water ran down his chin to his shirt.

"I've had it!" he yelled to the empty break room. "I'm going home! I dare anyone to try stopping me!"

He threw the remains of the cup at the sink and marched out into the hallway. "To hell with all of you!" he growled at the small crowd standing around Alisha. He stomped across the office to the elevator while ignoring the looks of amusement from the people whose cubicles he passed. "To hell with all of you, too," he snapped, pointing a finger at each mocking face.

He stood at the elevator and jammed the down button with his thumb. He was wearing more coffee than he normally drank. Sweat poured off him like he was a perspiration fountain. Even his hair was soaked.

Turning around, he noticed every cubicle in sight had a space heater.

"It must be 85 degrees in here!" he whined in a high-pitched voice. "What the hell is wrong with you people?"

Every eye in the room stared back at him with mixed looks of amusement, irritation, or indignation. He shook his head. "For this, I'm still paying on student loans," he mumbled.

He stepped into the elevator when it finally arrived. The vomitous smell of flatulence, left by someone who was clearly in need of immediate medical attention, assaulted his nostrils. He pushed "G" for the ground floor, then pinched his nostrils together. The doors slid shut. The elevator rushed down two floors, then jerked to a stop. The doors slid open to admit two overly perky teenagers. They wore pristine white tennis dresses and carried racquets. They stared at him judgmentally as they noticed the unfortunate odor.

"Rude," said one of them in a drawn-out, sing-song voice.

"It wasn't me," Sidney snapped.

"Sure, dude," said the other one, turning to whisper to her friend.

The doors slid shut. The elevator rushed down four floors, then stopped suddenly a second time. A man with a white service dog got in. The dog sniffed the air and howled in abject misery.

The doors slid shut. The elevator rushed down three more floors, then stopped. Three women wearing business suits got in, and the teenagers got out. Sidney felt nauseated. He looked at the elevator's digital display. Seventeen floors to go.

Once again, the doors slid shut. Sidney tried convincing his stomach to settle. He shouldn't have eaten that third donut for breakfast, but he knew he wouldn't have time for lunch.

The elevator picked up speed as it descended.

The dog continued to howl. Sidney seemed to be the only person who noticed it.

After ten floors, the elevator stopped so suddenly one of the businesswomen lost her balance and fell against her colleagues. The women rushed through the doors the instant they opened. Four pale, dark-haired men, all dressed in black suits, stepped in. The quartet stood in a row and stared at Sidney with vacant eyes. Sidney looked straight ahead at the doors and tried not to squirm. The uncomfortable situation didn't help his nausea.

When they finally reached the ground floor, Sidney stepped forward, but the four men didn't move.

"Excuse me," Sidney said testily.

"You're excused," they replied politely.

"Move apart!" he demanded.

Sidney shoved past them, took two steps out of the elevator, and ran straight into Andrew Lentil, the building's superintendent. As he opened his mouth to apologize, his stomach succumbed to the morning's stress. Sidney vomited on the man's freshly shined and obviously expensive shoes.

Lentil, who stood 6’4” and weighed about 250 pounds, looked down at the decorative remains of Sidney’s last couple meals.

Last night’s chocolate fudge strawberry supreme pie wouldn’t be adding to his waistline, at least.

“You’re coming with me, you degenerate thug,” grunted Lentil as he grabbed Sidney’s arm.

Sidney, feeling somewhat better after the sudden, violent purge, blurted the first words that came to mind. “Sorry! Wrong floor!”

The superintendent yanked him away from the elevator. “I don’t care! You’re coming to my office and cleaning off my—”

“Can’t, my man. I have to give a presentation!” Sidney twisted out of the giant man’s grip and fled back into the elevator.

“Hey!” yelled the indignant superintendent.

“Look at his pants!” yelled someone on the ground floor.

Sidney leaned against the farthest corner of the elevator and smirked as the doors closed. Getting away from his cubicle for a bit had put everything in perspective, and he relaxed a little. Storming out of the building would’ve cost him his job. He’d give a killer presentation, and everything would be fine. He wasn’t the first person to ruin their clothes before a big meeting. With any luck, he’d have a chance to dim the lights in the boardroom before any of the bigwigs noticed his pants.

A small, frail-looking, silver-haired woman with a cane stood in front of the number panel. She pressed the button for the 40th floor. Sidney collected himself and asked politely, “Could you please press 26?”

She raised her crooked, wrinkled middle finger and didn’t budge.

His moment of relaxation ended as quickly as it began. Feeling his last thread of self-control snap, he grabbed her by her narrow shoulders and shoved her away from the control panel. With his attention fully focused on reaching the circular button, he failed to notice the woman’s hand digging into her pocket. With astonishing speed, she pulled out a small, black aerosol bottle and sprayed him in the face.

Sidney fell to the floor as he coughed, gagged, and screamed.

“That’ll teach you, ya fat creep,” the old woman shouted in a crackled, long-time smoker’s voice.

Sputtering, he managed, “I’m just trying to get to my office!”

The elevator stopped on the second floor, and the doors slid open. For the first time since he was twelve years old, Sidney began to sob. The tears stung his already violated face. A young, professionally dressed couple looked from Sydney to the snarling old woman.

“We’ll take the next one,” they said together.

The elevator wobbled up to the third floor. As Sidney got to his feet, a man with pale skin, a long black cape, and teeth filed down to sharp points came through the doors. Sidney wiped his watering eyes and wondered if the blood on the cracked corner of his mouth was from a human being.

On the fourth floor, a woman with elegant makeup and a parrot on her shoulder strode in and stood to the right of Sidney.

"Jackass," the parrot said pleasantly. Its beady black eye met Sydney's. "Jackass," it repeated, as if expecting a response.

Sidney ignored the bird. His still-stinging face was undoubtedly red and blotchy. His right eye was beginning to swell shut. *Maybe that'll keep the Directors' attention off my torn pants*, he thought. *Ironic.*

A delivery man was waiting on the fifth floor. He wheeled in a cart that held a wooden box shaped like a coffin. Sidney was suddenly certain it held the remains of the Corvette driver from this morning's accident. The delivery man turned the cart around and backed up to stand right in front of Sidney. Sidney yelped involuntarily as the man stomped on his feet.

"Move it!" the delivery man demanded.

"I was here first!" Sidney snapped.

"Jackass," said the parrot.

Sidney didn't bother responding. He just shook his head.

The elevator proceeded to stop on every floor. Sidney realized that although people were getting in, no one was getting out. The air became stale, and Sidney wondered how many more people the elevator could hold. It had to be approaching the weight limit.

He'd been standing there for at least twenty-five minutes. At this rate, he'd miss his meeting with the Directors. Restless and panicky, he glanced at his watch.

8:55. Damn, he forgot the battery was dead.

"Does anyone have the time?" he asked.

"Jackass," replied the parrot. No one else responded. The parrot's owner wore earbuds and was oblivious to her bird's vulgar comments.

On the tenth floor, two middle-aged women joined the group.

"I'm telling you," said the first one. "That boy is bad news. He'll have Sabrina knocked up in no time."

"Sabrina, ha!" answered the second woman. Sidney cringed at the shrill tone of her voice. "That little slut deserves what she gets. She's slept with half the boys in town and a few of the girls! I've even heard she's had *abortions*."

"Absolutely *scandalous*!"

"Jackasses," said the parrot. This time, Sidney agreed with it.

The elevator lurched to a stop. Sidney's nausea returned with a vengeance, and being forced to listen to the judgmental gossip session didn't help.

A girl with a large boa constrictor wrapped around her body squeezed in next to the pair of women, who looked at her disapprovingly.

"People who bring exotic pets into public spaces are rather rude, don't you think, Marla?" Miss High and Mighty said to her friend.

The girl turned to glare at the women, and the snake hissed. Sidney didn't think Snake Girl looked like someone to mess with. Marla sniffed. Vampire Guy checked out Snake Girl with obvious interest.

The elevator stopped on the twelfth floor. A big, burly man with a toolbox was waiting to get on. He smelled of acrid sweat, cigarette smoke, and alcohol. Incredibly, no one else seemed bothered by the horrendous, suffocating blend of odors.

The tennis girls would've passed out, he thought.

Marla asked, "And what do you do for a living?"

Sidney wasn't paying close attention to the conversation, but he could swear the smelly guy said he was on his way to flip some breakers.

You're losing it, Sidney told himself.

He decided to get out on the next floor and take a different elevator. This one was definitely over its weight capacity. He just had to figure out how to get by Delivery Guy. He shifted his weight to the left and tried to see over the man's shoulder. He would have to shove his way past a few people, but he didn't care. With the exception of Snake Girl, anyway. Sidney would give her a wide berth.

Sidney waited. The loud, groaning motor made him nervous. After several more seconds, the elevator stopped. Sidney figured they'd reached at least the 20th floor. However, when the doors opened, the digital display overhead flashed the number 14.

Maybe someone was playing a practical joke on him. Maybe he was on one of those reality shows where they pranked unsuspecting people. What if one of these weirdos was filming him? Could there be a camera in the elevator?

He closed his eyes. *I will not succumb to paranoia.*

A man with a spiked mohawk and a wide, toothy grin strode into the elevator. He carried a butcher knife. His leather jacket had silver spikes sticking three inches off the shoulders. To Sidney's horror (but not surprise), the man pushed his way to the back of the elevator and stood at Sidney's left side.

"Suck my cock," commanded the parrot.

The man leaned down until he was inches from Sidney's face.

"What'd you say to me?" He continued grinning like a maniac.

This is it, Sidney thought. *A stranger is going to murder me in an elevator because of a rude bird.*

"I didn't. I mean it wasn't me," he stuttered.

"Suck my cock," the bird repeated. It hopped on Sidney's shoulder and relieved itself. Warm, greenish-yellow ooze slid down his shirt.

The man on his left continued to grin at Sidney with his horrible teeth. His breath was so putrid, Sidney gagged as he turned and shoved the bird off his shoulder.

"Jackass!" it cried. "Suck my cock!"

Sidney wanted to scream, but he was afraid if he started, he wouldn't be able to stop.

They arrived on the 15th floor. People were already packed together like sardines, but somehow a young mother with a crying baby and a wailing three-year-old squeezed in with them.

"Mama!" the toddler screamed. "Mama! Mama! Mama! *Mama*!"

"Suck my cock," the parrot demanded. "Your *mama* sucks my cock!"

Marla, speaking loudly so her companion could hear her over the chaos, complained about a neighbor's dog who kept digging up her flower bed. "At least the bitch doesn't *swear*," she announced.

"Bitch!" cried the bird.

Grinning guy sneezed on Sidney. The stench nearly made his heart stop.

On the 16th floor, an Elvis impersonator got in. The old woman with the pepper spray and a bad attitude held the door open for him.

"Thank you," he said in a perfect imitation of Elvis. "Thank you very much."

Sidney couldn't take anymore. His sanity had been slowly deteriorating for about seven floors now. He roared, the adrenaline-fueled burst of anger exploding from his lungs in an almost visible cloud of energy. Startled passengers raised their eyebrows or giggled. Sidney shoved his way through the wall of bodies. The doors slammed shut just before he reached them.

They stopped on the 17th floor. The doors opened, revealing a brick wall. Hysterical laughter erupted from his mouth. Tears and snot erupted from other orifices, and the others on the elevator began shirking away from him. He clapped his hands.

"Good one, guys! Good one!"

By the time they reached the 20th floor, he'd managed to pull himself together. He used his handkerchief to clean off his face, taking great care to avoid his swollen eye and irritated skin. The elevator doors opened, and he flung himself into the lobby. He landed on his hands and knees in front of a group of men and women in military uniforms. They looked at him with distaste, then walked around him and got in the elevator.

As the elevator doors closed, he heard the bird cheerfully shout out, "Sayonara, Jackass!"

He stood up, checked that his pants were still somewhat repaired, and looked at his surroundings. The immaculate hallways, leading in three different directions that formed a "T," looked the same as those on the other floors he'd been to. Closed doors lined the plain walls. The hum from a cluster of vending machines was the only sound. An acquaintance from the purchasing department strolled by and nodded at him. Sidney walked to the lone window and looked out at the dreary day.

Maybe the constant stress of the job was finally breaking him. He knew the human resources office hadn't moved from the 17th floor. He'd obviously hallucinated the brick wall. Maybe it was time to think about switching careers.

The stairwell was on his left. Walking up the six floors would probably be the fastest and least stressful option. He wasn't sure he could bring himself to get in another elevator. Sidney pushed against the metal bar on the door and went in, half expecting to wind up in another elevator or maybe outer space. He laughed nervously when he saw the stairs. They appeared to be much steeper than any stairs in a public building should've been.

By the time he reached the 22nd floor, he was feeling the effects of his lack of regular exercise. His breath came in wheezy gasps, and colored spots danced through his field of vision. His heart fluttered like the wings of a panicked bird.

Gulping air as he passed the 24th floor, he leaned forward and half-crawled up the stairs. When he reached the 26th floor, he wondered if he could get to his desk before he passed out.

With his eyes watering and still half-shut, his rubbery legs made their way uneventfully through the office to his cubicle. He collapsed into his chair, which rolled out from underneath him, dumping him on the floor with a graceless *thud.* The remaining staples in his pants dug into his skin, and he felt tiny spots of warm blood soak through his underwear.

He crawled back into his chair. His computer screen showed that his presentation file was 98% loaded. Swiping at his eyes, he looked at the time on his desk phone's LED display. It showed 9:15 AM.

That's simply not possible! he thought. *I've been in this building for at least three hours.*

But the phone, his digital clock, and the computer system all agreed. He hadn't even been here an hour.

Looking again at his expensive watch, he noticed one of the diamonds was missing from its setting. He began to laugh and found himself unable to stop. Melissa, the girl next to him, told him to shut up so she could concentrate.

A male voice chimed in. "Wallace! Keep it down over there!"

His supervisor appeared out of nowhere and hovered over him. Sidney wanted to respond with a scathing insult, but he saw the title slide of his presentation pop up on his computer screen. It read: "How to Increase Productivity and Avoid Wasting Time on the Clock."

The irony would have sent him into more gales of hysterical laughter, but he envisioned himself standing unprepared in front of all the suits in the boardroom and came back to his senses. His supervisor scoffed and moved on.

He scrolled through the slides, familiarizing himself with the information. "We could increase productivity by 135%, simply by stretching out the length of an hour," he said to no one in particular. He giggled helplessly until he heard his supervisor's footsteps heading back toward his cubicle. He quickly cleared his throat and continued looking through the file, until the shrill ringing of his telephone interrupted him.

"Wallace," he answered.

A deep voice shouted, "You're late! The Directors are waiting! Get your ass down here, or you're fired!" The line went dead.

"But that's impossible!" Sidney cried, looking at the time. It read 3:02. Had he fallen asleep?

No. He hadn't. Standing up and looking around the office, he saw everyone diligently working at their computers or talking with coworkers. Why hadn't anyone else noticed weird things happening?

He didn't have the luxury of taking time to find out. Quickly, he resaved his presentation to his flash drive and raced to the boardroom. He pulled open the heavy wooden doors. Twelve sets of eyes stared at him coldly.

"I, uh, apologize for my appearance. It's been a... strange day."

"You were late to work, and you were late to this meeting. What do you have to say for yourself?"

demanded his boss. He put out a cigarette in the ashtray in front of him.

"I'm sorry. Let me get the presentation started, so I don't waste more of your valuable time," Sidney said. He struggled to keep the sarcasm out of his voice.

He dropped the flash drive on the plush red carpet, and they laughed. He felt an angry flush heat his face as he picked up the tiny device. He inserted it into the laptop on the table and opened his file. The title page of his presentation appeared on the giant screen at the head of the room. He cleared his throat.

"Today," he began, "I'd like to present to you the findings of my study on how to increase productivity."

He clicked to the first slide. Anger swelled in him as everyone in the room began to laugh again. Looking behind him, he saw that someone had tampered with his file. A gory photograph replaced the chart he'd painstakingly created.

"Hey! Who changed my file?" he yelped in a high-pitched, panicked voice. "What the hell is that?" He gestured forcefully at the photo displayed on the screen.

"Don't you recognize it? Look more closely," instructed a man sitting at the far end of the table. Sidney couldn't make him out in the dim light, and he didn't recognize the deep, crackly voice. He looked at the screen.

"Oh god!" Sidney gasped as he gaped at the slide. "That's the scene of the accident on the Interstate this morning! That's the reason I was late!"

The Directors laughed harder. A few laughed so hard they gasped for breath. Finally, the man shrouded in darkness spoke.

"No, Wallace," the deep voice said. "That accident is not the reason you were late. That accident is the reason you are dead."

Sweat poured from Sidney and stung his widening eyes. Realization struck him like a thousand volts of electricity. Stumbling, he ran toward the door. As he reached for the door handle, it disappeared. A brick wall stood where the door had been. As he whimpered, he heard more shrieking laughter from the Directors.

His boss composed himself enough to ask, "What's the matter, Wallace? Do you have a problem with Hell?"

JUST ANOTHER HALLOWEEN

Isabella craved a gin and tonic. She hadn't needed a drink this badly since the day they found cancer in her liver. When she started chemotherapy, she was far too nauseous to even consider consuming alcohol. Hell, she hadn't even *thought* about drinking for a good nine months or so.

But now, the Halloween party was stirring up bittersweet memories, and she needed a distraction.

"Mateo?" she called.

"Yes, love?"

"Talk to me, would you? Help me get my mind off having a drink."

Mateo said nothing at first.

She listened to the heavy bass beat of the latest song. She loved all kinds of music, but those car speakers were blaring loud enough to wake the dead.

"You still get those cravings?" he asked.

"Not often."

"Okay. Well, let's see. My kids came to visit yesterday. My youngest daughter is pregnant again. I think she's trying to populate a small country. Don't get me wrong; I love my grandkids. But there's too many damn people on this planet as it is."

Isabella wanted to tell him he should be grateful to have such a large family. But she wasn't going to criticize what he was saying when she was the one that asked him to talk.

"How many is this, now?"

"Counting Marlaine, it's six."

Mateo's granddaughter, Marlaine, had drowned in a river at the age of five. Her body was never recovered. Isabella had mourned the child's death as if she'd been her own granddaughter.

"Well, congratulations! Another grandchild! That's very exciting news!"

Mateo hummed.

"Sometimes I still crave cigarettes, and I quit 46 years ago," said a familiar voice. It was Lars, butting in on their conversation. Isabella didn't mind, honestly. She knew the old guy was lonely. His estranged wife lived in Tucson, and his kids never came to see him.

"Yeah?" she answered. She'd never smoked, so she wasn't sure how to compare that kind of craving with her own. She supposed addiction was addiction, no matter what the poison.

The music lagged, and the friends overheard the teenagers by the car talking.

"Guys, did you hear that?" a young female voice asked. She sounded timid, as if she'd had to work up the nerve to ask that simple question.

"No one's falling for that shit, Chloe," said a know-it-all male voice. Isabella had always despised know-it-alls.

"Shut up, Cole! I heard something, too," said another girl.

"Think about where we are," added the timid girl in a slightly more confident tone.

"Where we are," said Cole in a lilting voice, "is the best place ever for a Halloween party."

Isabella didn't want to listen to teenagers. Lord knew she'd already listened to enough of them over the years. Most of them hadn't even been hers, biologically. Probably explained the alcoholism, now that she thought about it.

"Did you all hear what happened to Floyd?" asked Lars.

"No," Mateo said.

"Tell us what happened," Isabella encouraged.

He didn't speak right away, and Isabella wondered if he was trying to create a dramatic effect or if he was simply collecting his thoughts.

"He was forced into helping solve the murder. As if he hadn't already suffered enough trauma," Lars said.

"How'd they force him?" asked Troy, a twenty-something who should've been hanging out with an entirely different social group.

Lars said quietly, "They took him right outta his home. It wasn't like the poor bastard could fight them off. They used to say, 'a man's home is his castle.' Even a tiny home, ya know? Nobody's got respect for their fellow man anymore."

"Fellow *person*," Troy corrected.

"I had jury duty once," Mateo said solemnly. "For a murder trial."

The party music began blaring again. The song was "Werewolves of London," one of Isabella's Halloween favorites.

"This guy shot his whole family," continued Mateo. "Did his wife in the head. Shot her five times, *in the head.* They had to identify her by her dental records. The defense lawyer accused the dead wife of cheating on his client, as if that made it okay to splatter her brains across the wall. They found a piece of her skull stuck in the drywall. Guy also killed his twin boys. Then he shot his dog."

"Who the hell shoots their dog?" Troy asked, baffled.

"Who the hell shoots their *kids*?" Isabella asked incredulously.

"Who the hell shoots *anybody* five times in the head, for God's sake?" Lars exclaimed.

"They made us look at pictures," Mateo continued solemnly. "I saw those images in my sleep for years afterwards. Those poor little kids..." He paused, then spoke in a tone as authoritative as that of a drill sergeant. "When I looked at the killer, I was looking into the eyes of the Devil. He was pure evil. Not an ounce of goodness in him."

"What about the dog?" Troy asked. "Did he shoot it in the head, too? More than once?"

"Who cares about the damn dog?" Isabella exclaimed. She no longer wanted a gin and tonic, she decided. Three or four fingers of whiskey would be good right about now.

"Did the jury convict the creep?" Lars asked.

"Course they did," Troy said confidently.

No one spoke.

"Didn't they?"

"It was a hung jury. In the end, the bastard walked."

As the group fell silent, Chloe, the nervous girl across from them, yelled, "Did you *see that*?"

"She's damn irritating," Mateo mumbled.

"Fuck all the way off, Chloe!" shouted a third girl. Several male voices snickered.

"Anyway, he walked, but he didn't get away," Mateo continued. "Dude broke into someone's house, and the homeowner shot him at close range. Poetic justice is better than no justice, I guess."

The others mumbled their agreement.

"Uh, hello?" said an unfamiliar voice.

"Well, hello, my dear!" Isabella said, startled. "Are those your friends over there?"

"No. I don't know anybody. I'm new here."

"I am too," Troy said, almost cheerfully.

"Well, I'm Isabella. Now you know someone."

"Thanks. I'm Jean. I… I'm scared. I don't think I'm gonna like it here. I don't have any friends."

"Aw, give it a chance. The neighborhood is beautiful," Troy said soothingly.

Isabella knew Lars would roll his two glass eyes had he been able.

"It seems loud."

"Only once a year, my dear. This group, they've partied here for several years. They're harmless," Isabella assured her.

"Something just touched me," shrieked the twitchy teenager.

"You're such a baby! I'm sick of you crying wolf!"

Isabella recognized the voice as belonging to the one she had called 'Cole.'

Another girl screamed.

"What's happening over there?" asked Jean. She sounded nervous. Isabella wondered what on Earth she could possibly be worried about.

"I don't know," Mateo asked. "Hey, Red, you still over there?"

"Of course I am, you asshole," answered the gruff voice. "Where else would I be?"

"Can you see what's going on?" asked Mateo, ignoring the man's rudeness.

For a moment, all was silent. Isabella didn't expect the crotchety old fart to answer. Red was a pretty big asshole himself.

The voices of the teenage friends broke up their uneasy silence.

"What the fuck did you do?" cried a hysterical girl, the one who'd told Chloe to 'fuck off' earlier.

"I didn't mean to!" shouted Cole. "How was I supposed to know she'd fall?"

"You pushed her, dumbass! What did you think would happen?"

"I just wanted her to stop being such a chicken. Do you think she's okay?" Cole asked in a soft, frightened voice.

"No, she's not okay, dude!" shouted one of the guys, as another one cried, "What's wrong with you, Cole? You broke her neck, you freak! You killed her! Chloe's dead!"

"We gotta get out of here!"

Several sets of vehicle doors slammed, and tires peeled out.

"At least the party ended early," Lars pointed out.

"Because somebody died!" exclaimed Jean, as if death wasn't something that happened to everyone, eventually.

"What's happening?" Chloe's voice cried as she joined the small group. "What's happening to me? Where are my friends?"

"You died, sweetheart. How hard is it to figure out?" Red answered.

"Well don't sugarcoat it," Mateo snapped.

"What? What do you mean, 'died'?" Chloe exclaimed.

"I mean *died*! Dead! You've been killed. Your body's gone. You're just a spirit in a graveyard now. Like the rest of us."

"Honestly, Red," said Mateo in disgust. "You could show a little kindness."

"But I don't want to be dead!" Chloe cried.

"None of us do, my dear," Isabella said. "You get used to it."

SIDE EFFECT

A cockroach skittered across Marisela's kitchen floor. As its tiny legs hit the hardwood, they sounded like long, manicured fingernails tapping nervously on a table. The insect disappeared under the refrigerator.

For three months, roaches had been gallivanting about her kitchen like they owned it. No matter what she tried, she couldn't get rid of the damned things. She'd stomped on them. She'd poisoned them. She'd captured them in glue traps. She'd flattened them with frying pans. She'd even hexed them. Marisela had tried every commercial bug killer on the market. She'd hired exterminators. The critters would disappear for a few days, but they always returned.

After every conventional killing method failed, she'd searched the web for alternative ideas. After scrolling through countless listings and only finding more of the same, she came upon a site that looked promising. She'd sent an admittedly ridiculous amount of money to someone called "The Practitioner". In return, an unmarked box was delivered to her door. The can inside was as small as a stick of deodorant, but according to the ad, one use was all she'd need.

For the first time in weeks, she felt hopeful. This attempt would be different. This time she would clear out the infestation once and for all.

She wasn't just concerned about the filthiness of roaches, or even the food contamination and health risks they created. Their invasion was a personal insult. It was an orchestrated attack by a cunning enemy. She'd swear in a court of law the little bastards laughed at her every time she tried and failed to kill them. Eradicating every last one of them had become her sole mission in life.

Marisela grabbed the spray can containing the new bug killer. The black can bore a white skull-and-crossbones on the front. Red letters proclaimed it would 'Permanently End Cockroach Problems.' There were no warnings or markings of any other kind on the can.

She didn't have to wait long for another cockroach to appear. One crawled out from behind the bundle of bananas on her counter. She slipped off her shoe and used it to send the bug flying across the kitchen. The instant it hit the floor, Marisela fired a steady stream of poison at it. The spray burned into its shell, and it squealed in pain.

"Take that, you little bastard," she said smugly. "You're not laughing *now*, are you? Let's find your friends."

She kicked the detested creature out of the way. It continued to shriek as it slid across the floor upside down, with its legs clawing uselessly at the air. She could stomp on it and put it out of its misery, but she was enjoying the show far too much to end it. She didn't consider herself a cruel person, but after the hell those bugs had put her through recently, they deserved to die horribly. Besides, she thought, there was nothing wrong with taking a little pleasure in a job well done.

She shook the can, reassuring herself it still contained plenty of poison. She began to actively search for the rest of the colony, starting with the cabinet over the oven where she stored her candy. A few cockroaches dove for safety as the door opened. She shoved her candy out of the way and sprayed. The direct hit from such a short distance dropped the insects that hadn't escaped in time. Marisela shuddered to think of all the carcasses she'd have to clean up.

The writhing bug on the floor, however, refused to die. Rolling her eyes, she sprayed it again.

The potent smell erupting from the aerosol was saturating the air, nasty enough to be death itself. When Marisela accidentally inhaled a bit of spray, it plummeted her into waves of dizziness. She stumbled backward. Colors danced in front of her eyes as she sat heavily on the floor. Soft chuckles echoed through the air above her before everything faded to black.

* * *

When she regained consciousness, sunlight was streaming through the kitchen's west window. She'd apparently slept the entire night and half the day on her kitchen floor, thanks to that damned bug poison. The website hadn't mentioned any side effects of accidental ingestion, but her head was throbbing, and her stomach hurt like she had food poisoning. She must've fallen hard enough to cause a head injury, at the very least.

Looking around, she realized she could have a severe concussion. As she lay flat on the floor, her vision switched from double, to triple, to quadruple. Even stranger, everything in the kitchen looked black and white, like all the color had been sucked out of the world.

She'd had head injuries before, but none of them caused the kind of visual disruption she was experiencing. She decided to call an ambulance. She'd left her phone on the counter, but it might as well have been on Mars. Her arms wouldn't move.

Oh god, please don't let me have a spinal cord injury, she thought. How long would she lay on the floor before someone found her? She wanted to cry, but no tears came to her eyes.

When she felt better, she'd go through her browser history and locate "The Practitioner's" contact information. She wanted her two hundred dollars back, and she fully intended to give the jerk a piece of her mind. Bug spray shouldn't cause humans to pass out. Maybe she'd report him to the

Environmental Protection Agency while she was at it. And she would *destroy* him on social media.

Gathering her willpower, she lifted her head. She couldn't see her body, but she could see a bunch of tiny legs sticking up in the air. It was no wonder she couldn't move her arms; she no longer *had* arms. With dawning disgust and horror, she looked around her kitchen. She gaped at the sight of her own body leaning against the kitchen counter. She screamed, but the only sound that came from her mouth was '*hsssssssss*.'

From across the room, her body clumsily, slowly walked toward her. She recognized the look of excitement on her own face. Numbly, she watched her own hands pick up the can of bug spray that had dropped to the floor. Her own body, apparently occupied by the cockroach she'd tried to kill, was about to spray poison on her. As it leaned over her, her own long, dark brown hair dangled above her. A droplet of spittle landed on her thorax. She curled up the cockroach legs in a futile attempt to protect herself.

After a few failed attempts, the bug occupying her body figured out how to shake the can.

Marisela suddenly realized when it sprayed her with the poison, she and the bug should, theoretically, return to their own bodies. The poison was what made them switch in the first place, after all. When that happened, the first thing she intended to do was make this bug suffer. She'd pin it by its useless wings to her corkboard and let it starve.

She braced herself for the poison's horrible smell.

Everything will be okay. Hell, this is probably just a concussion-induced hallucination, anyway.

Her relief was short-lived. Just as it was about to spray her, the bug froze. It held up the can, then looked down at her. It must've come to the same conclusion about the poison. It staggered awkwardly across the room and set the can on the counter.

The noise Marisela made would've been a whimper, if she hadn't been trapped in a cockroach's body. Instead, the sound that issued from her mouth was *"hsssssssss,"* and it almost destroyed her sanity.

The damned bug smiled at her with her own mouth.

Panicking will only make things worse, she told herself. She needed to focus on getting to that counter. It occurred to her that she'd have to find a way to manipulate the spray nozzle while standing in front of the stream of poison. She didn't know if she'd be able to coordinate the movement. Maybe some of the poison had gotten on the outside of the can, and inhaling even a little bit would be enough to send them back to their own bodies.

One step at a time. I'll find a way.

She was not letting a damn cockroach get the better of her.

She rocked back and forth, trying to roll over. Coordinating six legs and a segmented body was challenging, but she managed to flip the bug's body upright.

Her body waddled toward her. Hopefully the bug didn't fall and break any of her bones, she thought, as she watched him wiggling her arms.

Hurry.

Two long antennae stretched ahead of her, and she realized they were attached to her head. Her moan of revulsion made the same monotonous, dreadful hiss as before.

Moving one leg at a time was the wrong strategy, she realized. Using the back legs to propel her forward and the other legs to maintain balance, Marisela inched toward the counter. She was so focused on staying out of the reach of her own body that she didn't hear her front door open.

The bug ignored the noise, too. It was concentrating on getting to Marisela, but it struggled to fully coordinate her limbs. It couldn't react quickly enough to keep up with her skittering movements.

"Mari? Where are you? Are you okay?"

Marisela recognized the voice of her sister, and waves of relief washed over her.

"What happened to lunch? I waited at the sandwich shop… for… an hour." Her words slowed down as she looked at Marisela's body.

The cockroach either hadn't figured out how to speak yet, or it didn't know a response was expected.

"Mari? Uh, are you sick? You're acting… really weird." Her sister grabbed her chin and stared into her eyes.

Marisela worried again about injuries to her body as the cockroach lost its balance and fell into her sister.

"¡Hijole!" She grunted as she helped the bug balance Marisela's body. "Do you need a doctor?"

"Help me!" Marisela shouted, but her words came out as "*hhiiissssssssss*."

Her sister turned to look at her with disgust.

Oh god, she doesn't know it's me. She doesn't know it's me!

"Honestly, Mari, if you can't get rid of these disgusting bugs, you need to move." Marisela's sister picked up the can of bug spray and walked over to her. "Gross," she muttered, and sprayed her with the rest of the poison.

* * *

Marisela opened her eyes. It took a moment for her dizziness to subside. She looked down and saw two blurry but definitely human hands. Her sister had saved her. She was a human being again.

Time to decimate that cockroach.

"Sis, you are never gonna believe what just happened!" she exclaimed. She rubbed at the tears forming in her eyes. Marisela wasn't fond of hugging, but now she turned to throw her arms around her sister.

Instead, she screamed. Marisela staggered backward. “No. No, this can’t be right. No! Oh god, *no*!” Her unsteady feet managed to stumble to the bathroom, where she looked in the mirror over the sink.

Her sister’s face stared back at her.

From the kitchen, the cockroach still occupying Marisela’s body laughed. Marisela ran into the kitchen just in time to see her own boot stomp on the cockroach in the middle of the floor.

THE SPECIALIST'S FACE

Lau's taut, blue-tinged lips twisted into a scowl as she watched the Cleanup Specialist materialize. Skin, feathers, fur, and scales from various creatures he'd slain had been assembled into a barbaric covering for his eight-foot frame. He wore the pelt of a silver ice-fox over the dark cavity where his Face belonged.

He knows pelt masks are illegal, Lau thought, irritated. Then again, he also knew anyone he came into contact with would be too terrified to challenge a Cleanup Specialist's lack of morals.

Clawslayers were the fiercest race to arrive on Earth after the mass extinction left the planet vulnerable to colonization. Out of desperation, Earth's few remaining governments formed an uneasy alliance with the aliens. In return for undisputed control of Earth's barely habitable land and polluted oceans, the Clawslayers agreed to protect the planet when nastier, more dangerous alien species attempted invasion. While every remaining intelligent species now fell under their rule, Earth's native inhabitants were still allowed to attempt to survive. The Clawslayers diligently kept their end of the bargain; they seemed to enjoy violence.

Lau lived and worked on the edge of an island in the Arctic. She provided services required by Cleanup Specialists, the deadliest of the Clawslayers. This one's abrupt arrival in her ice cave caused more chaos than she'd expected. Lau's soothing enchantments had little to no effect on the panicking group of replacement Faces. She needed them to be calm and ready to act. Still, she could hardly blame her precious creations for scattering at the sight of the Clawslayer. They knew what he wanted.

This particular Cleanup Specialist had already consumed eighty-one replacement Faces. Once installed on his body, a replacement Face was doomed to a torturous, hellish existence. Its future included mutilation, abuse, and a painful, drawn-out end – if it was even allowed to die. Cleanup Specialists were notoriously careless while using their Faces to coax and bait their alien adversaries, even though they, too, felt the pain when their enemies slashed and pummeled them.

The physical agony wasn't even the cruelest part of a Specialist's Face's ultimate fate. Many Cleanup Specialists (present company included) kept their depleted Faces as trophies, immortalizing them and preventing them from entering the afterlife. Whatever they did to those Faces at the end, after they'd used them up, kept them just functional enough to inspire terror in others. The "trophies" could hear, feel sensations, and understand what was happening to them. They couldn't speak words, but their moans and tortured expressions spoke volumes.

* * *

A short time after the Clawslayers established themselves on Earth, Lau had been sought out by an ambassador from the Specialists' Guild. They needed someone to produce replacement Faces, and she'd been honored to accept such a prestigious contract. Although breeding intelligent creatures solely to live a life of torment seemed cruel, the Faces were necessary for the Guild's Specialists to operate efficiently.

She never could've imagined she'd become so fond of the damned things. Over time, Lau found it increasingly difficult to see Face after Face destroyed by reckless, heartless Guild Specialists. Cleanup Specialists were the most savage of all.

Saving at least one generation became an obsession for her. She'd supplied the Guild's needs faithfully and flawlessly from day one. The Faces were *her* creations, and she was going to keep some of them for herself, just this once. The Guild owed her that one small request, in her opinion, although she knew they wouldn't see it that way.

Her plan to hide and keep the Faces had only one drawback: it would almost certainly cost the lives of a few of them. Lau explained to the group that the casualties, while tragic, would be necessary, and really didn't matter much in the grand scheme of things. She'd gently assured her babies that sacrificing two or even three of them, out of a batch of thirty, was an acceptable arrangement.

After all, it wasn't as if Lau could put *herself* in peril. Cleanup Specialists were ruthless fighters, and Lau knew she didn't have a chance of winning against one in a scuffle. If she attacked him and lost, he'd see to it that she suffered eternal agony.

If her Faces attacked him using their new enhancements, however, they could almost certainly take him down.

* * *

"Give me my Face," the Cleanup Specialist said by way of greeting. His speech was slightly muffled by the pelt.

Lau hoped her terrified creations wouldn't lose their courage. If the sight of the tormented Faces hanging on chains from the Clawslayer's cobra-skin belt didn't motivate them to fight, nothing would.

She'd spent years developing the tiny mutation she'd woven into this generation's DNA. A Cleanup Specialist would never expect to be attacked by Faces. The element of surprise would give them the precious seconds they needed to settle their teeth into the one vulnerable area on a Clawslayer: his empty, Faceless head. They'd destroy him from the inside out before he even realized who was attacking him.

When he failed to contact the Guild, the others would assume he'd been killed on the job. He'd be written off as incompetent. No one would come looking for him. The Guild would assume he'd destroyed Lau's Faces in battle. This generation of Faces, her creations, her *children*, would be safe. The Guild wouldn't miss a generation they didn't know about.

In theory, anyway.

The Faces who survived the attack on the Cleanup Specialist would be rewarded with the love, safety, and purpose of a life with Lau.

Although Lau hadn't personally created any of the members of this Clawslayer's collection, she pitied her predecessor's destroyed children. The doomed Faces were grotesque. Their beauty had been stolen from them by the reckless, thoughtless actions of a being who existed solely to murder and mutilate. Expressions of unfathomable terror were permanently etched into the Faces' marred features.

Boslo, Lau's favorite Face from her current batch, floated back toward its tiny cage in an attempt to slip past the Clawslayer.

Damn you! Lau screamed in her head. *It's not time to move yet! You're jeopardizing everything!* Out of the entire group, Boslo was the last one she'd expect to lose its courage. What a disappointing turn of events.

The Faceless creature's clawed hand pointed at Boslo.

"That one will come with me," his muffled words announced. "As you know, under Guild Decree 7.3a, the punishment for any slave attempting to flee an Immortal is permanent impalement through the mouth to the Wall of Deserters."

Boslo wailed.

"Of *course* it's attempting to escape!" Lau cried in its defense. While she was furious over Boslo's cowardice, she couldn't afford to lose a Face to eternal punishment. Not now. Her other babies' morale was fragile enough without seeing one of their own captured. Without positivity and confidence, they wouldn't stand a chance of completing her objective.

"You cannot punish it for feeling fear," she declared, reining in her emotions. Lau glanced sideways at her creations to monitor their reactions. "They'd rather die than go with you! Can you blame them? You're an abomination!"

Arguing with a Cleanup Specialist, not to mention insulting one, wasn't the smartest thing she'd done in her very long life.

With no emotion, with no inflection in his voice, the Clawslayer responded, "We are exactly what we were created to be, as you well know."

Her frightened children watched as the Clawslayer effortlessly captured Boslo. He stuffed the terrified Face into the prisoner transport bag that hung from a strap over his shoulders.

"I have no time for sentiment. There is much work to be done." He then grabbed the nearest Face out of pure spite and added it to his bag. He moved much too fast for Zawol, a kind Face with a serious expression and tidy facial hair, to have any chance of evading him.

Lau bared her mouthful of sharp, claw-like teeth. He had no right to take two Faces. He could take his Guild Decrees and stuff them. Her Faces needed to act *now*.

"Go-o-o!" she bellowed. Her deep, vibrating voice resonated throughout the ice cave.

Her plan to destroy the Clawslayer was flawless. The weapon engineered into this generation of Faces was foolproof (for those who had a chance to use it, anyway).

The Faces flew toward the Clawslayer in a tight formation. A special set of teeth, claw-shaped like Lau's own, erupted from their mouths. The new set dislodged the Faces' original teeth, which clattered loudly as they hit the floor.

Success! Lau thought euphorically.

The surprised Cleanup Specialist, hindered as expected by his current lack of a Face, stumbled backward. As Lau cheered, the snarling Faces stopped and turned away from the creature. They moved into an O-shaped formation and flew toward Lau.

"What are you doing?" she cried.

Too shocked to react, Lau stood motionless for a millisecond too long. Her Faces, her *babies*, descended on her from all sides. Hundreds of teeth clamped down on the crusty, wrinkled skin of her centuries-old Face, until it tore free from her head with a *shloop*.

"Bring it to me," said the Cleanup Specialist as he casually adjusted the moaning Faces hanging from his belt.

Lau's Face shrieked in pain and terror as it was flown slowly across the room by her very own creations. She watched in horror and disbelief as the Clawslayer removed the ice-fox pelt from his revolting head. Tiny rose-colored tentacles, equipped with suction cups that emitted a gluey substance, reached out from the darkness in the hollow of his head. Her children's teeth dug deeply into her skin as they spun her Face around. They lowered it onto the Cleanup Specialist's head, allowing the creature's suction cups to attach themselves to the back of it. Tentacles burrowed their way into the muscles and nerves of Lau's Face, securing their positions with a chemical secretion.

She watched in fury and disbelief as the Faces attacked her body. Several chomped on her hands, the very hands that produced them. Others slowly gnawed on her torso and legs, emboldened by their terrible new teeth. Her body couldn't defend itself from such a large number of attackers.

Their leader, the rosy cheeked Kyle, guided them through their work in a calm and organized manner. This attack must've taken months to coordinate. The betrayal was unfathomable. Lau couldn't understand what she'd done to cause the batch of ingrates to turn on her.

"You're unlikely to survive my next assignment, but I have a place already picked out for you on my belt."

Before she could respond, the Cleanup Specialist assumed control of her voice. He laughed, and Lau's Face laughed with him. She was helpless to resist his movements. Her facial muscles now followed his body's commands.

"You should be honored," said the Cleanup Specialist. "You've just become the first member of our species to surrender your own Face as a replacement to a fellow Clawslayer."

REPRODUCTION

He had no face.

I didn't realize that at first, of course. The upper part of his body was hidden from view. I didn't understand the full horror of what I was looking at until it was too late.

I caught my first glimpse of the man while jogging in the Safe Zone through the dried-up remains of the southern territory. The blackened skeletons of trees burned up by the drone strikes stood against an orange sky. Deep crevices lined the lifeless ground where there once had been lush green vegetation, vibrant flowers, and abundant wildlife. The planet's human population had been decimated during the first wave of attacks, so I rarely encountered other people on my daily run.

My first reaction upon seeing a human being standing in the Forbidden Zone was horror. The horror was almost immediately replaced by anger. Why would anyone put their life in jeopardy on purpose after surviving an assault that killed billions of others?

I slowed my jogging pace. The man stood fifty feet or so off the running trail. Although very few people traveled anymore, it was entirely possible that he was new to the area. I wanted to give him the benefit of the doubt. He might genuinely be unaware that he'd stepped outside the Safe Zone.

"Hey!" I yelled, slightly out of breath. "Get out of that sand field! Get back on the trail!"

The man didn't move.

I could see he wore expensive running shoes and teal jogging pants with a blue stripe running down the side of the leg. A matching jacket was tied around his waist. The top part of his body was obscured by the dead tree branches hanging near him.

"Hey, mister! You're in danger!"

I rounded the curve on the trail. I could finally see the full height of his body, and two things became apparent. One, he wasn't alone. And two, my warnings were pointless.

A smooth, greyish-blue skin with a rubbery-looking surface encased his head. He stood completely still. The device pointed at his temple looked unlike anything I'd ever seen, but there was no question about its purpose.

The owner of the hovering weapon appeared to be a conglomeration of entities trying to occupy the same physical space at the same time. They disrupted the surrounding air, causing it to waver and sparkle around them. They flashed in and out of existence, but the weapon remained completely tangible. Watching their constant, desperate struggle to wiggle into this dimension hurt my eyes, but I couldn't look away.

I assumed they were alien bounty hunters, fighting over who would be first to claim the subject of some lucrative contract. That was a common occurrence in this territory these days. I wondered what this ordinary looking guy could've done to warrant interdimensional attention.

Several of the creatures finally emerged and solidified. I could see they were all members of the same species. They grabbed the weapon simultaneously. The faceless man made no effort to escape as he was fired upon. Green pulses blasted his head to bits and pieces. As his body fell to the ground, chunks of the grey-blue substance, mixed with flesh, blood, and bone, slid horizontally through the air in slow motion. It was as if gravity was an inconvenience to them, and they refused to yield to its unreasonable demands. After several seconds, the remains dropped to the ground and splattered. The range of impact was wide; some pieces even made it as far as the trail. The tiny globs crawled across the barren earth, spreading across the area like a virus.

The small group of creatures ignored my horrified screams. Maybe they weren't far enough into this reality to pick up sound, or maybe they didn't have organs that processed noise. Maybe I simply wasn't interesting enough for them to notice or acknowledge.

They faded back out of this dimension, leaving the corpse and the gruesome, animated remains of its terrible head.

So much for the "Safe" Zone, I thought, as I carefully stepped over the five or six pieces that had landed on the trail. I'd seen a lot of strange things happen since the world started dying, but this was by far the most terrifying event I'd witnessed. I needed to get out of this wasteland.

I ran. I didn't look back when I heard the slithering sound, but I did reach up to scratch the sudden itch on my head. A tiny, revolting bit of oily, bloody flesh had landed unnoticed in my hair. I gagged as my fingers sank into the rubbery goop. I tried to pull them free, but they were stuck fast. The thick goo crawled across my scalp, spreading like someone was pouring glue over my head.

The nasty stuff expanded and seeped onto my forehead. I tried to wipe it away with my free hand. I shouldn't have been surprised to find that I couldn't. Even worse, now both hands were stuck to my head. I stopped running and started panicking. I inhaled huge gulps of air as the gummy detritus oozed down the back of my head in rivulets. My nose and right eye disappeared beneath the smooth surface.

Grunting, I tugged as hard as I could to pull my fingers away from my head. It was like trying to free them from drying cement, but I eventually succeeded. The thick layer of goop didn't loosen at all from my scalp, however. It tore, allowing the alien substance to wiggle its way beneath my skin. It reached my skull and took root even more firmly. I now had warm streams of blood running alongside the cool trickles of goo.

I fell to my knees as the agony of having the skin peeled from my fingers seared through me. With the eye that remained uncovered, I saw my fingerprints were gone. Only the pinkish-yellow fatty tissue underneath remained. I gagged again, and this time I vomited.

The air next to me wavered, like heat waves in the distance looming over a black tar road. Familiar creatures struggled against each other as they tried to enter this world. I wondered why they hadn't just stayed here. Maybe they hadn't expected to snare someone else this quickly with their otherworldly trap.

A young, muscular kid with a blond crewcut jogged toward me on the path and froze when he caught sight of me. *Two people in one day,* I thought. *What are the odds of seeing two people in one day?*

I tried to move, to chase him away, but I was as frozen as the guy in the sand field had been. I tried to scream, to warn him he was in danger. The slimy substance flowed into my mouth the instant I opened it, coated my tongue, and ran down my throat. My efforts to tell the jogger to save himself ended before they could begin. He screamed, but he didn't run.

My attention was drawn to the creatures in the wavering air beside me. They slithered across each other like snakes, fighting to become corporeal. A familiar looking weapon appeared and aimed at my head. I couldn't watch it fire at me.

My uncovered eye slid back to the other jogger. He was frantically kicking his leg, trying to dislodge the bluish-gray blob already crawling over his ankle.

The weapon made a high-pitched whining noise as it fired.

I was rather shocked to discover I was still alive and in one piece. I opened the eye I'd squeezed shut and saw the interdimensional portal disappear. The weapon disappeared with it. I was standing on the trail with the jogger. The blob on his ankle shriveled up and fell to the ground.

I coughed, dislodging the goo that had crawled into my mouth and down my throat. The rest of the substance on my head remained unchanged, but at least I was able to speak again.

"Run!" I yelled. That should've been the kid's automatic response to what he'd seen, but incredibly, he stayed where he was. "Why are you still here?"

"You okay, dude?" he asked, ignoring me. My face and head were still mostly covered, but the substance was no longer spreading. I still had one eye free, and the stuff hadn't gone into my ears. And I was alive. I looked at my hands, and was about to respond, when pulses of green light fired behind me. I dropped to the ground automatically and watched as the corpse and every trace of the substance on the ground was obliterated.

"He should be fine, and so should you," said an authoritative voice behind me.

I scrambled to my feet and found myself face to face with a woman wearing a jogging suit that matched the unfortunate victim's.

"What was that?" I asked, still numb with shock.

The jogger walked closer to where the woman and I stood.

"We've named the race '*Volatilian Expatarian.*' This," she said, gesturing to where the mess had been. "It's how they reproduce. They absorb the brain from a human victim. Once they've internalized it, the resulting entity splits into smaller pieces. Those pieces multiply. Each one grows into one of two variations. One kind continues to reproduce. The other kind becomes a colonizer."

"Why did the bounty hunters show up, fire on that guy, and disappear?"

"To speed up the process. They work with the colonizers. We don't fully understand their relationship."

"How do we stop them?" asked the jogger.

"We don't," she said. "At least not yet. We're constantly experimenting, learning, trying to understand how they take hold of a person. How they get inside the skull and reach the brain." She looked at me.

"I felt it go under my scalp," I whispered. "Did it get in *my* brain? I thought you said I'd be okay!"

"You will be. Our experiments are painless."

"What?"

"We take very good care of our test subjects. After all, it will be you who ultimately help us learn how to destroy our enemy."

"Wait. How… how long have you been here?" I suddenly felt very, very sick. "Were you watching? Did you *let it* attack me? *So you could experiment on me*?"

"It's necessary," she said simply.

Three men walked up behind her. One held a syringe the size of a salami. They didn't look like the type of people who would "take good care of" their "test subjects". I couldn't believe how close I'd been to falling for her spiel.

The jogger turned and ran. Finally.

"It's much simpler if you don't make us sedate you," the woman said. I hadn't realized before how incredibly cold her eyes were. "Just come peacefully. You will be a hero."

Mentally, I quickly mapped out a path through this part of the Safe Zone. I knew this area like the back of my hand, and I knew where the terrain was the roughest. I'd been running this trail every day for several years now, and I was in excellent physical condition.

"Humanity is doomed, don't you get it?" I asked. "No experiments can save us."

I thanked whoever was listening that the gooey globs hadn't touched my legs. I raised my blood-soaked middle fingers, then ran for my life.

PORTRAITS IN THE ATTIC

Accepting this project was a mistake, in Willie's opinion. The house needed a lot more work than the others they'd flipped. She didn't mind the extra work, but she did mind the extra expense. Sinking money into an old house could prove disastrous. Their profit might not cover the cost of repairs if they ran into unexpected problems. And in this line of work, there were *always* unexpected problems.

Willie loved remodeling houses. It was incredibly satisfying to transform an unlivable disaster into a home. She and her partner, Katie, had met on a jobsite. They discovered their talents complimented each other perfectly, so they decided to go into business on their own. Over the past eight years, they'd bought, restored, and sold twenty-one houses. They'd developed a reputation for quality work. They'd also developed a romantic relationship.

Katie had been drawn to this house from the instant she saw it. While the place had tremendous potential, Willie had concerns about its local reputation for being haunted. The realtor assured them once they transformed the house from its current condition to someplace livable, they'd have buyers fighting over it. Willie deferred to Katie's judgment, and they bought the house.

As Willie guided their truck through the tiny town of Banded Rock, her misgivings returned with a vengeance. She wished she'd tried harder to dissuade Katie from jumping on this contract.

They did a quick run-through of the house, taking specific notes and making a list of things they'd need to buy from the hardware store. The kitchen had to be gutted, which was common in most houses they took on. They'd already ordered cabinets; they were getting delivered in three days. They had a lot of hideous wallpaper to remove, subfloors to build, tile to lay, and three windows to replace (which were to be delivered in six days). The hardwood floors needed to be sanded and stained. There was a banister to repair, and bathroom fixtures to replace. Several rooms needed new sections of drywall.

The master bedroom was at the end of a hallway on the second floor. Willie examined the light fixture. *This thing is so old, we could probably sell it to a history museum.*

"Hey? Do you remember this room having two closets?" Katie asked.

"No. I thought it just had one really big one."

"Huh. I hope it doesn't have wallpaper like the other one," she said.

Willie looked across the room and saw Katie open a door that stood in the middle of the back wall.

"What the hell? It leads up. I don't remember the disclosure mentioning an attic."

"It's probably just a tiny storage space. Let's check it out later."

* * *

Katie eased the truck into a parking stall on the main street of Banded Rock. Aside from a few other vehicles, the street was empty of any sign of life.

"This place gives me the creeps," Willie muttered.

"You just aren't used to small towns."

"Whatever. Why don't we split up to save time? You get the groceries, and I'll go to that hardware store across the street."

Willie walked over to the small, locally owned business. A sign in the display window announced this was their 50th year of operation.

A bell chimed over the door when she walked in. A half dozen customers were milling about, and two or three of them turned to stare at the newcomer. They caught Willie's eye, then quickly turned back to what they were doing. As she walked up and down the aisles, people made an obvious effort to ignore and even avoid her.

Creepy. But at least it's not deserted.

The store was tidy and well-organized, and it didn't take long for her to find what they needed. As she stood in line to check out, a woman approached her. She was easily six inches shorter than Willie. She had a young face, suggesting she was maybe in her mid-twenties, but her dark hair was streaked with silver.

"You bought the old Mason place," she stated. It sounded like an accusation.

"Yes," Willie responded, startled by the sudden, thousandfold increase in tension in the air. Conversations stopped as the other customers turned to look at them. The employee stocking shelves dropped the box of nails he was holding. The man at the cash register stopped ringing up his current customer so they could both pay attention to whatever was about to happen. When the woman next to her remained silent but continued to watch her, Willie cleared her throat and said, "We're looking forward to fixing it up. We can do wonders for the place." She smiled, determined to stay positive and ignore the stares now aimed at her from every eye in the store.

"You need to find out what happens in the attic," the woman finally said. "Find out, and put a stop to it." The woman looked around at the other townspeople and wrung her hands. She was obviously paranoid, Willie thought. "Don't let them take your picture," she added.

With that cryptic warning, she fled the store.

The cashier said nothing as he rang up Willie's order. She felt a sudden desire to pick up Katie and drive to the Interstate without looking back.

Instead, she thanked the man who handed her the bags of supplies she'd bought. She walked as quickly as she could without looking like she was fleeing. While she was tossing her things into the truck, Katie walked up behind her.

"Hey, that was good timing!" she exclaimed.

Willie jumped.

"Everything go okay in there?" Katie asked, looking concerned. "You seem a little freaked out."

"Yeah. Well, no, but I'm fine. I just ran into some locals who tried to scare me with the town gossip. How about you?"

"Well, people around here are very nosy and a little – I don't know." She frowned. "I'm excited about this house, but I'm not really excited about the town. Someone asked me if we planned to attend church this Sunday. I told them we're not religious. They said we better find religion fast."

Willie swallowed. "Did they say why?"

Katie looked at her oddly and snorted. "Because this is a conservative Christian town? I don't know. Maybe they don't approve of our lifestyle."

"That's not it. Did they mention the attic?"

"The attic? No? Why?"

"We need to go up there when we get back and see what's there."

Katie shrugged. "As long as we don't waste a lot of time."

* * *

Willie and Katie stood in the attic's single room. Bare drywall covered the walls, but the ceiling was just rafters. The floor was bare wood. There were several metal cabinets, and a light fixture jutting from the wall like an afterthought. The rest of the room was empty.

"We could throw a quick coat of paint on the walls and maybe cover this floor with an area rug," Katie suggested. "A big storage room is a great selling point; we know that from experience. But for now, we need to focus on the kitchen. If you want to start—"

Willie was already standing in front of the cupboards.

"What are you doing?"

"I just need to see something." She opened one of the doors.

Katie grabbed her shoulder. "What happened at the store? There's something you're not telling me."

She sighed. "This woman came up to me and said something about the attic. She said we need to check it out. She said there's something up here."

Katie rolled her eyes. "I can't believe you're letting ghost stories get to you."

"She said nothing about ghosts." Willie turned to look at her. "Humor me."

The cupboards were filled with random junk. There were some old clothes, rusty hand tools, several pairs of broken eyeglasses, half-filled jugs of household chemicals, pieces of costume jewelry, and knick-knacks. Instead of just pushing them aside, Willie took them out and examined them.

“For God’s sake Willie. I know you don’t want to do this house, but seriously? You’re going to worry about local rumors? What do you expect to find in an empty attic?”

“Wait a second,” Willie said as she knelt. After pulling out an empty cardboard box, she crawled inside. She knocked on it and heard a hollow thud. “There’s something behind this.”

“Yes. A wall.”

“Give me your flashlight.” Willie reached a hand back out.

Katie sighed. “Take it. I’m going downstairs to work on the kitchen. When you’re done messing around, perhaps you could join me?”

Willie ignored her. The left edge of the cabinet had hinges. About two and a half feet to the right, her fingers ran into a lip running from near the top of the cupboard to the bottom. She’d discovered a tiny door. She pulled it open and crawled through the back of the cabinet.

She stood carefully, unsure of the height of the ceiling. She reached up and was pleasantly surprised to find it was high enough her fingertips could barely reach it. *If someone bothered to put up a ceiling, they must’ve put in lights,* she thought. She felt along the wall until she found a switch and flipped on the overhead light.

The room was completely finished. It had an out of style brown shag carpet that must've been laid in the seventies, although it was in near perfect condition. The walls and textured ceiling were all painted light brown.

She turned off the flashlight. Finding secret rooms wasn't unprecedented. They'd found a hidden room under a floor in one of the other old houses they'd worked on.

They could move the cabinets and build an actual doorway, she supposed. The shag carpet would have to go. She noticed some portraits hanging on the opposite wall. The first was an eight-by-ten inch black and white photo of a man screaming. His eyes were wide open, and as Willie studied it, she saw the outline of a person reflected in the irises.

She stepped back in horror. "Why would anyone take a picture like that?" she asked the empty room. She hadn't seen the photos hanging on the walls when she crawled in. She shone the flashlight on the closest one and saw a woman with the same expression as the man in the other photo. Her eyes were full of terror, and her mouth was wide open in a scream. A child was the subject of the portrait to the right of that one. She was screaming also. They all wore Victorian clothing, Willie noticed.

The row of photos had to be a prank. A sick, disturbing prank. *The woman in the store was probably the one who thought it up. That's why the whole store turned to stare. They're probably having a good laugh right now.*

She felt compelled to look for portraits on the other wall, although she was certain the wall had been bare when she came in. She saw four of them hanging at eye level, all full color. All were screaming.

"Katie!" she screamed. She crawled back out the room, slammed the cupboard door, and ran down the stairs.

* * *

Katie was knocking shelves out of the cupboards with a sledgehammer. She'd stripped down to her tank top, displaying her well defined muscles. Her brown hair was pulled back in a bouncy ponytail. Her cutoff shorts clung to her hips like they were painted on. Willie barely noticed. She was too frightened.

"Katie, I found something," she said with a trembling voice.

"Damn it, Willie, I need your help. Stop messing around in the attic."

"Please just come look."

"I have actual work to do, and so do you."

"Come up and look. If you aren't concerned, I promise I won't mention it again."

Katie turned to her, holding the sledgehammer, sweat dripping down her face. She swore. "Fine."

She followed Willie up the stairs. Willie opened the door to the cupboard and crawled inside.

"You have *got* to be joking."

"Come *on*."

Katie finally followed her.

"See? Secret room." Willie walked to the wall with the photos.

Katie looked around and shuddered. "Okay. I admit it. This is creepy. Hidden rooms are never used for anything good."

"Now look at this." She shone her flashlight on the photos.

"Oh my god," Katie said quietly. She moved from portrait to portrait, lightly touching the frames. "What exactly did the person at the store tell you?"

"You believe me now?"

Katie grabbed the light from her hand and looked at the portraits. "I believe this is someone's idea of a sick joke. Hell, they probably have a camera stashed somewhere up here, running a live feed," Katie said. "It's probably some sort of town prank. Let's get back down to the kitchen."

They worked on the kitchen in silence. Katie tore out the old cabinets while Willie tore down wallpaper. After a time, Katie said, "huh."

"'Huh,' what?"

"The attic. It wouldn't take too much to turn both those rooms into bedrooms."

"Bedrooms? Are you insane?*"*

"Come on. It's not that hard to take pictures off the wall. We'll have an electrician put brighter lights in both rooms. We'll need to have egress windows built in, of course. We can do the rest, and we can build a couple of closets in the corners. That'll cut into our budget, but I think it would be worth it. We had a little more in our windows budget than we used, anyway."

"Jesus, Katie!"

"I'll go talk to the city engineer tomorrow and see what we need to do about a building permit."

Willie remained silent. Katie would argue until she got her way. There was no point in trying to dissuade her from what had to be the worst idea in their history of flipping houses.

The next day, Willie tore out the living room carpet while Katie went to talk to the city engineer. She didn't want to be alone in the house, but she wasn't about to admit it.

When Katie got back to the house, she was pale as a ghost. Warning bells rang in Willie's head. "What's wrong?"

"I talked to Bob Bellman, the city engineer."

"Yeah? Is he gonna give us our permit?"

Katie leaned against the kitchen doorframe and looked into the living room. "He can't."

"Why not?"

"Because… Willie…" Her mouth stayed open, but she didn't say anything. It was like the words were stuck in her throat. She opened the cooler they'd brought with them and pulled out a bottle of juice.

"Because what? What did he say?"

"He pulled out the blueprints of the house. He showed me. He..." She took a large drink of the juice.

"He *what!?*"

"This house doesn't have an attic, Willie. It can't. He showed me the dimensions. The house isn't tall enough for there to be one. Are you hearing me? It can't possibly be there. The attic we were standing in doesn't exist."

"Well, the blueprints are wrong. It's obviously there."

"There's something else."

"You're shaking." Katie didn't get shaken up easily. Maybe this place was getting to her, finally, too.

"A woman came up to me while I was getting into the car. She said, 'You need to find out what happens in the attic.'"

"She said what? Were those her exact words?"

"Yes. Then she turned and walked across the street. A car came around the corner and hit her. Then it... it backed up and drove over her body. Like it wanted to make sure she was dead. Another witness asked me if I got the license plate. I had looked, but it didn't have one."

Willie put her arms around her girlfriend. "That's awful. I'm so sorry you had to see something like that. But I need to ask you something. What did the woman look like?"

Katie buried her face in Willie's shoulder.

"She was short, with dark hair."

Just like the woman in the hardware store.

"Let's go have another look at the attic," she said in a solemn voice. "We were so focused on those creepy portraits, we didn't really look at anything else. Rooms don't just appear out of nowhere. We'll take measurements and photos and get that engineer to come check it out. Okay?"

Or we could just take the truck and get the hell out of here.

"Okay. I love you, Willie."

Willie winked at her, unsmiling. "I know."

They went to the attic, walked through the first room that supposedly didn't exist, and crawled through the cupboard doors into the second.

"Bellman thought I was screwing with him," Katie said softly. "He got mad, Willie. Really, really angry. He practically threw me out of his office."

"The people in this town are weird. Seriously… maybe there's something in the water," murmured Willie. She squinted at the walls as she ran her hands along them. "Unless there's another secret door in this room, I don't see anything but those creepy pictures."

"Oh my god, this is morbid," Katie muttered, staring at the portraits. "If this isn't part of the house, then where are we?"

"I don't know. I'll tell you right now, if we find a body, I'm out of here."

"We're not gonna find a body."

Her hesitant voice told Willie she wouldn't be surprised at all to find a body.

"There's something the woman in the hardware store said. She said, 'Don't let them take your picture.' Kind of creepy considering all these." She shone the flashlight from one end of the row to the other.

"Who do you suppose 'they' are?"

Willie shrugged. "I don't know." She took a closer glance at the wall. A new portrait had appeared. "What the hell is this?" she murmured.

Katie walked toward her. "What is it?"

"I think – I think maybe we need to get out of the attic. Right now."

Katie looked over Willie's shoulder. "Oh my god," she said as she stared at the portrait. "That's the girl I saw. The dead girl."

"It's the same girl I talked to in the store. I think she tried to warn us, and the house killed her."

"A car killed her, Willie."

"Then why is her picture *here* if the house wasn't involved? What if these are all photos of people it has killed? She's screaming in the photo, just like the others!"

Katie looked at her, unsettled. "That's impossible. Houses don't kill people. Houses don't have a reason to kill people. They're just… just *houses*."

"Look at the damn picture! It's not only possible, it's right there staring us in the face!"

Katie wrung her hands, something she only did when she was afraid. "There's got to be a logical explanation. Tomorrow we'll go into town. I'll talk to that engineer again and make him tell me the entire history of this place, no matter how angry he gets. We'll get to the bottom of this. In the meantime, can we just get back to work? We have a lot to do yet before the cupboards get delivered."

Willie gaped at her. "You're insane. We're leaving, Katie. Now." She reached for her hands and pulled.

Katie's feet stayed planted to the floor. "Why did you shut the door?"

Willie turned to look. "I didn't."

Not only was the door closed, the doorknob was missing.

Willie swore. She went to the wall where the door was. She tried to pry it open, but it wouldn't budge. "Help me."

The overhead light exploded, sending shards of glass flying.

Katie screamed.

"Are you alright?" Willie pulled the flashlight from her belt and shone it toward Katie.

"Great," she snapped. "Never better. Maybe if you'd stayed out of the damned cupboards—"

"You're blaming me? I told you we should stay away from this house in the first place! If everyone says a house is haunted, you don't buy it! You get the hell away from it!"

Katie took a deep breath. "I admit it. I screwed up. You were right and I was wrong. Yell at me later."

"At least we still have our flashlights. It wasn't that bright in here anyway. Just watch it so you don't cut yourself."

"Where did that come from?" Katie asked. They each pointed their flashlight at the wall.

A new picture frame had appeared. Inside it a photo slowly developed, like it was in a darkroom. It showed two human heads, with long necks connected to the same body. Neither one had hair, and they both grinned slowly from ear to ear as the girls watched.

The flashlights' batteries died. They heard a chuckle from the area where the portrait was.

Katie put her arms around Willie. "I'm sorry," she whispered. "I'm so sorry."

A male voice whispered in their ears. "Welcome," it said.

"So, you have big plans for our house, huh?" said the monster in the portrait. "They all do," the thing sighed. "We like things just the way they are around here."

"We'll leave," Willie said. "Right now. We'll go right out the front door."

"Ah, but it's so difficult to leave when there's no door to get out of the room!" the two-headed thing commented.

As Willie and Katie clung to each other, they heard the click of a camera.

* * *

When Willie woke up, she was still in the attic, but the light had been replaced in the room. It was brighter than it had been when she first discovered it. Broken glass no longer littered the floor.

"Willie? Where are you?"

"I'm right here. I can't see you. I think I passed out. I had a nightmare about a monster."

"Unless we're sharing nightmares, I don't think it was a dream. Look, the door is open. Let's go."

Willie ran face first into a pane of glass. She heard a *thud* next to her.

Katie grunted. "I can't move. What's happening?"

"Allow me to show you," said the creepy voice of the two-headed monster.

A mirror materialized on the opposite wall. Willie looked at the reflection of two new framed portraits. The only difference between these and the others was that she and Katie weren't screaming.

The monster disappeared.

"Katie?"

"Don't start."

"Do you think we're dead?"

"No. I mean we can still talk, right? And we're not frozen in terror, screaming. We can get out of here. I mean, the door is back, right? We just have to think."

Willie thought of the first portrait she saw. The man had a reflection of something or someone in his eye. It didn't have two heads, so it must've been something else.

"Something else is coming. The thing that will make us scream. The thing that'll kill us."

"Don't borrow trouble," she snapped. "Let's just figure out how to get out of here."

Willie heard *thud thud thud thud*. "What are you doing?"

"I'm trying to break the glass." *Thud.*

"How? By pounding your head into it?"

Thud. Thud.

"Katie, stop! Listen. I saw something in one of the portraits."

Across the room, their reflections faded. The mirror was replaced with a tunnel, stretching farther and farther back until it disappeared. The sides of the tunnel wavered as they formed walls. Watching it was a bit like looking in a curvy funhouse mirror. As soon as the walls solidified, framed portraits appeared, hanging in neat rows that stretched back toward the end of the tunnel. Dozens of photos became hundreds. Hundreds became thousands.

And then it appeared. Katie and Willie watched a mess of tornadic swirls take on the form of a person. With its wobbling legs, it walked toward them. As it passed each portrait, the person inside screamed audibly.

The noise level rose and rose, until it nearly pierced their eardrums.

"Don't scream!" Willie hollered, without any real hope that Katie could hear her over the unbearable cacophony. *"Once you scream, it's over!"* She didn't know why that made sense, but deep inside she knew it was true.

Katie screamed.

"No! No, Katie, stop! Stop!"

The creature stepped out of the mirror.

Willie finally succumbed and screamed, too. She couldn't help it. The sound was being ripped out of her. She felt her face forming the same expression as the people in the other portraits, and she couldn't make it stop. The corners of her mouth cracked as her jaw was pried open by a force she couldn't see. Her eyes were stretched open in a terrified stare by invisible fingers. She tried to blink, but she might as well have been trying to move a mountain by blowing on it.

The creature plucked a photo off the wall and held it up in front of them. The woman inside screamed. Grinning, the thing tossed it into the tunnel, where it slammed onto one of the tunnel walls.

Willie and Katie watched in horror as photo after screaming photo were thrown into the tunnel. The portraits were added to the row inside. And then the monster stepped out of view. Katie would be next.

A baseball bat slammed into the glass in front of Willie's face, and she fell through a barrier onto the floor of the attic. She could move her facial muscles again. She heard another smash of glass, and Katie landed on the floor next to her.

A man stood in front of the creature. He held the baseball bat, ready to swing. The creature lunged, losing its shape as it stretched toward him.

"Bob, look out!" Katie screamed.

The man swung the bat, but not at the creature. He struck the mirror, which disintegrated, taking the creature along with it. The noise of screams coming from the tunnel was cut off.

"Who the hell are you?" demanded Willie. She saw the portraits on the wall fade away.

"Why aren't they being released like us? What's happening to them?" Katie asked.

"They've already crossed over. They're part of the tunnel now. There's nothing we can do."

The man tossed the bat to the ground and reached down to help Willie up.

"I'm Robert Bellman," he said, and Willie recognized the name of the city engineer. He held out a hand to Katie next and pulled her up. "Go," he said, grabbing each girl by the shoulder and steering them toward the little door.

He doesn't have to tell me twice, thought Willie. She crawled through the opening and out the cupboard door into the attic's main room. She reached back in and dragged Katie out, and Bellman followed.

"We need to leave. Go!"

The group ran down the stairs. Willie expected the front door to slam shut like it always did in horror movies. Or maybe one of them would trip and fall down the stairs. But those things didn't happen. They ran out the front door, not even bothering to close it.

* * *

The trio settled around a table at the town's only café. They drew a few judgmental stares, but Willie ignored them. The townspeople's opinions about newcomers didn't interest her in the least. Especially since they'd be leaving here forever, just as soon as Bob explained to them what the hell just happened.

A server poured them some coffee. Katie's hands shook too hard for her to open her plastic cup of creamer, so Bob took it from her and did it himself.

"How did you know to come up there? How were you able to find a room you said doesn't exist?" Katie asked as she watched him stir her coffee.

"And how did you know what to do?" Willie added.

"I didn't. I acted on instinct. And the room – I knew it existed. Here's what you need to understand. That house is so old, no one even knows when it was built. There are no records. But the whole town claims it's haunted, and not by an ordinary ghost.

There have been rumors about people dying in there over the years. The local cops have checked it out, and they swear up and down people get trapped in pictures. People accept that explanation. Folks around here are superstitious.

"After talking to you, Katie, I realized it was about to happen again. I'd always thought the rumors were ridiculous, but when I looked back through the town's obituaries, I saw that many of the locals' bodies were never found. Considering what you had asked me about, I figured you could be in trouble."

"And what about the next owners?" Willie asked.

"There won't be any next owners," Katie answered. "We're not selling."

"Not selling?" Willie and Bob asked in unison.

"Not selling," Katie repeated. "Demolishing. Think we can get a permit for that?"

"I don't think it'll be a problem," said Bob. "At least, not from a city or legal aspect. If anyone tries to prevent its destruction, it'll be the house itself."

MIRRORS DO LIE

At first, Charlie thought his wife had finally driven him insane.

On the night his life changed, he stepped out of the shower and dried himself off. He pulled the shower curtain closed, grabbed his pajamas from their hook behind the door, and got dressed. (Charlie preferred to sleep naked, but Andrea refused to allow it). He took his toothbrush and toothpaste from the medicine cabinet. When he shut the cabinet door, he dropped them both in the sink with a clatter. He whirled around to look at the shower curtain, grabbing his chest as his heart began pounding furiously. He looked back at the mirror, and again saw something that couldn't possibly be there.

Charlie jumped when his wife stuck her head through the doorway. "What are you doing in here? You've been in this bathroom for thirty minutes! And look at how much water you dripped on the floor! You are *such* a slob! I can't believe I've put up with you for all these years."

He ignored her. Tuning her out was a self-defense mechanism. "Do you see that?" he asked. "There, in the mirror?"

She scoffed and rolled her eyes. "Why don't you stop spending so much time staring at yourself in the mirror and pay some attention to me for once?"

"Andrea, *look in the mirror*." He couldn't take his eyes off the reflection of the shower curtain. Wrapped around the edge were four delicate fingers, with impeccably manicured, cherry red fingernails. "The mirror is *wrong*!"

His wife huffed. She ran a hand through her hair. "Are you ever going to get over your ridiculous fear of mirrors? Why can't you be afraid of dust? Maybe this house wouldn't be so filthy if you'd clean it occasionally."

One of the lovely fingers in the mirror beckoned him to come closer. "Is this some kind of joke?" Charlie demanded. He whirled around and ripped the shower curtain from the bar, exposing an empty shower stall.

"Why did you do that?" his wife screeched. "Look at what you've done!"

Her bulging eyes were roughly the size of beach balls, Charlie thought, and her voice rang out at a high enough pitch that every dog within a three-mile radius most likely had bleeding ears. He turned back toward the reflection and gasped, staggering backward into the wall.

Part of a woman's face joined the fingers in the reflection. A brown eye, a sliver of a nose and half a smile emerged from behind the shower curtain.

Charlie's wife ventured into the bathroom. He bumped into her as he slammed his hands against the mirror. It was completely solid.

"I don't know what you think you're trying to pull off, here. But it's not working. Clean up this mess! I need to shower so I can get Muffy to her grooming appointment! We can't be late!"

Mesmerized by the face that had now fully emerged from behind the shower curtain, Charlie said, "You know what? I hate that damned dog."

"How dare you talk about my Muffy Poo that way?" exclaimed Andrea. "Have you lost your mind?"

He let her ranting and raving turn into a gray blur of sound. His attention was fully focused on the leg stepping out of the shower. The woman wasn't especially beautiful, but she wasn't unattractive, either. She had a kind smile, and a graceful way of moving that reminded Charlie of a swan on a lake.

At this point, Charlie briefly feared for his sanity. He had to be hallucinating. There was no other explanation.

"You're not hallucinating," said a soft voice. The woman in the mirror winked at him, and her smile grew wider.

"Did you hear that?" Charlie asked, interrupting Andrea's complaining.

"Are you even *listening to me*?"

"Yes, dear. So is everyone else on the block, I expect." He touched the mirror again, and this time his fingers pushed into it slightly.

"You can't talk to me like that!"

"Like what?" he asked, his eyes locked with those of the woman on the other side of the mirror.

"Like I'm some floozy off the street! Like I'm an annoyance you have to put up with! I'm your wife!"

The woman in the mirror gestured again for him to come to her.

"I want to come to you," Charlie said. "I don't know how!"

"Oh my god, you're having a psychotic breakdown! You're talking to a mirror! I'm going to call my sister!" With that announcement, she stomped off like a crabby three-year-old.

"I didn't think we'd ever get rid of her," said the soft voice.

"I've wanted to get rid of her for years. You have no idea," Charlie said.

"Then take my hand."

The woman reached her hand through the mirror, into Charlie's bathroom. He glanced out the doorway, but didn't see his wife in the bedroom. He looked around the rest of the bathroom, checking again to make sure no one else was with him on this side of the mirror.

He shrugged. "What've I got to lose?"

He slid his fingers into her grip, and she pulled him off the floor and through the mirror.

The woman let go of his hand as he crossed the threshold of the mirror, and he landed with a thump on his hands and knees. He stumbled a bit as he got to his feet. He was standing in a bathroom like his own, but he'd expected there to be a doorway leading to an exact copy of his bedroom. He'd expected to fall into the arms of the woman on the other side. But this… wasn't that at all.

"Hey! Lady! Where are you?" He threw back the shower curtain, but the shower stall was empty. "What is this? What's happening?"

Charlie frantically looked around the confines of the bathroom. It was a mirror image of his own, certainly, but that's all it was. There was no door, and there was no way back through the mirror. He was trapped inside.

"Thank you, Monica. You have no idea how grateful I am."

"You're quite welcome, Andrea," answered the soft voice of the woman in the mirror.

VITAL TO YOUR SURVIVAL

"Please pay close attention. What I'm about to tell you is vital to your survival."

Their unwavering stares, which didn't quite meet my eyes, disturbed me. I didn't want to show fear before the house's new owners, and I didn't want to say anything that could be construed as an admission of guilt. My husband Tyler and I technically hadn't lied, but we hadn't exactly disclosed information about the events leading to the sale of the property, either.

Now these ladies owned the place, and they were in trouble. They'd asked me to come and speak with them about the house. I had a moral responsibility to tell them the truth. My conscience insisted I warn them, no matter how uncomfortable or difficult it was for me to speak to them.

They'd introduced themselves as Teri and Simone, two sisters who moved to the Midwest from Seattle in search of a quiet life. Both appeared to be just as nervous as I was, and I suspected they wouldn't be surprised by some of the things I had to say.

"Everyone has heard ghost stories about houses haunted by the spirits of past occupants who don't want to leave, or victims of car accidents hanging out on the road they died on because they don't realize they're dead. There are many moving tales of those who wait to move on until they make sure their loved ones are safe. Many of these accounts are based on fact. Ghosts aren't as uncommon as you might think, and usually they're harmless.

"Occasionally, a living person attracts a poltergeist or demon. Now those? Those are manifestations of pure evil. And if the demon latches on to a place, it fouls the land for eternity.

"This house has none of those problems," I said. I wanted to start our conversation on a positive note, even if I had to stretch the truth a little.

"We were beside ourselves with excitement, Tyler and I, when we found out our bid on this house was accepted. After twenty long years of living in apartments and run-down rental houses, we were finally buying our own place.

"The house had gone through six owners in twenty years. Seven, now, I guess. None of the previous owners lived here more than four years. We should've suspected something was wrong when we were given that information."

Teri glared at her sister as if trying to bore a hole through her head with her eyes. *She*, apparently, had suspected something was wrong.

“How was I supposed to know?” Simone muttered.

“The place was in excellent condition, as far as we could tell,” I continued. “It was by far the best house we’d seen in eight months of looking. It had so much personality, such an amazing layout, and such beautiful landscaping; we knew we’d never find another place like it. Even though it was a bit out of our price range, our mortgage application was approved, and we moved into the house three weeks later.

“At first, we didn’t think too much about the random repairs the house constantly required. Even brand-new houses could have problems, after all. It’s a simple fact of home ownership. So, when the dishwasher broke, and a window leaked, and an electrical outlet stopped working, we chalked it up to everyday homeowner woes. These were easy problems to fix, although not inexpensive. But we were so excited to have our own home, it didn’t cross our minds that something sinister could be causing our problems.

“Our three cats were just as thrilled to be in the new place as Tyler and I were. An open floor plan after six years of running around in a cramped townhome was heaven on earth for them. Merlin, our orange kitten; Crowley, a sleek black terror on wheels; and Charge, a beautiful tabby, warmed up to the house right away. And Tyler and me? For the first time in our marriage, we lived in a place that didn't make us claustrophobic.

"As the weeks went by, we unpacked, we organized, we settled in. Then things started to disappear. Little things, like earrings, shoes, keys, and small tools. We'd find them later, in places we didn't remember putting them. At first, we chalked it up to carelessness.

"But then, things began to show up in *impossible* places. One time, Tyler found his phone under the sink, balanced on a pipe. We found forty cans of cat food stacked in a corner in the basement. We located a beef roast that had gone missing from the freezer when it spoiled under the basement stairs. Let me tell you, from that day forward, we began exclusively eating white meat."

"*We* are *vegetarian*," Teri announced, lifting her head.

"What does that have to do with anything?" Simone asked, baffled.

I continued. "Tyler and I suspected each other of playing pranks on each other, of course, until the day we walked into the kitchen and saw all three cats hovering near the ceiling." After a pause and an awkward silence, I continued. "Tyler and I both worked from home, so we spent almost all our time in the house. We were frightened. By now, we both knew we weren't imagining what was happening. We started nervously joking that we must have a ghost."

Both ladies shifted uncomfortably on the couch, and I knew their discomfort had nothing to do with the furniture.

"You just said there aren't ghosts here," Teri accused.

"There aren't, but we didn't know that yet. We hadn't discovered what kind of entity we were dealing with."

"What does that mean?" asked Simone, who I'd begun to think of as the quiet one.

"Have patience. You'll understand by the time I'm finished."

Simone crossed her arms and pursed her lips. I wanted to get this over with. It was surprisingly more uncomfortable than I thought it would be. And irritating.

"Like I was saying, we joked about it. But we didn't know what to believe. It's not that we didn't believe in ghosts. We just thought they must have better things to do than move someone's stuff around and bother house pets. We convinced ourselves that we'd shared a hallucination about the cats. After all, they acted no differently than they had before the incident. They didn't act like they sensed evil.

"Then we became sick.

"We had symptoms of a cold, or of allergies. But our sneezing, dripping noses, and endlessly watering eyes didn't respond to the usual over-the-counter medications meant to lessen these symptoms. We were sick for days, then weeks. Our condition continued to worsen, so we went to the doctor. She wasn't worried; she gave us shots of antihistamines and assured us we'd feel better soon.

"We didn't.

"That's when everything began to spiral out of control, I think. We were both in the upstairs office working on our laptops one morning. From downstairs came a sound like a freight train thundering through the kitchen. We rushed down the stairs and saw the ceiling fan in a crumpled-up mess on the floor. Its live wires hung from the ceiling like spiders' legs and danced around like lit firecrackers. Tyler ran to the basement and flipped the breaker.

"We heard squeaking, hissing, and chattering sounds coming from the attic, after the electrical sparking and sizzling noises stopped.

"'That explains it,' Tyler said. 'Those sounds are coming from mice. Or maybe rats. They must've chewed through the wiring.'

"It was a perfectly logical explanation."

Teri stood up and began to pace. "The seller's disclosure document said nothing about rats. "What else haven't you told us?"

I ignored her.

"We bought some traps since we couldn't use poison around our pets. When we climbed up to the attic to lay them out, we discovered black, green and white mold growing in great swirls on the walls."

"It said nothing about mold, either," Teri said.

"Please stop interrupting me.

"A few days later it rained, and streams of water leaked in through the bathroom skylights. We put buckets and bowls under the leaks and dumped them every twenty minutes for over five hours. It was exhausting, filthy, and frustrating. When the rain stopped, Tyler climbed onto the roof to put a tarp over the leaking glass. He—"

I stopped. Of all the things we experienced, this was the most difficult to talk about. This was the moment we realized we were in over our heads.

"He what?" demanded Teri.

I looked away. "He found scratches on the roof by the skylight. Like something with giant claws tried to dig the skylight out of the roof."

Both sisters stared blankly at me.

"We didn't even know who to call for help. Tyler dragged the tarp over the roof, covered the skylight, and we… we just tried to rationalize it.

"The house grew darker after that, like something was sucking the light out of it. We bought a couple of standing lamps, and a couple table lamps. We put higher wattage bulbs in the fixtures. We even painted the bathrooms and bedrooms lighter colors. Nothing changed. It was like a permanent layer of film covered the lights.

"By now, the jokes about having a ghost in our house were becoming serious conversations.

"I called a metaphysical store to ask for some advice. I bet you know the one, since you have those very distinctive candles." I gestured at the white candles shaped like winding staircases that were burning on either side of the coffee table.

"The Crystal Empire," said Simone.

"Yes. I was afraid they might not believe me. As I briefly described our situation, I half expected them to try and sell me incense, or charms, or spells. Instead, the person I talked to offered to send someone to our house to do a blessing. She didn't charge anything, the person on the phone assured me. She did it because she had the ability and felt it was her responsibility to use it.

"A few days later, she arrived at a prearranged time. We invited her in. She told us about her background, and her process, and asked if we'd show her around the house so she could get a feel for it.

"Her face was expressionless as we led her from room to room. We went downstairs, and she stopped in the middle of the family room.

"'What do you know about the prior occupants?' she asked us.

"We replied that we didn't know anything, except that there'd been a lot of them over the years.

"'Homes can soak up psychic energy, either positive or negative. It affects the house's personality. When a lot of people have come and gone, the house is bound to feel rejected and uneasy.'

"Tyler looked at her and chuckled nervously. 'Houses can't feel rejected. That's preposterous.'

"'I'm afraid you're wrong, Mr. Diver. Houses absorb psychic energy. In a manner of speaking, all houses are alive.'

"She wrinkled her forehead and looked at the floor, almost like she was trying to hear something. Tyler and I glanced sideways at each other. He looked as panicked as I felt. Did this woman honestly think our house was alive? I wondered if I'd made a mistake by inviting her here.

"We both jumped when she asked, 'Have you ever tried to record EVPs? Electronic Voice Phenomena? If there is something here, you might be able to communicate with it that way. The house may even now be trying to speak to you.'

"We had discussed it, we told her, but quite frankly we were afraid of what we'd hear.

"'Hmm,' she responded. She walked over to the circuit breaker box. 'How's the wiring in this place? This box looks ancient. If there's a lot of EMF activity, it could explain your feelings of unease. EMF, as I'm sure you're aware, stands for electromagnetic frequency. Too much household EMF can cause paranoia.'

"Tyler and I, who both had more than a passing interest in the paranormal, had used an EMF meter when we first moved in. It spiked throughout the entire house.

"'I suggest having an electrician check out your house. I'm not blaming old wiring for all the experiences you've been having, but it's definitely contributing to them.'

"With that, she started to walk back up the stairs. She stopped suddenly and cast a strange glance toward the area she'd been standing in, but said no more about the basement and continued to the main floor.

"She proceeded with her blessing, walking through our home with burning sage, opening the windows so the bad energy could leave. She had us ring bells to fill the rooms with sound. As we walked through again, room to room, she told whatever spirits might be listening that they were to live in harmony with us, and any who couldn't do that were not welcome here.

"When she finished, she said, 'I don't sense a foreign presence here. There's nothing here that… shouldn't be.'

"'What's that supposed to mean?' Tyler asked as he crossed his arms and glared at her.

"She ignored him. 'Call about the wiring,' she said. 'I must go. I'm not meant to be here.'

"I thanked her and closed the door behind her. 'What the hell was all that about?' Tyler asked, but I had no answers. 'She thinks our fucking house is alive.'

"Tyler rarely swore, so I knew he was angry. I think he was starting to have the same suspicions I did, and it frightened him. The truth was, even though I hadn't accepted the whole living-house thing, I felt like *something* was… waiting. Waiting to do something horrible to us. It was the most intense feeling of foreboding I'd ever had, and having this blessing done seemed to make it worse, not better. I didn't think it worked. I thought it pissed something off.

"We decided to have an electrician come out. We found a company online with a decent service rating and made an appointment for the following week.

"The next morning, I went to the cupboard and got out a couple cans of cat food. Crowley wove in and out of my legs, Charge was nowhere to be found, and Merlin went straight to the patio door and yowled. I let him out so he could prowl the perimeter of the fence that sectioned off the backyard from the rest of the land."

"That fence is falling apart," Teri complained.

If you didn't see that when you looked at the house, that's your fault, I thought, but didn't want to start an argument. I just wanted to finish this nightmare discussion.

"Oh my *god* Teri! Shut up!" cried Simone.

"We never saw Merlin again," I continued. "I started the coffee machine and looked down at Crowley. His fur, which had been completely black the day before, now had tips of gray in it.

"I pointed it out to Tyler as he walked into the kitchen, towel drying his hair. 'Something must've really scared him, to turn him gray like that,' I said.

"After a pause, he answered, 'That cat's fourteen years old. He's just aging, and we haven't noticed till now.' He poured himself some coffee. I no longer wanted any. I went upstairs to shower.

"As for the attic, the mold mitigation people came and left. We expected relief from our symptoms, but they intensified instead.

"'You know, we never went up there after they left,' Tyler pointed out. 'Maybe they didn't get it all.'

"'We should go up and check the rat traps anyway. We can have a look around.' Armed with flashlights, we climbed the pull-down stairs.

"We carefully stepped from floorboard to floorboard till we were in the corner over the kitchen. Tyler shone his flashlight around the floor. 'I'm sure this is where I put them. Right over the kitchen, where the noises are coming from.'

"We glanced at the walls, and as I turned my flashlight beam to another wall, I screamed. Tyler turned his flashlight to where I was looking.

"'What the hell?' he muttered. The mold was gone, but now blood stained the wood, the insulation, the floor beams. In the midst of the blood, laying on the insulation between the floorboards, were all the rat traps. They hadn't caught any rats, though. Instead, they'd caught Charge, our cat. It was as if he'd stepped on every single one of them. I won't go into detail. I think you can imagine."

Both sisters looked up at the ceiling, as if they could somehow see through it to the attic.

"We couldn't even bring ourselves to move the tiny corpse. We were too horrified. We just needed to get out of the attic.

"Tyler went back up the next day with work gloves, a garbage bag, and a scarf wrapped around his nose. He was up there a long time, and when he came back down, he looked like he'd seen a ghost.

"Charge was very much alive, his body untouched, and he was lying in Tyler's arms and purring.

"'We must've imagined it,' Tyler said, his voice high and hysterical. 'It was dark, we only had flashlights.'

"'You think we both imagined a dead, mutilated cat?'

"'Maybe it was a pile of rats. We've been really stressed lately, and Charge was missing, and we were worried about him. We could've both dreamt it up.'"

Teri, who didn't have her priorities straight at all, in my opinion, asked if they would find dead rats all over the attic.

"Don't you think your home inspector would've found them?" I asked. The truth was, I didn't know. When in doubt, I'd learned, evade.

"So what happened with your cat?" asked Simone.

"Tyler put Charge on the ground, and he went to the kitchen and lapped up an entire bowl of water.

"'What should we do with him?' Tyler asked, as if I were some sort of expert on undead cats.

"'I don't know, take him to the veterinarian?'

"'And then what? Ask the vet why our cat went from a mangled mess to a perfectly normal animal? What the hell is wrong with you?'

"'Well, we could hire an exterminator to take care of whatever is in the attic,' I suggested.

"'How? We're already behind on bills! Our savings is almost gone. Besides, how many exterminators do you know that take care of cat-attacking-and-reanimating pests?'

"He had a point. The next day was a Saturday and neither of us planned to work, so we decided to tackle some yardwork. I remember that day like it was yesterday.

"Tyler wanted to plant an herb garden in the wooden planter on the side of the house. We drove to the gardening store in town, picked up some hardy looking plants, and came back home. As we pulled into the drive, the tree in the front yard dropped a limb on the bed of our truck.

"Neither of us spoke. We didn't have to. Had we been under that branch, we'd have been crushed. Was it an accident? Was something giving us a warning? Or had something tried to kill us and missed?

"We got out of the truck and left it there, blocking the driveway, too stunned to deal with it. We carried the box of herbs to the planter, along with the gardening gloves and little trowel we'd bought to till up the dirt before we planted.

"We just wanted to do something normal. We wanted to create something that had order in the face of all the chaos.

"Tyler set the cardboard box on the ground. I handed him the trowel.

"'We were almost crushed, Ty.'

"'I was there! I noticed!'

"'Maybe we should sell the house,' I said, voicing what we'd both been thinking but neither of us had spoken out loud.

"Tyler threw the trowel into the dirt and whirled around to look at me.

"'And live where? With all the problems this house has, only an idiot would buy it!'"

I looked at the sisters, who were sitting so close together on the couch they were practically leaning on each other. "No offense."

Teri opened her mouth, so I quickly said, "Tyler argued there was no way we'd get back what we paid for it.

"'And we sure as hell can't afford a realtor!'

"'I – I don't know,' I answered. 'But we won't need to worry about money or a place to live if we're dead.' My fear was rapidly becoming anger.

"Tyler looked at me, and I barely recognized him. He scowled, and his eyes flashed briefly with something close to hatred. I'd never seen that look before. He turned back to the planter and began digging furiously, like he was trying to punish the soil. Dirt flew past my face. There wouldn't be any left in the planter at this rate.

"'What in the world is that?' He stopped digging and put down the trowel. He put a finger into the dirt and began to dig. I leaned in to see what he'd found. He pulled something out of the dirt and held it up for me to look at.

"Squinting at it, I asked, 'Is that…'

"'It's a damn *bone*, Brenda.'

"'What kind of bone?'

"'I don't know.' He held it up and examined it. 'From the size of it, I'd say it could be from a large dog, maybe?'

"'A large dog or a small child, isn't that what you're thinking?'"

Teri stood up. She shook her finger at me, and I felt like breaking it off her hand.

"Is that what's haunting this place? A dead child, murdered on this property? How *dare* you—"

I interrupted her. For the first time, I regretted agreeing to talk with them.

"As I've stated, there are no ghosts haunting this property! Do you want to hear the rest of what happened or not?"

Neither of them said a word, so I continued.

"Tyler looked at me before setting the bone carefully on the wooden edge of the planter. He stuck his fingers back in the dirt and carefully scooped and dug until he found another. 'God. It's a jawbone.' He held it up for me to look at, then put it next to the first one. After meeting my eyes, he continued digging. He methodically churned up all the soil in the planter, side to side and top to bottom. I watched in horror as he pulled up bone after bone. After forty minutes of churning up dirt, he'd uncovered a total of thirty-one small bones.

"'I'm calling the cops, Tyler.'

"'Wait,' he instructed while he consulted his phone. He glanced from the bones to the screen and back, then said, 'look at this. See this tooth here? And the one on this jawbone?'

"By comparing the bones to diagrams of animal skeletons he found online, we figured out we'd found the bones of a large dog, probably a Labrador Retriever.

"'These bones are completely clean,' I observed. 'They must've been here for a long time.'

"Tyler sighed, a sound of absolute defeat. 'We can't leave them like this,' he said. 'We have to bury them. In the ground.'

"'I know.' We dug a hole, put the bones in, packed it tight, and put some stones around it in a circle, to mark off its final resting place."

Teri demanded that I show her 'where we put it.' I agreed, even though I had no intention of showing her where the dog's little grave was.

"I don't want that on my land! I'm going to dig that disgusting mess up and throw it in the garbage!" she declared with an exaggerated shudder.

Simone looked at her with wide eyes and a wrinkled forehead, like maybe she was starting to think her sister was insane. "Do you really think that's a good idea? I don't think we should disturb it."

"It's not even a whole body, Simone. It's not like digging up a human corpse!"

How wrong you are, I thought.

"Well? Then what happened?" Teri asked.

"The electrician showed up a few days later while Tyler was at the grocery store. I followed him around with dreadful resignation as he checked the circuit breaker box, the outlets, and the meter outside. He mumbled to himself while he wrote some notes on a pad.

"He went back inside and studied the breaker box again. 'You've got some problems here. Basically, from the look of this wiring, your house is a toaster. It's a ticking time bomb. It needs a new circuit breaker box, and most of the wiring is ass-backwards. I'll have to go in through the walls to replace and reroute it, and in a house this size, that ain't gonna be cheap.'

"'How much are we looking at?' I asked, afraid to hear the answer.

"The electrician looked at me. 'I'll have to figure up an estimate. Off the top of my head, I'd say you're looking at fifteen grand.'

"'*What?* We can't afford that!' I burst out.

"'Hope you have good homeowner's insurance, then. And buy some more smoke detectors, cause sooner or later, you're gonna need 'em. Having a couple of fire extinguishers around would be a good idea, also.'

"I put my hands on my head and grabbed two fistfuls of hair. I couldn't believe our bad luck. 'Please get us the detailed estimate as soon as you can,' I said.

"Tyler came in the house a few minutes later juggling several bags of groceries. 'Hey, I saw the electrician driving away. How bad is it?'

"'Bad.'

"After pacing around the kitchen, he said, 'Maybe once we fix the electrical problems, some of these other problems will stop.'

"'Oh, definitely,' I replied in the most sarcastic voice I had. 'We won't have to worry about bad wiring killing and burying dogs in the backyard anymore.'

"He glared at me and shook his head. He left the kitchen, and I followed. I almost ran into him when he came to a dead stop.

"'What the hell are you doing?' I asked irritably.

"'He put a hand over his mouth and walked into the dining room. The room's four electrical outlets had been completely shoved out of the wall. Piles of colored wires lay on the hardwood floor in front of each one.

"Tyler didn't say anything. He just turned and walked out of the room.

"'Uh, do you want to call the electrician back?' I called after him. 'Or should I?'

"'And tell him what? That the local poltergeist didn't like him checking the wiring, so it threw a temper tantrum? I think we can safely assume—'

"'We can't leave it like that!'

"'We'll just eat out from now on!' he snapped, then stormed down the basement stairs.

"I went to the basement door and hollered after him. 'What are you doing?'

"'I'm getting a beer. That okay with you?'

"'No! Call the damned electrician!'

"He didn't answer. I threw up my hands and tried to ignore the chill creeping up my spine. I didn't want to be alone anywhere in the house. I waited anxiously for him to come back upstairs, but he didn't return.

"Our marriage had been on shaky ground before we bought the house. Now it was crumbling. I decided at that moment that if he wouldn't agree to sell the house, I'd move out on my own.

"We had turned an alcove in the family room downstairs into a mini bar. We'd intended to have football parties down there. We had a large screen tv, a plush sofa, a couple chairs, and the bar. We'd had too many problems with the house to entertain friends yet, and our hopes of being able to do that were dwindling with every passing day.

"After five minutes, when Tyler didn't come upstairs, I was fuming. I knew he could guzzle a beer in ninety seconds flat. Maybe he'd decided to just drink the entire twelve pack. After thirty minutes, I stormed downstairs, intending to give him a piece of my mind, and maybe crack open a bottle of wine. Or two.

"He wasn't there. As you know, there are no egress windows in the basement. The only way in or out is up the stairs.

"'Seriously? You're hiding from me?' I decided to skip wine and go for whiskey. I walked over to the bar, poured a shot, and tossed it back. Then I threw back another, relaxing as the warm burn of whiskey ran through me. I thought maybe he'd gone into the guest bedroom we had down there. He probably drank too much too fast and crashed on the bed. In all fairness, that didn't sound like a bad idea.

"But he wasn't there, either.

"The only other place he could be was the utility room. I threw open the door, but he wasn't there. He couldn't have gone up the stairs without me seeing him.

"'Tyler?' I started feeling goosebumps popping up all over my skin. 'Tyler? Where are you, you jerk?'

"I knew he hadn't left, but I also knew he wasn't down there, and I suddenly felt overwhelming terror. I went to the stairs, and I glanced at the bar. The bottle of whiskey sat on the bar where I'd left it. I decided to bring that upstairs with me, because if I was alone with this house, I was gonna need it."

"Why didn't you leave?" asked Simone. "Why didn't you go somewhere, or call someone for help?"

"Because the truck was still under the tree branch. We hadn't decided what to do with it yet. We worked from home, remember, and we had put it out of our minds because we hadn't needed it."

Teri rolled her eyes. "That is the most ridiculous thing I've ever heard. Who forgets their truck is crushed in the driveway? Besides, you know how to walk, don't you? Town isn't that far."

I wanted to smack the woman.

"No, town isn't that far. But it was irrelevant."

I paused to gather my thoughts. The next part was hard to think about, let alone share with anyone. Especially strangers.

"As I was saying, I walked to the bar, grabbed the bottle, turned around… and the stairs were gone."

"How could the stairs be gone? I walked down them this morning," said Teri. "That's just ridiculous."

If the woman said the word "ridiculous" one more time, I was leaving. I'd had enough. If not for my concern for Simone, I'd have been gone already.

"That's exactly what I thought," I said, trying to be diplomatic. "I went to the solid wall that now stood where the stairs had been. I felt along it with spread out palms, looking for a way to get through it. But there was none.

"I turned around to look at the window, the only other possible way to get out of the basement. It was much closer to me than it should've been. The furniture was gone. Disoriented, I looked back to the bar. I could've reached out and touched it. The walls shrunk as I watched. They literally closed in on me.

"I screamed. I called out for Tyler. I called for my friends, my parents, anyone within hearing range. No one heard me.

"The room continued to contract, with me in it. I pounded on the walls. The window disappeared. The bar disappeared. I looked up and the ceiling was immediately above my head, like I was in a tomb. The lights went out, and that's the last thing I remember."

Teri figured it out first.

"This house isn't really a house, is it?"

"No. Not exactly."

"There aren't ghosts here, or demons, or poltergeists," Simone said. "You were right about that. But this is something worse, isn't it?"

"Yes."

Simone grew frighteningly pale. I was afraid she'd faint.

"What is it, then?" demanded Teri impatiently.

"The terminology doesn't really exist. I think of it as a black hole of evil."

"You sold us a *black hole of evil*?" Simone cried.

Teri opened and closed her mouth several times. Finally, she said, "So it's a portal to hell."

"Not at all. The house doesn't let its prisoners go to hell, no matter how much they beg."

"They beg to go to hell?" she asked incredulously. She didn't look frightened at all by this tidbit of information. She could see on my face that I wasn't joking, and she leaned back on the couch. "Huh."

"Now. Listen to me, and you might still save your souls. You might have a chance at survival."

I looked at their faces. Simone's was pale and horrified. Teri's wore an expression of interest and curiosity. Something was definitely wrong with her.

"Don't let the house kill you. If the house kills you, it claims you. You must stay alive."

"You're crazy. I'm getting the hell out of here." Simone got off the couch and ran toward the entryway.

"Simone! It won't let you leave."

When she flung open the front door, there was no sunshine or grass. There was only darkness. She screamed.

"How long until someone rescues us?" Teri asked.

I should've been ashamed of laughing, but I wasn't. I disliked Teri.

"No one's going to rescue you, my dear. You are already part of the house, in a sense. It will supply your basic needs, but the two of you are otherwise on your own. You must stay alive until you die of natural causes."

The noise Simone made sounded like someone was strangling a kitten. She buried her face in her hands and began to cry. "How could you let us buy this place? Why didn't you tell us? Were you that desperate for money?"

"No one told *us* when we bought it," I snapped. "What makes you special?"

My response shocked them into silence.

"I have one more warning to give you before I go. By summoning me with a Ouija board, you've made yourself known to every entity that is stuck here. I cannot shield you from all of them, although my sense of duty compels me to try. You must find a way to protect yourselves and do it quickly. It won't be easy. They're already fighting over who gets to keep you."

TRANSGRESSORS

Meeting of Senate Subcommittee regarding Teleportation of Energy Pulse (TEP) Weapon
Present Day

"Wilson, a space weapon is a waste of taxpayer dollars, and you know it! My voters don't want their hard-earned money spent on science fiction!" The large, red-faced Chairman lost his balance and nearly toppled over with the force of his maniacal fist shaking. He grabbed onto the podium and regained his footing. He looked around at the other six Senators, who were crammed uncomfortably around a metal table. He was hoping for a show of support, but he wasn't getting one. Each person wore the same carefully crafted, neutral expression.

"Threats from outer space?" he continued desperately, his voice rising. "Aliens? Don't any of you understand how pointless this is?"

Your face is pointless, Wilson thought silently. From his position at the head of the table, his cold, coffee-colored eyes scanned the government committee members. The elected officials had about as much interest in being there as Wilson, which was to say, none. Two of them covertly scrolled through their phones, one was texting, and two were having a quiet discussion about sports cars. The remaining Senator kept dozing off.

If Wilson could somehow combine all six of them, they'd still be less useful than the table they were sitting around.

The youngest looked up from his phone. "Absolutely ridiculous," he stated after an uncomfortable moment of silence. The others murmured their noncommittal agreement.

Wilson hated politicians. Leaving something as important as planetary defense decisions in the hands of a bunch of civilians with no military or science background was the stupidest practice he'd encountered since he arrived. He would've happily strangled them all right there, but someone might notice their absence.

He doubted it, but he couldn't afford to take unnecessary risks.

At the edge of his field of vision, the Chairman briefly clutched his chest. His wince of pain was subtle, but Wilson noticed it. Wilson was a predator. He had an extensive array of skills, and observation was one of his specialties.

Should the Chairman persuade the other Senators not to support the TEP weapon project, his job would become unnecessarily complicated. The last thing he needed was a bunch of politicians interfering with his operation. They couldn't prevent the deployment of the weapon, but they could delay it, and that could prove just as disastrous. Wilson had a timetable.

The national population was aware of the true nature of the project now, thanks to a security breach. People were protesting its existence in the streets, holding up cardboard signs with messages like "No Space Nukes!" and "Protect E.T.!"

The ignorance was astounding. The project had nothing to do with nuclear munitions, and extraterrestrials didn't need protection from this weak planet.

Wilson took a cigarette from the silver case in his jacket pocket. "What makes this program any different from all the other ones you lie about?" he asked casually. The man who'd been sleeping sat up straight in his chair, suddenly wide awake.

"Your voters don't need any more information than they already have. Tell them you're developing technology to blow up asteroids if that's what it takes to satisfy them. I don't care what you say. Just keep them out of my way." His quiet, authoritative tone filled the room. "Frankly, I'm surprised by your lack of support, Holland. The two things your political party consistently, overwhelmingly approve of are lying and building more weapons."

Wilson lit the cigarette with a flick of a match and inhaled deeply. He pinched the tiny flame between his thumb and forefinger to extinguish it, enjoying the disconcerted expressions he saw around the room. Wilson knew smoking was outlawed in government buildings, but such trivial laws didn't interest him. Democracy in general didn't interest him. He suspected he would've had fewer complications had he gone with his second choice of developers.

Immediately upon his arrival, he'd sought out the most resourceful, devious government he could find, and gave them the technology to build, store and launch the weapon. There had been several contenders. Most of them mistakenly thought he cared about money. What he truly cared about was quality, and efficiency, and only one government promised both.

It amused Wilson tremendously that this very committee had approved the weapon's funding, although they weren't aware of it until now. If the damned whistleblower had kept their mouth shut, they would've stayed in the dark until it no longer mattered.

Wilson intended to find the person who'd leaked the information about the true nature of his "geological surveillance satellite" program. If that person proved to be human, he'd find out their agenda and dispose of them. No human could hide from him forever. They all had the same weakness: they had to sleep.

If the snitch was extraterrestrial, finding them could prove difficult.

He'd spent years setting up this operation. Now, with success imminent, this unexpected and very inconvenient inquiry into the project's specific details wasted his valuable time. The scrutiny and attention that now surrounded his every move were two variables he hadn't even conceived of.

His greatest advantage was that only a handful of people knew the weapon had already been built. At this very moment, a high-level military commander and his team awaited Wilson's order to test launch. Wilson planned to give that order, no matter how much these self-serving pricks protested.

He'd handled more complicated situations than this one. Getting things done was another one of his specialties.

"The very idea of the need for such a weapon is preposterous," raged the oblivious Chairman, who dabbed at his sweaty forehead with a blue silk handkerchief. Wilson's cigarette smoke reached him, and he coughed violently.

Chairman Rodney Holland was a slightly balding man in his late fifties who, Wilson guessed, had downed two or three shots of whiskey before this meeting in a failed attempt to calm his nerves. Raising his voice, the man bellowed his objections with the righteous indignation that, in Wilson's opinion, only the truly ignorant could muster.

"How dare you lie to this committee! How dare you waste our time and resources with this fantasy of yours! We are alone in the Universe!" he shouted, spreading his arms wide. Focusing again on Wilson, he added, "Your insistence on implementing this – this *Planetary Defense Shield* is a product of your own spiritual insecurities and overactive imagination! We have no need to defend ourselves against a threat that doesn't exist. There aren't any little green men running around waiting to attack our planet."

Seven hundred and three known species are green, Wilson wanted to tell him, *but you're right. None of them are men.*

Holland continued ranting, and a few cautiously emboldened committee members muttered their agreements and nodded their heads. Wilson's patience was at an end.

He stood from his chair. Instantly, the room became silent as a tomb. Wilson had a certain reputation, and he knew his very presence made them apprehensive. With no expression whatsoever on his face, he smoothed down his expertly tailored black suit. He approached the frozen Senator, who eyed him with distrust and fear. The man stood so still he appeared to have forgotten even to breathe.

Wilson dragged heavily on his cigarette. He pulled it from his mouth and grabbed Holland by the back of his head. Briefly regretting the waste of perfectly good tobacco, he pushed the lit cigarette into the man's chin.

Paralysis broken, Holland slapped uselessly at Wilson's arms and howled. The smell of burnt skin filled the air. No one else in the room moved, spoke, or tried to help Holland, unwilling to draw Wilson's attention or wrath down upon themselves.

"Allow me to offer a different opinion," Wilson said calmly, his face inches from the scarlet face of Holland. The man stopped grabbing Wilson's arms and once again clutched his chest. "I have personally assessed the threat you say doesn't exist. And while you pander to your voters' whims, I have a much larger agenda. Like it or not, you pointless skin sack, the TEP weapon will be deployed. The Planetary Defense Shield will be activated."

"You… will pay… for your sins," gasped Holland as he sank to the floor. With three mostly clogged arteries, a heart trying to pump blood through 270 pounds, and the shock of Wilson's attack, the Chairman didn't stand a chance. A thin tendril of smoke rose from the charred skin on his chin as he lay unmoving in a graceless heap by Wilson's feet. Wilson dropped the cigarette butt on his dead face.

"Does anyone else wish to add their *insight* to this discussion?" Wilson asked, his stone-cold stare unwavering as it fell on the others. The utter silence, downcast eyes, and pursed lips of every person in the room gave him his answer.

* * *

Bunker, Secret Military Installation, New Mexico
Twenty-four hours after Rodney Holland's death

"Sir? May I, uh—"

The officer awkwardly cleared his throat. He was nervous, despite his training and years of service.

He currently stood at the controls of a prototype weapon whose destructive capability was inestimable. He had a God-given right to be nervous.

Garcia, the commanding officer, glanced across the control panel at his second-in-command. "I've asked you to always speak your mind, Terrell. Especially now."

Terrell cleared his throat and briefly surveyed the command station. Seven people were squeezed into the claustrophobic and heavily fortified room. The physicist responsible for telemetry was checking her data against a three-dimensional map of orbiting satellites. The two men responsible for launching the bomb stood on the opposite side of the room, their profiles eerie against the blue flashing lights of the machinery. Dr. Porter, the lead physicist on the First Strike team and primary designer of the pulse weapon's teleportation device, sat leaning into his computer, his face so close to the screen Terrell thought it might suck him in.

He'd seen stranger things happen on this assignment.

Finally, his eyes landed on the creepy bastard standing across the room. According to hushed theorizing and discreet whispers heard around the base, the man had appeared, literally, out of nowhere. No agency claimed him, yet every agency bowed to him. Mr. Wilson, the man in black, with ultimate authority, unimaginable motives, and unnatural intelligence, currently stared back at Terrell as if he could hear the very thoughts in his head. Since Wilson wasn't wearing a headset, Terrell doubted he could hear anything over the thrumming roar of the teleportation machine. So, he took a deep breath and spoke, hoping Wilson couldn't read lips.

Or minds.

"Sir, I believe test firing this weapon is a grossly irresponsible act."

His commanding officer straightened in his chair. Terrell didn't miss the man's furtive glance in Wilson's direction. "Continue."

Terrell leaned forward. "So many things could go wrong, Sir. The pulse weapon could fail to teleport once we ignite it. The navigational system could fail, and we could hit the moon and knock it out of orbit. We don't know the quantum level effects of disrupting space with Wilson's magical light beams, or whatever the hell they are. And what if we actually *attract* an alien presence by test-firing such a monstrous weapon?"

The commander stared at him. "Don't you suppose they've evaluated these scenarios already, and put safeguards in place?"

Terrell glanced over at Wilson, who stared unwaveringly back at him. Terrell figured the bastard had been one of those kids who plucked wings off flies or focused the sun's rays through a magnifying glass to burn ants. He doubted the guy had much concern for safety, and he doubted he'd take responsibility for any unexpected repercussions. Now that he thought about it, he doubted he'd ever been a kid. Hopefully, Dr. Porter had at least a modicum sense of self-preservation.

Terrell put his hand near his mouth to hide his lips from Wilson. "Of course, Sir. But no one has actually seen the thing work."

"That is, in fact, the purpose of a test fire, soldier," Garcia said dryly.

"Yes, Sir. I don't mean to overstep, but is the risk necessary to ensure humanity's safety? Do you really think there are aliens out there who know about Earth and plan to attack us?"

The commander studied him. "I *think* our job is to oversee the test firing of a global defense weapon. And that's what we're going to do." The man sighed. "Your objections are noted. Complete your electronic security scan of the facility. We'll be launching soon."

Terrell ran a hand over his clean-shaven head. "Yes, Sir. Thank you, Sir."

He looked over the technology laid out in front of him. He had enough engineering education to know the military was at least a hundred years from developing this kind of tech on their own. Terrell glanced at Wilson, who continued to focus his unnatural stare on him. He looked back at the control panels and began to scroll through the security camera footage covering the installation. He forced himself to maintain a neutral expression as he thought, *He knows something he's not telling us. I swear that guy isn't from Earth.*

On further consideration, if Wilson was an alien, a disturbing number of Terrell's questions about this project suddenly had answers.

Jesus. I should've joined the Navy.

Forty-two minutes later, Wilson gave the order to launch the Teleportation of Energy Pulse Weapon. The two men responsible for the duty went to work. Terrell initiated the power source to raise the Planetary Defense Shield.

The order was successfully carried out.

* * *

Earth

Two Earth-days after the test-fire of the TEP weapon

Wilson, as he called himself on this planet, assessed the destruction caused by the weapon he'd commissioned. Its effect on Spacetime was as devastating as he and his alliance had hoped. Once the ripple effect of the damage it caused reached their enemies, the threat to his home planet would be eliminated.

His final objective was to find and eliminate the traitor who exposed his project's true purpose. Then, at last, he could get off this rock and go home. It wouldn't be long before someone noticed his handiwork and came to punish this planet, and he did not want to be here when that happened.

* * *

Warship Knight's Blood, traveling through the Oort Cloud
Two Earth-months after the test-fire of the TEP weapon

"I am unable to continue Pushing the ship along this course." The Monk withdrew her injured appendages from the Space Winder propulsion system. She then plunged one of her left tentacles into the ship's sensors above her. Perhaps the data could tell her how Space itself had become damaged.

The Warrior paced the Bridge of his ship. He'd already sensed there was a problem, he just wasn't able to identify it. His ability to communicate telepathically with the Monk had developed so recently, he hadn't yet learned to decipher his pilot's extraordinarily complex thoughts.

"What is wrong?" he asked, answering her silently. Her feelings of frustration pulsed through his mind as she searched for a way to explain what was, obviously, a catastrophic predicament.

"The fabric of Space is... bent," she finally said.

"And? You bend Space around the ship to create propulsion. What difference does it make if Space is bent to begin with?" The Warrior tried and failed to hide his irritation. Their war campaign was finished. They'd successfully reestablished their claim to the planet Thora7693, but their supplies were low, and the crew was exhausted. Home was still light years away.

"If I attempt to bend corrupted Space, I cannot predict our arc of travel," she explained. *"We could end up farther from home than we are now. And I can't even begin to predict the effect of this damage on Time. We could end up so far in the past that your grandchildren's grandchildren wouldn't live long enough to return to your home."*

The Warrior swore viciously across their telepathic connection and felt the Monk flinch. *"What is responsible for this corrupted Space?"*

There was a pause. *"The sensors can't tell. They were created to explore events in Space, not diagnose damage."*

The Monk pushed her upper right tentacle back through the access point of the ship and into the Space Winder. She melded her appendage back into the distorted fabric of Space, and the Warrior tried to feel what she was experiencing. He wasn't successful. He supposed the skill would come with time.

"Space, normally, is a flowing ebb of particles and energy," she explained.

The Warrior had no problem at all feeling the sudden onslaught of agonizing, paralyzing pain. The tentacle she'd pushed out of the ship and into Space was being squeezed, as if something was shrinking around it.

"Something is creating random energy spikes. Foreign, unstable particles are creating and destroying miniscule realities within ours, and it's... Warrior, our ship is in trouble. Even our section of

Space is in trouble." She barely managed to convey the message before crushing pain cut off her thoughts.

"Is this something you've encountered before? Can you counteract the effects? Surely there are precedents for this kind of thing."

"Based on the steadily increasing chaos I've felt as we've approached this resting point, and the severity of the changes in the structure of Space, I believe this instability was caused by the discharge of a sophisticated energy pulse weapon."

The Warrior swore again, audibly this time.

"Such weapons were outlawed after the Sezu-Tahk Surge!" he responded in rage. *"All sentient life forms, even those in the outlying regions, are aware of this. For anyone to disobey this law – it's unfathomable!"*

The Monk's mood shifted to panic. Her words formed in a precise rhythm.

"I cannot retrieve my tentacles, not from Space, not from the sensors. They're trapped."

He forced himself to ignore her extreme physical distress and her struggle to control her pain.

"You can't lose focus," he said. *"We'll figure this out."*

He just needed time to think. With her pain leaking into their telepathic connection, forming thoughts was a struggle. He knew she was trying to prevent him from feeling her agony, but she'd have to learn to do better.

"Where did the damage originate? A ship? A planet? Can you extrapolate? Per the laws of the Imperial Galactic Alliance, we have the responsibility to punish the transgressors."

"Warrior, I don't believe you understand the severity of our situation. We need to reverse course and hope I can follow the echoes of my energy back to safe Space."

The Warrior ignored her. Despite his weariness, his crew's exhaustion, and her warning, he knew he had to destroy the offenders. He activated the alarm that would alert his Fighters. Immediately they woke, and, burned out as they were, prepared to undertake whatever duties the Warrior assigned them.

"What are you doing?" demanded the Monk. *"Warrior, I am unlikely to survive the course of action you are considering."*

Hiding his emotions within a telepathic connection was difficult, but he was learning. With forced but convincing indifference, he said, *"Despite your pain, you must determine the origin of the problem. This – situation is much bigger than we are."*

"Acknowledged," the Monk replied coldly.

As she twined two more of her tentacles through the ship's propulsion system and into Space, the Monk vindictively drew the Warrior's mind completely into her own. As her pain filled his consciousness, he collapsed to the floor on the Bridge. His brain struggled to interpret the onslaught of sensory information she released into their telepathic connection. Inside a body that wasn't his, he felt layers of Space rolling over him. Colors – millions and millions of colors – shattered and reformed in multi-dimensional patterns. Barriers he couldn't see pushed against the two of them, squeezing, tearing, mutilating, or obliterating anything they touched.

The Warrior had suffered a great many injuries in his time, but this feeling – it went far beyond misery or torment. Devastation, maybe. Consumption, definitely. It felt like Space was eating the Monk alive. The Warrior wondered how she could function, how she could even survive such torture.

She somehow maneuvered within, around, and parallel to Space, all at once. The Warrior saw flickers of color, and even the blackness changed. He dematerialized and was shot across all directions, directions he didn't even know existed, before being pulled back into one body. As he reformed, he understood at last the abhorrent wrongness of this part of Space. Her pain seared through every single one of his molecules.

The Monk pushed him away violently across their connection. He found himself sitting on the ground on the Bridge of his ship. He checked over his body, in awe that it was again in one piece.

Without acknowledging her actions, she said, "*I've discovered an intense concentration of damage.*

It is strongest near this system's water planet." She paused. *"Warrior... I believe I've discovered the origin of the energy pulses. But none of the species living on this planet appear to have the technology to have created them."*

"How is that possible?"

"I don't know. I don't understand why they would develop a weapon capable of such damage. The other lifeforms in this solar system are not a threat to them. Something about this feels wrong."

Two of his crew joined him on the bridge and prepared their stations for attack, pretending not to notice their leader as he struggled to get his feet back underneath himself.

"Someone must've given them the weapon," continued the Monk. *"From the chemical composition of the atmosphere, the debris orbiting the planet, the extraordinary wealth of untapped resources on the dark side of their moon... I am certain they are generations away from creating this technology.*

"It would explain their willingness to disobey the Holy Galactic Government's proclamation. They are ignorant of its existence."

"I don't care. Get us there," the Warrior demanded.

"Although it is but a small distance from our current position, the damage to Space makes it impossible to promise I can 'get us there.'"

If she had eyes, she likely would've rolled them, the Warrior suspected.

"I believe I can get us closer, however." The Monk suggested he warn the crew of her imminent attempt to Push the ship. She made sure he understood that her damaged body, as well as the churned-up area they were about to travel through, would make for a very dangerous and unpredictable journey.

"Agreed."

While he communicated the warning to the rest of the ship, the Monk violently tore the core of her body free from one of her tentacles. The horrified Warrior staggered backward.

"Don't panic," she said offhandedly. *"Even if I could eventually retrieve it from the Space Winder, it would be useless. The damage was irreversible."* She slid another of her tentacles into broken Space to replace the one she lost. *"Alright. Here we go."*

The ship didn't move.

"Monk?"

A scream spiraled through his mind. "*Warrior! I am—"* Her words faded into nonsensical white noise.

"What's happening now?" he demanded. *"Have they fired again?"*

"I don't know! I've become – trapped in different – threads of Time! My tentacles are split across realities—"

The *Knight's Blood* jolted as if hit by an asteroid. The Warrior's telepathic link to the Monk destabilized as she slowly became indistinguishable from the Space she was trying to navigate through. This damage to Space would destroy her, and she'd take all of them with her.

Before he could figure out what to do, the ship reversed, shooting back in the direction it came from.

The Warrior raced to the back of his ship. He reached the Monk's chamber as she fell backwards. The outstretched segments of her body shattered across fractured areas of Space. She collapsed on a pile of her remaining tentacles.

She would grow new tentacles, of course; her relief from the torment of damaged Space coursed through them both. Her body immediately began to seal its leaking wounds.

"Monk!"

"If I hadn't pulled away, we'd have been destroyed. A vortex appeared. I must be more careful." The Monk spoke calmly, as if she hadn't just nearly disintegrated. Even telepathically, the Warrior wasn't sure he'd ever get used to her sudden, inexplicable mood changes.

Reeling from every part of the current situation, the Warrior forced himself to focus. An innocent race of people. If they hadn't explored the important part of their moon, their entire species likely existed on this single planet. They may not even know other species existed near them.

"They don't need the weapon." The Warrior's system of stomachs clenched. This was starting to make a sick kind of sense. "*Someone wanted to test the weapon without bringing consequences upon their own world. They needed a scapegoat planet to test it from. Monk, can you tell if there are any dominant species on this water world? What sort of life dwells there?"*

The Monk didn't respond for several minutes. He felt fear and anger grow inside her.

Although she didn't have lungs, she made a sound in his head like gasping. She'd picked up the habit from him, and he normally found it endearing. Right now, however, fury coursed through her, and the strength of her emotions unsettled him.

"I believe at least seven intelligent species exist in the water. I am most concerned by one of the land species. They look far too much like the Traitor from Thora7693, Wilschegt Sonenvert. He could've infiltrated their society easily and gained the help and resources he'd require to create an energy pulse weapon."

"Then our duty is clear," he stated.

"Warrior, no. This planet – through the sensors I've estimated the existence of over a hundred thousand different species. Thousands of them are self-aware. We can't risk obliterating so many because of the actions of a few," the Monk said.

"Nor can we allow Wilschegt Sonenvert to destroy Space."

"We don't even know if he's still on the water planet! Or if he was ever there! We need to find out what happened before we make rash decisions. They may have been unwilling participants. By now, he's probably returned to whatever base of operations he might be using. Destroying countless innocents will solve nothing! There is no honor in this!"

"This is not about honor! *Do you not understand our ways at all?"*

"I understand right and wrong!"

"Our weapons are ready for use, my lord," spoke a crewmember the Warrior forgot was even on the Bridge with him. "What is our target?"

Anger matching the Monk's swelled up in him. His homesick, hungry, weary crew followed him with complete loyalty. They did their jobs as ordered, trusting him to do the right thing. They didn't accuse him of making 'rash decisions.'

The Monk didn't experience hunger or weariness, and her home was Space. Yet *she* questioned him. The *Monk,* with whom a physical relationship was impossible but unnecessary. The *Monk*, who knew him on such an intimate level they'd spontaneously developed telepathic communication.

"Do you really consider these creatures helpless?" he asked finally. "*You know nothing about them. They could have built thousands of energy pulse weapons!"* The Warrior's six glowing eyes shone with changing gradients of orange as his anger

bled into their connection. *"Do you care more for aliens than for our civilization? Our responsibility to the Galactic Government—"*

The force of her emotion startled him into silence. Through their connection he felt her frustration and pain become even more unbearable.

"They are a young intelligence. They made a mistake."

"And what about the damage they've caused?" he asked, flabbergasted. *"Why do you doubt me? How can you consider letting them go unpunished?"*

She didn't respond.

He checked on the rest of his crew. They were fine. The ship was fine. The Monk would hate him, but he had to follow his conscience.

"Monk," he began gently. *"I understand your objections. We will report the Traitor and see that he comes to justice if he doesn't die on the water planet. But these creatures have already launched one devastating weapon. They could destroy this entire region of Space."* He closed his many eyes and sighed. *"I know Space is fighting you, but I must ask you to pinpoint the specific source of the launch. Where on the water planet did this weapon originate?"*

The Monk was controlling her physical agony, but her mental agony lingered. *"These land creatures are surrounded by Time fractures. I didn't expect that. They're experiencing slight variations in their reality."*

She paused as her mind began contemplating the shape of a new tentacle for her left side. *"This has never happened before. I can't detect the weapon's exact origin. Space is too damaged in the area. I won't be able to ascertain the location until they launch again."*

The Warrior grunted, making the second audible sound of the conversation. *"These Time fractures... were they caused by their weapon or another Space phenomenon?"*

"The weapon. I feel no evidence of other fouled Space."

The Warrior braced himself for her reaction and spoke. "*These beings, naïve or not, benevolent or not, are not complying with the Accord. We cannot allow them to damage any more passageways through Space. And – we both know Time fractures will eventually spread throughout the Galaxy and beyond. The Council would insist we destroy all life in the area."*

The Monk bristled.

"Monk—"

Bitterly, she responded, *"I will be risking the ship and all our lives to* maybe *get us within attack range. The damage to Space increases as we get closer to the water planet. However, assuming I can get us there in one piece, destroying these helpless creatures will be an easy campaign with minimal use of resources."*

The Warrior relaxed. *"Monk, we are doing the right thing. Your physical sacrifices will be noted in my report, and I will see to it that you are rewarded."*

"Keep your blotzing rewards!" she yelled. *"The blood of trillions of lives is on your conscience!"*

"My conscience is not your concern," he said resignedly, hating himself and knowing he'd crossed a line in their relationship from which they wouldn't return. *"Begin your manipulation of Space. Take care not to draw us into the fractures as you close them. I will omit your objections in my report of the incident to the Holy Galactic Government.*

"I'm – sorry for the pain you will endure."

She didn't answer with words, but the wall that suddenly materialized in her mind said plenty.

He returned to the Bridge. The ship wobbled and shook as they crossed the deformed space. Moments later, the Monk Pushed them as close to the Earth as the damaged Space would allow.

"To be clear, we cannot determine the weapon's exact point of origin. You must destroy the entire surface of the planet to ensure we destroy every trace of the weapon. You are cleared to fire."

The order was successfully carried out.

RUN

The first sensation Larson felt upon waking was water lapping over his face. Sputtering, he inhaled, and immediately began choking.

He pushed himself up onto his hands and knees. Hanging his head, he coughed for what seemed like days.

When he was finally able to pull full breaths of air into his lungs, he got to his feet. Images flashed in front of his eyes like a slide show, each bringing with it a sear of pain in the back of his head. The crash. The bodies. The slow escape over dunes of black sand. Losing Rainmaker when he fell through the sand into a ravine that shouldn't have been there.

He turned his head, but in the near darkness he could see only shadows. "Help!" he yelled. His voice crackled and barely made a sound. He cleared his throat and tried again. *"HELP!"*

Lightning flashed, followed immediately by thunder. It must be close, and he was standing in water. He estimated the depth of the water to be eighteen inches, give or take. The air was musty, and the lightning showed him cylindrical walls with a staircase winding around the inside of them.

Squinting, he saw an opening overhead. It had to be fifty stories up.

"He's awake!" screamed a staticky voice in his ear. He hadn't noticed the earpiece, and the sudden noise in his head nearly made him jump out of his skin. He put a hand to his face to feel for a microphone. If there had been one, it must've gotten lost when he fell.

Drops of rain pelted his head.

"You have to *run*!" shouted a panicked woman. Her voice was indistinct. She could've been a child or an elder. He couldn't remember having children on the mission, but sometimes they came along on tours to act as interpreters.

"He's mine! You are all mine!" rumbled a deep, crackling, metallic voice. *"There's nowhere for you to hide."*

Larson heard automatic weapons fire, then silence.

His head throbbed. The raindrops fell faster, tapping against his scalp. A powerful light beamed down on him for a few seconds. He folded his hands over his head.

"Don't just stand there! Run!" yelled a voice, male this time. The static from the speaker and the yelling tortured his ears. "Get moving!"

Larson splashed over to the side of the cylindrical staircase. Getting up these stairs would take forever. How had he gotten down here in the first place?

Lightning rippled through the sky again.

"Run!" hollered the male voice again. Larson flinched. "Move, damn you!"

It occurred to him suddenly that he might not be alone down here. There could be something hiding in the water, or even on the staircase.

Another flash of lightning taunted him with a view of the winding stairs.

"You have to run!" yelled the first girl.

He heard an explosion.

"There's another one! Give me that gun!" yelled another voice.

Larson heard more gunfire.

"There's three ships landing on your six, three to four miles out," someone else announced.

Larson's head was pounding like it was keeping time to a song. *Throb. Throb. Throb.*

"Then we're out of time," said a new voice, answering a question Larson hadn't heard.

"RUN!" the voices yelled in sync. "Why are you just standing there?"

The noise in his ear made his head scream in pain.

"Maybe he's hurt," someone said.

Larson shivered as he climbed up the stairs and out of the water. His soggy clothes clung to his skin.

"We need help!" one of the men called. "Delta Base isn't responding! For God's sake, Larson! What are you doing?"

"I'm coming!" Larson yelled. They couldn't possibly hear him, but he didn't care. If only he had his scope, and he could see them as well as they could see him.

If they were under attack, he'd never get to them in time. Surely they knew that.

He began to run. He vowed not to look up at the impossible distance he had to climb.

Larson was in excellent shape, but by the time he'd run up one hundred fifty stairs or so, his breath was coming in gasps. He heard nothing but static in the earpiece. What if they were all already dead?

Larson realized he didn't even know who 'they' were.

They obviously knew him, though, and expected him to help. Expected him to run. Up thousands of stairs. Nothing about this made sense. The throbbing in his head made it difficult to think.

Had he agreed to come down here? He couldn't remember.

He stopped after another twenty steps. His legs were shaking, and his muscles burned.

From the top of the hole, he heard, "What are you doing, Larson? *Run! RUN!*"

He took a couple deep breaths and began climbing the stairs again, although not at the furious pace he'd started out with. This time, the machine gun fire above was accompanied by the familiar sound of a laser firing.

Larson quickly identified the weapon. *That's my laser.*

He heard screaming.

Something was falling down the hole.

"SARAH! NOO!!" screamed the woman at the top.

"Larson, whhyyyyyyyyyy?" cried a female voice, apparently belonging to Sarah, as she fell past him. Her body hit the water. The splash wasn't loud enough to drown out the horrible thud and the crunch of bone.

Why *what?* He couldn't possibly have run up the stairs that quickly!

The sounds of weapons ceased.

After forty more stairs, his muscles failed, and he collapsed forward. Every breath stung. His lungs felt like they were being stabbed.

He sure as hell wasn't going back down, but he didn't think he could go up anymore, either.

"Larson! God damnit! What are you doing?"

One man was still alive, anyway. One man who was yelling angrily at him.

One step at a time, he told himself. *One step at a time.*

He pulled himself up using the railing. The stitch in his side made him double over and fall back onto the stairs.

Gotta go. He'd help them, or die trying.

He put one foot in front of the other. He wasn't moving fast, but he was moving. The stairs had metal grated floors. He hadn't noticed before the clanging of his feet as they stomped their way up. Having metal stairs in an open hole where it rained wasn't a great idea, Larson thought. They were probably rusty. They could even be damaged. For that matter, there could be some that had rusted all the way through. Falling in a hole and breaking an ankle could be deadly. Falling through missing stairs would definitely be deadly.

Lightning struck, and thunder boomed.

"Larson!" came the sharp voice of the remaining woman. "We're all gonna die, don't you get it?"

"Run, you asshole!" someone chimed in.

He opened his mouth to respond, but remembered they couldn't hear him. He didn't have enough air to waste on words that no one would hear.

How dare they? he thought. He was taking the steps as fast as he could.

The smooth bar of the railing under his hand tempted him. It tempted him to climb onto it and slide all the way back down to the bottom. It'd be a hell of a ride. If he got to the top and everyone was dead, he thought he might do just that.

A scream from the top of the hole grabbed his attention. It was the woman, and for some reason, Larson felt urgency in a way he hadn't before.

What if he was in a relationship with one of those people? He hadn't even considered that. He got his second wind, and began running up the stairs, not at full throttle, but fast enough to make steady progress.

Her scream doubled in intensity. He didn't think it was a scream of pain. It was a death scream. He'd heard them before, far too many times.

Something swooshed by him. In the dim light he could make out a limb as it went past him. He didn't think it was long enough to be a leg. An arm, then. Not a whole body. She could still be alive.

His muscles were tight enough to tear, and from the little burns he was feeling in random places by his legs, he thought maybe they were. By the time he got to the top, he might not be able to walk, let alone help anyone. Especially if they expected him to fight.

He could see the top. It was, at most, one hundred feet away. He could see the grey, darkening sky. He heard thunder, but this time, he didn't see lightning.

The woman stopped screaming.

Larson's heart pounded. He felt like he was heaving in razor blades. He couldn't feel his feet. He saw people moving at the top of the hole. He also saw something that was much too large to be human. That something picked up the woman and threw her into the hole.

Nooooo!

Larson didn't know if he screamed out loud or in his head. But this time he was close enough to the top that he could see her. It was as if she fell in slow motion. He thought she was screaming, but maybe that was in his head too.

"Nooooooo!" hollered the man at the top. He opened fire.

Larson's entire body screamed at him to stop running. But he knew if he stopped, he would never start again. He'd just lay down on the steps and wait to die.

The man stopped firing his weapon and looked down the hole. Larson couldn't make out the details of his face, but he could see the outline of his body.

"I oughta shoot you, too, you dumb son of a bitch!" he shouted. He pointed the weapon into the hole.

Larson was surprised to discover he didn't actually want to die, in spite of what his body thought about the matter. And he was only fifty or so stairs from reaching the top. Then he and this guy were gonna have words, after taking care of whatever was hunting them, anyway.

Larson was close enough to the top now to see the spotlight that stood another twenty feet off the ground.

"Whose bloody side are you on?" yelled a new voice.

He wasn't in a hole, Larson realized. He was in a beacon tower, the equivalent of a lighthouse to a spaceship.

What were they doing on top of a beacon tower? Maybe they were no longer in the sand dunes.

The top was within sight. He saw the guy. He wore the same thing Larson was wearing: camo pants and an olive-green shirt, only his was shredded. He was bleeding from so many places, Larson couldn't tell how many wounds he had. He looked familiar, but he couldn't put a name to the face.

As Larson crawled up the final stairs, the man growled at him.

"You'll burn in hell for this, asshole."

Larson lay flat on the ground, too tired to move another muscle. Looked like he was too late, anyway. All that pain and effort for nothing.

"I got here as fast as I could," he croaked.

"Yes, but why? Don't you realize we are all dead, now?"

"What do you mean, *why*?"

"Why didn't you leave? Why didn't you go for help? We got you down there, all you had to do was find the door to the ground exit! You could've gotten to base! You could've gotten them to send reinforcements! Now it's too late!"

The man fell to his knees, then flat on his face. He didn't speak again.

THE FACILITY

As Devin stopped to swipe his badge at the screening station, he issued yet another warning: "I know you, A. You're gonna see things, and you're gonna be curious. But listen. No matter what happens, don't snoop around. Promise me."

Angel snorted. Devin had nothing to worry about. While he was gone, she'd be pulling sixteen to eighteen hours a day trying to cover both their workloads. Even if she wanted to go 'snooping,' she wouldn't have time.

The two lab assistants submitted to retinal scans before entering the transport station. They located an empty capsule, programmed their route into the transport's computer, and set out for the civilian researchers' complexes.

Angel and Devin worked on a floating city called the Facility. The structure's official purpose was to test the viability of moving some of the Earth's population onto the oceans. Unofficially, the remote location was perfect for conducting ethically questionable research without oversight.

"Hey!" Devin snapped his fingers in front of her face. "Focus!"

She rolled her eyes. "Don't worry! My team is already pissed that Creepazoid's needs are getting priority over theirs. I'm not gonna linger."

Devin groaned. "And stop calling him 'Creepazoid.' If you slip up and call him that to his face, I'll have to go deep sea diving to find your body."

"I'll risk it."

He glared at her mischievous grin. "I mean it, A. You don't want any part of what he's got going on."

"Dev, relax! I'm not going snooping!" She looked him over with a critical eye. "You look like you slept in a garbage disposal." He shook his head and looked away.

"Look, you know LaDania in Operations, right?" Angel asked. "She already told me to watch my back. She told me Creepazoid was suspected of kidnapping two of his own assistants when he worked for Military Intelligence. They went into his lab for their shifts one day and didn't come out. Their bodies were never found."

Devin looked at her wearily. "Everyone knows that's just a rumor."

She crossed her arms. "Really? The word LaDania used was 'coverup.'"

"My job isn't much different than yours," Devin said, changing the subject. His eyes flashed between Angel and the capsule's smooth metal floor. "Get his notes transcribed as quickly as you can. He mumbles a lot during dictation, but don't ask him to clarify. Just slow down the recording and figure out what he's saying.

"We have separate servers down here, so I've set you up a temporary user ID. I've also left instructions for sorting his snail mail. Follow them to the letter, if you'll excuse the pun. Oh, and he might give you lists of bizarre things to order. Don't question it, just do it."

Finally, he focused his gaze on her. "Dr. Crofton has some strange hang-ups."

She raised her eyebrows and put a hand over her heart. "I'm shocked."

"Be sure to check all the soap dispensers several times a day," Devin instructed. "The guy from Environmental Services doesn't always fill them completely. If Crofton runs out of soap, your day will end badly."

"Okaaaaay. Soap. Got it. What else?"

"We're almost there. I'll show you the rest as I give you the tour."

Devin's off-site mystery assignment was set to begin the next morning. Crofton had told him he'd receive instructions upon arrival, but he had refused to reveal the destination or purpose of the trip.

Dr. Crofton's research involved establishing communication with a newly discovered form of life. The heavy secrecy shrouding his project led Angel to believe something of worldwide significance was going to happen. She suspected (and hoped) he'd established contact with extraterrestrials, but she had no basis for her hunch.

Whatever he was doing, he couldn't be without an assistant for two weeks. In Angel's opinion, he should've thought of that before deciding to send Devin off to who-knows-where.

The capsule hissed to a stop in front of Complex One. The entrance looked like an ominous barrier separating Crofton's lair from the rest of the world.

They climbed out of the capsule, and Devin swiped his keycard at the door. Devin's fingers went to the distinctively thick, gold chain around his neck, as they so often did when he was nervous. Angel knew his son gave him the necklace for his birthday, two days before a minivan crushed the kid's car on I-35.

"Welcome to the eighth ring of Hell," Devin muttered as he ushered her through the entrance. "Try to avoid drawing the attention of Satan."

The door closed behind them with a whoosh. They stepped into a narrow entryway, lit only by red bulbs in cages on the walls. They walked past a closed door on their way to the end of the hall. Devin swiped his keycard again, and they entered the strangest office Angel had ever seen.

Intricately detailed statues of sea monsters, ancient gods and goddesses, and other mythical creatures stood in a line against the far wall. Standing from three to seven feet high, they appeared to be made of an iridescent plaster. Angel recognized a few of the forms from Greek mythology, but some were completely unlike anything she'd seen before.

To her right sat a cherrywood desk, flanked on both sides by matching bookcases. Hundreds of books had been packed onto them, with more stacked on the floor. The desk held two 34-inch computer monitors and a keyboard. Where most people might've had pictures of their family or pets, Creepazoid's desk had a framed diagram of the human nervous system, a display of tiny fish skeletons, and a bobble-head monkey.

A floor to ceiling aquarium spanned the left wall. Behind the thick glass, a decorative pirate ship and a castle standing twice as high as Angel stood next to corals and plants. Colorful fish swam lazily in and out of view. Something with a flat, purple shell and several eyes on the ends of stalks studied her through the glass.

Devin sneezed. In the quiet, she'd almost forgotten he was there.

"What does he have in there?" Angel asked, staring back at the purple critter.

After a pause, Devin said, "It varies. The aquarium connects to the open ocean. Different fish come and go. Sometimes there's… other things."

He cleared his throat. Angel watched him twist the gold chain back and forth as he looked around the room.

"Dev, you're freaking me out."

"Sorry. Let me show you the lab." He led her to the entrance, near Crofton's desk. "To get inside, punch this code in. And for the love of donkey snot, do not forget it: 837401292684."

"Donkey snot?"

"Angel!"

"Okay!" She shook her head as she looked at the keypad, then pulled out her phone. "Tell me again so I can make a note for myself."

"NO!" he shouted, as if she were about to jump from the top of a building. He put his hand on her arm. "Just enter it! 837401292684!"

"I'll never remember that!" She paused, thumbs hovering over the notetaking app on her phone. She flinched as she met his intense stare. "Dev, seriously—"

Growling, he grabbed the phone away from her. He scrunched over, hiding it from view, and entered the number.

"Don't ever let him know this number was on your phone," he whispered. "Go back to your quarters after your shift, memorize it, and delete it."

"Um, okay." At Devin's nervous look, she added, "I promise!"

Devin's features were drawn tight as they entered the lab. To Angel, it looked like every other lab she'd been in. The mandatory eye wash station and fire extinguishers hung on the wall near the door. Packed into the room were microscopes, a centrifuge, computer equipment ranging from state-of-the-art to outdated ("he's sentimental," Devin told her), and a few unidentifiable devices that must have been custom built for use in Crofton's research.

"Always assume he's watching you. Don't ever come in here without permission, unless you have a jug in your hands to fill the soap dispensers. Don't ever do anything you wouldn't do if he were standing next to you."

Incredulous, she turned to him with wide eyes. "I'm not four years old!"

"Shut up, A!"

She raised her eyebrows and glared at him.

"Sorry." He sighed, running a hand across his forehead. "Oh, see that door over there?" He pointed across the lab.

"Yeah. Fire exit?"

"No!"

Angel flinched. "What the hell is wrong with you?" she demanded, putting her hands on her hips.

He closed his eyes for a moment and took a deep breath. "That's the door to his secret work area. Don't go near it. Don't ask about it. If you have any questions while I'm gone, call Dr. Meisner in Biology."

Angel huffed and crossed her arms. "Why don't I just call you?"

"Because apparently, where I'm going is so top secret they don't allow outside communication."

"Woah." Her voice lowered. "Do you get hush money? Hazard pay?"

"Look, I've got to get up early, and so do you. Let me show you the files I need you to update so we can get out of here."

Afterward, as they walked back to the capsule, Devin stopped short in front of her. She barely avoided running into him. Turning around, he said, "Angel – no matter what – if Crofton tells you to do something, drop what you're doing and take care of it. Don't give him any reason to—"

"Dev, for the last time! I'm an adult and a professional. I can handle Creepazoid."

* * *

Angel snuggled into her light cotton blankets and opened her book. She had one hundred and eighty pages left in the seventh and last volume of the romantic fantasy series she'd been reading. She'd waited years to find out what would happen between Tracy and Maurice, and she sure as hell wouldn't have time to read while Devin was gone.

After reading exactly twelve pages, the doorbell outside her quarters buzzed. Groaning, she dragged herself out of bed. At the door stood Devin, leaning against the wall. He held a bottle, and the smell of alcohol wafted from him.

"What happened to turning in early?" she demanded.

"You gonna let me in?"

Angel sighed. "Of course."

She climbed back under the covers onto the bed and leaned against the headboard. She slid her legs under the blankets as Devin settled on the edge of her mattress and lifted the bottle to his lips.

"What're you doing?" Angel asked, nodding at the alcohol. "You look like crap. In fact, you look worse than you did earlier, and that's saying something."

"There're things you need to know that I couldn't tell you in there. For your own safety. He has hidden cameras, and I bet there are far more than even the ones I know about. Even here I should be careful, and so should you. He's paranoid enough he may have had your quarters bugged."

"He may have what? Why? The only person who comes in here is you."

"Exactly. Me. You see, I found out what the statues really are," Devin whispered. He took a sizeable swig of the clear liquid. Angel assumed it was vodka, his usual drink of choice. She'd never seen him take it straight from the bottle, though.

"The statues. Are they aliens?" she asked hopefully, leaning over to grab a ponytail holder from her nightstand. "Please tell me they're aliens."

Devin snorted and took another swig from the bottle. "You're fucking nuts."

She let out a sigh. She'd really, really hoped for aliens.

"I wish it were something that simple." He paused for several seconds, staring at the floor. "Crofton has this crazy obsession with mythology."

"Yeah, I noticed the cyclops. Hey, do you want something to eat? Or a water chaser, maybe? You're gonna get sick drinking like that. And so help me, if you puke on my bed, there will be consequences."

"He believes creatures from old mythologies really existed," Devin interjected. "He thinks they've survived to the modern era and are living undetected in unexplored parts of the ocean."

"Okay, yeah, that's creepier than aliens, actually."

"Sometimes when I get to work in the morning, the statues have moved."

Angel stared at him blankly. "You lost me. You think, what, that Creepazoid's creatures have entered the Facility and are masquerading as statues during the day? And they walk around at night? Maybe they work in the lab?" She chuckled. "Even that scenario is less terrifying than that monkey sitting by his computer screens. Who knows what that thing gets up to at night? I mean, where do you even get a bobble-head monkey? What the hell is that about?"

"Forget the fucking monkey!"

Angel blinked at the uncharacteristic swearing. This twitchy, cryptic version of her best friend was irritating, not to mention unnerving. "They're just statues! Strange, ugly statues, but statues, nonetheless."

Devin took another drink, then breathed in deeply. “You need to take this seriously. Sometimes they have puddles of water under them.”

“Yellow puddles?”

“This isn’t funny!” he exploded. “What will it take to get it through your thick skull that you are in danger!?” His normally brown eyes darkened to almost black with the depth of his fear.

“Dev,” she replied soothingly, “we all know your boss is crazy. He probably showers with them.” She shuddered and mumbled, “Gross.”

“He’s right about the creatures, Angel. They’re out there. He’s actually capturing mythological beasts. I’ve personally seen one, and I know about others. He’s studying them. I think he’s planting the statues in the ocean and using them to lure the creatures to him,” he said, his voice slurring a bit. He looked at his bottle of vodka with confusion, like he’d forgotten he was holding it.

“Lures, huh? And that works? Those things are ugly as fu—”

He silenced her with a look.

Angel studied his taut face, tense shoulders, and the hand holding his bottle in a vicelike grip. “Okay, Dev, okay. So that’s really what his secret project is? Making bait-statues for Medusa?”

Devin handed her the vodka, and she took it willingly.

“No, not Medusa. Not yet. Medusa lives in the Black Sea.”

Angel choked. Wiping her mouth with the back of her hand, she levelled her gaze at him. "Let me make sure I've got this straight. Creepazoid is catching mythological, yet real, sea creatures. Using statues as bait. And someone's actually funding this. Dev, mythological creatures are called 'mythological creatures' because they're myths."

"Not all of them. The overwhelming majority of myths are based on facts." He ran his fingers roughly through his hair. "The statues are sculpted in the image of whatever he thinks is out there. Then they – he and Meisner – create batches of artificial pheromones that they've adapted to work underwater. Then Crofton adds the pheromones to the statues and sticks them out in the ocean to pique the interest of his prey. When the creatures come to investigate, he traps them."

"That purple thing in the aquarium… that was one of them?" Angel pulled the sheets up a little higher with her unencumbered hand. "I kind of felt bad for the little guy. I mean, I know—"

"You don't know. Some of the creatures he's caught are humanoid. Sentient."

"Sentient? Creepazoid's trapping and studying sentient creatures? That's the most unethical – that's – isn't that illegal? If that's true, we have to stop him!" She tilted her head and stared at him with wide eyes. "Devin, how long have you known about this?"

He snatched the bottle from her trembling hand. "You remember that night a few weeks ago when I came over and said I didn't want to be alone?"

"Yeah. You ate the rest of my chocolate chip cookies." She narrowed her eyes and scowled. She hadn't entirely forgiven him for that yet.

"When I walked into work that morning, I saw this silvery-tailed mermaid inside the aquarium. A mermaid, Angel. Her hair was as silver as her scales. She had light brown skin and the greenest eyes, like emeralds, and they were intelligent. She was thrashing about, still tangled in the net he caught her with. That's how he catches them. In a wire net."

"A mermaid?" Angel looked at the bottle of alcohol. "What exactly are we drinking?"

"She saw me, and her face lit up. She pounded on the glass with her tiny fists. She thought I was gonna rescue her." Devin tipped the bottle back, taking a sizeable drink, then scrunched up his face and shuddered. "I could see in her eyes the exact second she realized I wasn't gonna help her." He fell silent and stared at the floor. "Her eyes, Angel. I don't sleep anymore. Her eyes keep me awake."

"What happened to her?"

"What the hell do you think happened to her?" he shouted. "It's not like he releases them back to the ocean where they could warn the others!"

After a pause, Angel said quietly, "I'd like another drink."

He handed it to her with a shaking hand, and she drank. Wincing, she put the bottle on the nightstand.

"So how does this work?" she asked, shuddering at the mouthful of alcohol.

"We're near some kind of underwater city. It's dark down there. These beings don't know the statues are a trap until they're ensnared. Then Creepa – Crofton – takes most of them to an offsite containment tank. A few end up in the lab aquarium, and believe me, they are the lucky ones. He does these experiments."

"What kind of experiments?"

"His dictation is sketchy, almost like he's speaking in code." Devin belched. Angel opened her mouth to say puke in the bathroom, damn it, but he resumed talking.

"I've figured out this much. He catalogs their physical characteristics. He's found a way to talk to them. One of his PhDs is in linguistics, did I ever tell you that? Anyway, he outlines what they talk about. Or rather, what he gets out of them when he tortures them into cooperating."

"How does he know when he's caught one? What keeps other ocean creatures from attacking the statues?" She paused. "Does he let them go when he's finished with them? Do they even survive?"

He groaned. "Angel, I don't know. He has notes from each one, but I told you, they don't make a lot of sense." His hand punctuated each word with a downward chopping motion. "And I don't know how he collects the data." He stood up and paced the tiny room. Grabbing the necklace around his neck, he twisted it between two fingers, back and forth, back and forth.

Neither of them spoke for a moment. "Look," he said, finally sitting back down next to Angel. "Don't try to impress him or make friends. Don't make small talk. Don't linger. Just do the job and get the hell out of there. The guy my predecessor replaced disappeared from this base, Angel. They covered it up. The rumor about his other assistants that LaDania told you about? Pretty sure that one's true, too."

"I'll be careful. Why haven't you told me any of this before?"

The terrified look he gave her answered the question. She reached for his hand and squeezed it. "Are you gonna be okay?"

"I don't know." He looked her in the eye before he got up and left. He forgot to take his vodka.

* * *

On her first day as Devin's temporary replacement, she walked into the complex to find Creepazoid standing next to his desk, frowning at the open book in his hands.

He wore a white lab coat over a black turtleneck and pants. A short, tight ponytail held his grayish-black hair away from his cleanly shaven face.

His skin was pale, like he'd never spent time in sunlight in his life.

Good god, Angel thought. *He even looks like a mad scientist.*

If he heard Angel come through the door, he made no effort to acknowledge her. She decided to at least introduce herself.

"Hi, Dr. Crofton," she said, proud to have kept her voice steady. "My name's Angel Tolliver."

"Yes, yes, yes," he grumbled, not bothering to look up. He waved a hand to brush her off.

She raised an eyebrow. Okay then.

She logged into Devin's computer and opened the list of instructions he'd left for her. At the top, bold capital letters demanded she CHECK THE SOAP DISPENSERS. Angel smiled.

Creepazoid left her alone at first as she worked through her list of instructions. She was diligently researching weather forecasts when he tossed a tiny cassette onto the desk. Angel jerked back in her chair when it landed with a clap.

"I fully expect you to be as efficient as Devin," snapped the scientist. Without another word, he stormed back over to his lab, punched the keycode in the reader with enough force to break his fingers, and disappeared behind the door.

"Nice to meet you too," Angel muttered. She glanced at the statues, and they stared back at her with plaster eyes. She shuddered.

With shaking hands, she opened the file Devin used to enter Creepazoid's transcription, picked up the earpiece he'd left by his phone, and got to work.

* * *

The first few days passed quickly. Working double duty took more out of her than she'd expected, both physically and mentally. She wondered how Devin was doing on his impromptu assignment, and hoped he returned soon.

When she let herself into the office on the fourth day, she noticed two things. First, a new statue stood with the group, replacing two others. Water dripped from it onto towels on the floor.

Maybe Creepazoid washed it for some reason, she told herself. Or, maybe, Devin's theory was correct. Maybe this one wasn't new at all. Maybe it had already served its purpose and been pulled from the ocean.

She whirled around to look at the aquarium, suddenly afraid of what she might see inside of it. An agitated eel, four feet long and metallic green, swam in circles around a lava rock. The purple creature that had checked her out the other day slept soundly on top of a pirate's skeleton on the deck of the ship. The stalks with eyes on the end were draped across the skeleton's ribs. Nothing else had changed.

With a deep breath, she went to find the cause of the other thing she noticed. After punching in the number code to the lab, she opened the door.

"Dr. Crofton? Is everything okay?"

As she walked through the lab, the smell that led her in there grew stronger. The normally locked door on the other side of the room, the one Devin said to avoid at all costs, stood slightly open. The stench of burning plastic permeated the air. Although she'd sworn to Devin she wouldn't go near the room, she decided to make an exception in this case.

"Dr. Crofton?" she called out, taking a few tentative steps forward. "Is everything okay? Do you need anything?"

He didn't answer.

Damn it all, she thought. Maybe she should call Dr. Meisner.

"Dr. Crofton? Are you here?"

No response.

Creeping closer, she peeked into the room. Smaller than the main lab, it featured a row of empty medical examination chairs. A deep blue glow emanated from an array of blank computer screens that faced the chairs. The opposite wall was lined with waist-high countertops. At the end of the room stood a podium.

"Holy crap," she whispered.

She gently pushed the door further open. Nothing in the room was burning. Creepazoid wasn't there. Time to leave before he returned.

Strong fingers gripped her shoulder from behind. Angel gasped as she whirled around to find herself face to face with Crofton.

"What are you doing in here?" he asked in a deathly calm voice.

Gracelessly, she stumbled backwards, farther into the room. She hadn't even heard his footsteps.

"Good morning, Doctor. I thought I smelled melting plastic, so I wanted to make sure everything was okay."

He stared down his nose at her. "You are not qualified to decide if everything is okay. Tell me, if you had found melting plastic, what would you have done?"

She had no idea. Crofton put both hands on her shoulders and squeezed. It felt like he was massaging them with rocks. "Did you go into the back room?" he asked quietly.

"What back room?" she asked, as adrenaline pumped through her. She hadn't seen another door, although the computer monitors emitted the only light in the room. Shadows falling on the wall could've easily hidden the entrance to another room.

He dug his thumbs into her collarbone.

"DID YOU GO INTO THE BACK ROOM?"

Angel didn't know a human voice could achieve such an incredibly high decibel level. Resisting the urge to stick her fingers in her ears, she said, "No, of course not! I told you, I wanted to be sure nothing was wrong."

Still not letting go, he said softly, "Do you know why I believe you?"

"Because I'm honest?"

His horrible smile, just inches from her face, sent chills up her spine. "I watched you on camera from the second you opened this door. Let me assure you, when it comes to what happens in here, I see everything."

Creepy bastard, she thought.

"Can you let go of my shoulders? You're hurting me," she said as casually as she could.

He let go of her. "Get out."

"I wouldn't have come in here at all if I'd known that foul odor was normal," she snapped, suddenly angry. She already felt bruises forming on her shoulders. "I would have no reason to."

"Make sure you never find one." Without another word, he brushed past her. He disappeared into the room and slammed the door behind him. Angel stared after him, wondering if she'd just made Creepazoid's hit list.

* * *

By the beginning of the second week, the horrific smell had faded away entirely. Creepazoid didn't mention their encounter again, so Angel hoped he'd forgotten about her seeing his super-secret villain cave. Or classroom. Whatever it was.

On day eight, she began her morning by topping off the soap dispensers. Crofton had left a new cassette with his cryptic research dictation on the desk. She'd developed a bit of familiarity with his nonsensical lingo, but some of his more bizarre phrases still baffled her. Spending the morning listening to his toneless, grating voice wasn't something she was looking forward to. The man could just as easily speak into the same dictation software used by the scientists on her team. Then all she'd have to do would be check it over and edit it.

He's sentimental, Devin had said.

Grating her teeth and wishing the man would get with the times, she got started.

An hour or so into the morning, a guy Angel had never seen before walked into the complex. Like she and Devin, he appeared to be in his thirties. He had the kind of face that wasn't exactly attractive but was still pleasing enough to look at. He carried a tool bag in one hand and a tablet in the other.

After five years of living and working at the Facility, Angel thought she knew everyone. This guy must've been specifically hired for Creepazoid. Devin hadn't mentioned to expect anyone but Environmental Services, which was strange considering his obvious paranoia.

"Where's Dev?" the man asked sharply.

Angel raised her eyebrows. She didn't know anyone else called him Dev.

"He's on a special assignment. I'm covering for him until he comes back. May I ask who you are?" He obviously had a keycard to access the complex, and he wore credentials in the form of an I.D. card around his neck. Still, if she let a stranger wander around, Creepazoid would lose his mind.

He chuckled. Angel wondered what he found funny.

"Name's Sampson. Don't worry, I'm just here to service the aquarium." He turned his attention to the statues and shook his head. "Hm. The doc sure doesn't have much artistic sense." He continued to study the statues long enough that Angel grew uncomfortable.

"I'm not a fan either," she said loudly. "I just ignore them, do the job, and keep my mouth shut."

"That's a good policy around here," Sampson said quietly. "I better get to work. Nice talkin' to you."

Angel watched him disappear into the electrical equipment room. She felt uneasy, like she'd just dodged a bullet.

"You're getting as paranoid as Devin," she muttered to herself.

By the beginning of week three, Angel woke up feeling happier than she had in weeks. She'd received a surprise email late last night from Crofton. After an unexpected delay, Devin would finally be returning in a couple days. She couldn't wait to see the look on her friend's face when she told him she'd seen inside Creepazoid's infamous locked room. Maybe she could bribe him for a bottle of sangria from his secret stash in exchange for the details, she thought wickedly.

When she reached the transport tube, she was surprised to see Dr. Meisner waiting for her at the capsule. The cellular biologist clearly wasn't happy to be there. Aside from saying the compulsory 'good morning,' neither of them spoke on the way to the complex.

After they went inside, Angel called out, "Good morning, Dr. Crofton!" like she'd done every morning since the day she started working for him. And, like every other morning, she felt relieved when he ignored her.

She sat at Devin's desk and started the computer as Dr. Meisner walked over to Creepazoid. Angel's attention strayed to a new statue with unusually creepy features. She hadn't seen one with fangs before.

"Do you have the data I asked for?" Crofton demanded without looking up from his desk.

So, Angel thought, Dr. Meisner doesn't get a 'hello' either. Against her better judgment, she watched them from the corner of her eye.

"Yes." She handed him a flash drive, which he practically tore from her fingers. She wiped her hands on her pants, like she was afraid some of his craziness might've rubbed off when he touched her. Angel could sympathize. "If that's all you need, I'm very busy—"

He whirled around in his leather chair that probably cost as much as Angel got paid in two months. "You're not leaving until I verify the data's on here."

She flinched. "I followed your instructions to the letter."

"I'll be the judge of that."

He plugged the flash drive into his computer as Angel tried to catch a glimpse of what came up on his screen. She could see it was a spreadsheet, but the words and numbers were too small to read. She looked back at her own screen before they caught her spying. She pretended to be absorbed in her work while listening to their increasingly heated exchange.

As Creepazoid clicked through the information, Angel marveled that someone could *aggressively* look through data. The more he mumbled, the twitchier Dr. Meisner became. Angel watched from the corner of her eye as Crofton turned to look up at the biologist.

"Where's the April data?" he asked in a flat voice.

"There's a separate tab for each month—"

"If April had a tab, I wouldn't be asking for the April data, would I?"

She stepped backward. Instead of putting space between them, it gave him room to get out of his chair and move closer to her.

"I compiled the raw data you gave me," she said quickly, backing away from him and past Angel. "I added in the observations from checkpoints three, seven, and eight. I noted all instances of interference, including seismic activity."

"None of that matters if an entire month of data is missing!"

His red, sweaty face made Angel wonder if he was having a heart attack. Crofton loomed over Dr. Meisner. She backed toward the statues, stepping farther into the complex. For a moment, Angel wondered absurdly if Creepazoid was a vampire. He looked ready, willing, and able to bite Dr. Meisner in the neck and suck out her blood.

She tried placating him. "I'll go back to my people and see if there's data that was omitted for some reason." She put up both hands, as if she expected to have to ward off a blow.

"Your people?" he raged. "No one should see this data except you! It's highly classified! Who saw it? I want names!"

Instantly realizing her mistake, she backed up more. "I can explain."

Creepazoid's blood pressure had to be somewhere between C4 detonation and volcanic eruption. Dr. Meisner stood just inches from the statues. If she took one more step backward, she'd run into the creepy new one. Angel couldn't believe Creepazoid wasn't stopping her.

"I will take down your entire department, and your staff will disappear," he threatened.

"For god's sake, Crofton! You're blowing this way out of proportion. No one could possibly understand the raw data. It's merely numbers and gibberish until it's decoded. And no one saw any of the real narrative. It's double password protected. And everyone here has signed a nondisclosure agreement."

"You will give me names." He advanced on her even more. "I will conduct interviews and decide for myself what they know. If I don't like their answers, I'll make sure every last one of you ends up at the bottom of the ocean. The project cannot be jeopardized."

As he finished his last threat, Dr. Meisner inevitably backed into the statue. Everything afterward happened in slow motion. Dr. Meisner twisted in the air, trying to keep herself upright.

Creepazoid's outstretched arms seemed to grow three feet as he reached for the falling statue, but he couldn't save it. It crashed to the ground, barely missing the one next to it, and shattered into thousands of pieces.

"Oh, god," Dr. Meisner said, as the blood drained from her face.

Creepazoid looked murderous.

"I'll, uh." She cleared her throat. "I'll clean it up. Where should I dispose of the pieces?"

Angel had never seen anyone so pale.

"That one was for the Arabian Sea Dragon." His voice rose with every word. "Do you realize what you've done!?"

"I of all people realize what I've done! What we've done!" She covered her mouth with her hands and stared at the mess.

"The Sea Dragon appears for a very specific time period every six months!" He crept closer to her. This time she didn't move away. "This lure had very specific properties! The teeth alone – I can't possibly have another set of teeth ready before the subject disappears again!"

While they argued, Angel slipped out of the complex. She'd return later, after taking care of her other responsibilities. Things were just a little too scary down there at the moment. Her only consolation was that the statue with the fangs wouldn't be staring at her anymore.

* * *

She finished up work in her regular department well after nine o'clock. Returning to Creepazoid's complex took every ounce of courage she had.

She wished she would've stayed that morning and finished the day's work, because Creepazoid would probably lose the remainder of his mind on her in the morning. Assuming he'd noticed she left, that is. If he gave her trouble, she decided she'd tell him she had to leave and check on an experiment for the Meteorology Department. Hopefully, he wouldn't look into her story.

Hopefully, she wouldn't find Dr. Meisner's body in the aquarium.

The complex was quiet and dark when she got there. Screensavers with mountains and sailboats lit

Creepazoid's computer monitors. Someone had cleaned up the broken statue and mopped the floor.

Angel started up her coworker's computer and went through the checklist to see what she needed to finish before Devin's return.

Angel clicked 'print' on a list of research projects so she could make some handwritten notes for Devin. An error message told her the printer was out of ink, so she went to the supply room for a new cartridge. Her hands shook badly. She felt like she was doing something illegal just by being in the complex alone.

Her jittery hands removed the cartridge from its package and dropped it on the floor. Swearing, Angel bent to pick it up, hoping it wasn't damaged.

Pull yourself together, she told herself.

As she stood, a glint of something shiny on the floor by the statues caught her eye. She put the ink cartridge down and tried not to look at the dozen or so renditions of sea creatures and not-quite-humans. Holding her breath, she walked over to check out the shiny object. The hair on the back of her neck stood on end as she imagined the statues' eyes following her.

She crouched near a statue that had neither male nor female anatomy. Gills ran from its cheeks to its ears. Next to the wall lay a length of Devin's gold necklace.

What the hell?

She picked it up and walked to the desk. Looking under the brighter light, she found crumbs of iridescent plaster embedded in some of the links.

He works down here. It could've snagged on something. He was probably busy and didn't notice he lost it, she told herself.

Except that she'd gone topside to see him off when he left, and he'd been wearing it. A uniformed officer had escorted him onto a transport boat. He'd been twisting it between his fingers until the officer frowned at him. He'd shot Angel a look and put his hand down, and she'd waved at him with a corner of her mouth curved in a smile.

So how had his necklace ended up here?

Glass shattered in the dark lab. She froze, listening.

After standing completely still for a full five minutes, she put the piece of necklace in her pocket. The entire complex remained silent.

A beaker full of volatile liquid probably exploded and sent glass flying everywhere, she rationalized. It was a weak explanation, but it was feasible. She certainly wasn't going to stick around and investigate. She picked up the ink cartridge again and installed it. She'd let the machine print her spreadsheet, then take it with her and finish the work in her quarters.

"Didn't anyone ever tell you curiosity killed the cat?" Dr. Crofton's soft, deadpan voice spoke from behind her. "You shouldn't be here this late."

"I was just finishing up some work from this morning," she said uneasily as she watched the printer. Her heart pounded like a bass drum at a parade. "What – ah – I'm not curious about anything."

"You shouldn't be here," he repeated.

"Where's Devin?" she blurted as she turned from the printer to face him.

After watching her for two or three seconds that lasted an eternity, he said, "I'd like to show you something. I believe you are – have – the solution to my problem. Come with me."

She froze. He was standing between her and the door, and she had nothing within reach to use as a weapon. "Look, I told you, I just came down here to finish up a few things since I had to, um, leave early this morning. For another project. I was just leaving. I'm really tired, and I'm just here to help out. I don't care what goes on here."

"You should."

Creepazoid grabbed her and wrapped her in a backwards bear hug. Screaming, she pulled on his arms while digging her nails into his hand, but instead of letting go, he tightened his hold on her. His arms were like an iron band around her chest. Squeezing her eyes shut, she slammed her head back and connected with his jaw. She cried out in pain, but so did he, and his grip on her loosened. Pushing free, she spun around and kicked between his legs. He blocked her kick before she made contact. He reached under her knee and flipped her on her back. He dropped down on top of her, and Angel saw a syringe in his hand. She tried to roll away, but he grabbed her shoulders and slammed her back to the ground. She felt the sharp stab of a needle pierce her neck, and a rush of warm liquid filled her veins. In a matter of seconds, she fell unconscious.

* * *

Angel dreamed of snow.

It was the perfect consistency: wet enough to stick to itself but dry enough not to turn to mush. She watched her eight-year-old brother and his friend as they built a snowman. Her brother shaped a crude football for the snowman to hold, while his friend traced the number '34' into the snowman's middle.

"Angel! Look! It's a running back!" her brother exclaimed.

"And when he melts, he'll be a runny back!" shouted the friend.

Angel laughed with them until the sun vanished. In the darkness, her little brother wailed. His friend had packed him into a ball of snow. His arms, legs and head were sticking out, but not by much.

"Help me Angel! Help!" her brother yelled.

"Don't worry," said the friend soothingly. "You get to be the quarterback."

Before Angel could react, marbles filled her mouth. Her eyes watered as she spit them out. More appeared to replace the ones she expelled. She scooped out dozens of the dime-sized glass spheres with her fingers, but she couldn't remove them faster than they materialized.

"Angel! Please help me! I'm sorry for taking your marbles! Don't leave me! I won't do it again!"

She couldn't move. Helplessly, she watched the friend pack more and more snow around her brother. Her jaw popped out of joint, and her front teeth broke off as the marbles pushed them away from her gums.

Her brother stopped screaming as his friend packed snow over his head.

"There!" exclaimed the friend. "See? You make a great quarterback! You'll be number '7.'" He drew the number on the snow entombing her brother's body. He turned to Angel. "You get to be the wide receiver!" he called out enthusiastically. When she didn't respond, his voice became demonic and threatening. "Quit playing with marbles. Come here."

Devin's face filled the dark sky. "WAKE UP RIGHT NOW!" his voice boomed.

Angel gasped as her eyes snapped open. Her swollen tongue pushed on her front teeth to make sure they were still there. She opened and closed her mouth, testing the function of her jaw. Her mouth was mercifully free of marbles, but her body was numb, and her thoughts were sluggish, fleeting. Whatever drugs Creepazoid had loaded into that needle were obviously still pumping through her system. The choking smell of burning plastic filled the air.

She fell back into a restless sleep.

* * *

The first thing she noticed when she woke for the second time was a dull humming noise. She blinked rapidly, trying to focus on her surroundings. The cold glare of fluorescent lighting filled the room. A statue, shaped somewhat like a person but with four eyes and four arms, leaned against the wall across from her. Next to it stood a cart with plaster residue on the bottom. A wooden worktable, covered with all kinds of clutter, took up almost half the room. To her right, a small row of white, metal cupboards lined the wall. A door to her left was the only way in or out of the room. Maybe she was in the secret room Crofton thought she'd seen during her first week.

Her groggy brain didn't immediately register the full horror of her situation. Trying to put thoughts together was like eating soup with a fork.

Without windows, she couldn't guess what time it was or how long she'd been unconscious. Her stomach growled and her throat was dry, so she must've been here quite a while. If she'd missed her shift, her coworkers might be looking for her. Maybe LaDania would suspect she was in trouble.

On the other hand, the crazy doctor could've formally requested her services for a couple days. If that were the case, her team would be angry, but not worried.

She couldn't wait around and hope someone came to rescue her. She needed to get to the infirmary. They could analyze her blood and figure out what she'd been injected with. The lab tech would report the results to the department head, and there'd be an investigation. The doctors could give her something to counteract the effects of whatever chemicals Crofton had poisoned her with.

Her legs wouldn't move. With a jolt, she realized she was standing upright. Looking down, she paid little attention to her unexpected nakedness. Angel saw iridescent plaster encasing her body from the floor to just above her waist. Her feet were melded to a circular base. Her arms hung at her side, but when she tried to move them, they were stuck. The plaster had already coated her wrists and solidified around each finger. Whimpering, she saw an extra three or four inches had been added to the end of each of her fingers. The plaster had formed a sharp, curved claw at the end of each one.

Is this what happened to his missing assistants? He used them to make statues?

Something else occurred to her. If he was making people into statues, had he done the same to Devin? Was Devin dead?

She fought back tears and forced herself to concentrate. There had to be a way to escape, and she needed to find it quickly.

"ANGEL. ROCK BACK AND FORTH. ROCK! ROCK! ROCK!" Devin's voice screamed at her the way it had in the dream. "BREAK FREE! ROCK!"

Shimmering plaster slithered up her forearm and encased her elbows. She tried in vain to shrink away from the horror climbing her body. It felt as if it were growing. As if it were alive.

There was one inevitable outcome to this situation if she didn't free herself: she would suffocate when the plaster inevitably enveloped her face.

Here goes nothing.

Rocking her upper body, she built up enough momentum to lift the base an inch or two off the ground. A couple more efforts and she'd be able to tip over. When she landed on the ground, the plaster would shatter. She'd be free. Getting a few bruises was certainly better than becoming part of the statue collection.

Part of the statue collection.

When Dr. Meisner knocked over the statue in the office, it had shattered.

With sudden clarity, she realized if she hit the ground, she'd break apart into thousands of pieces. In her mind, Devin laughed at her. Her brother and his friend joined in.

"Stop it!" she cried.

A door hissed open.

"Now, now, you can't be doing that," Creepazoid exclaimed, striding quickly to reach her. He grabbed her waist to steady her.

As soon as she was stationary, Angel spit in his face. He froze, staring at her with eyes that barely looked human. A dark bruise covered his chin where she'd head-butted him.

"You know," he said finally, wiping the saliva away with the back of his hand, "I can make this much, much more painful than it has to be."

With a wavering voice, she shouted, "Screw yourself, murderer!"

He grabbed her chin, digging his fingers into her jaw. "I could seal your mouth shut right now."

She stared, too frightened to speak.

"We've already been delayed, thanks to Meisner shattering your friend Devin," he growled. "I don't have time to construct another replica of the Sea Dragon's distinctive teeth. The pheromones may not be enough to get its attention, and if we fail to capture it, Meisner will wish she'd never been born." He let go of Angel's face and reached toward the table. "Time to move this along."

Hearing her friend's fate spoken out loud made it real to her, and it hit her like a punch in the gut. Angel whispered, "Dev… Oh god."

Creepazoid responded with a quiet hum. He held out a syringe with a six-inch needle. "The third phase will be unpleasant for you, I'm afraid. Quite frankly, it's still experimental, but it should accelerate the process."

"Third phase of what? What process?" Angel couldn't keep her voice from cracking. The plaster crept up to her armpits. “What process? Why are you doing this? I don’t want to die!”

“I hope you don’t whine like this the entire time. It’s quite irritating to listen to,” he said dismissively as he pushed another needle into her neck.

A chill shot through every inch of her body. She felt like bugs had been released inside her and were wiggling around in her organs. She tried to squirm and tighten her stomach, but even that potential bit of relief was denied.

“You won’t get away with this!” she yelled. “You can’t just do this to people!” The plaster inched its way up to her collarbone. It compressed her body, squeezing her lungs until she could barely breathe.

He laughed. “I’ve been ‘getting away with it’ for years. Why do you think the Facility’s board of directors hires people with no family, no connections, no ties to the rest of the world? The lives of a few random, ordinary people that no one will miss are a small price to pay for my discoveries. My research will change the world.”

“You mean… they know what you’re doing?” she said with effort.

He ignored her. “I’ve captured seventeen previously undiscovered creatures over the last six years. Entirely unknown species! The knowledge they’ve… offered to me has been incredible! Did you know there’s an entire city built from coral and populated by humanoids that breathe through gills?

The knowledge I'm gaining from the ocean's inhabitants is worth sacrificing a few common lives like yours."

"You crazy, sociopathic bastard," she whispered.

"I'd love to show you how I study them. I'm quite proud of my innovations. But alas—" He made a sweeping gesture toward her. "Trying to move you right now could prove damaging to the process, especially since your tail is still forming."

"Tail? *Tail*?" She could no longer blink back the tears. One slid down her face, and Crofton wiped it away with his finger. His neatly manicured but too long nail dug into her cheek.

"Oh yes. The Sea Dragon wouldn't look twice at you if you didn't have a tail."

He squinted at the syringe, as if making sure he'd used every last drop.

"Do you kill them, too?" She could barely manage to get the words out as the plaster crawled over her shoulders.

"Of course not! They're much too valuable. "I'm curious. Why do you think you're going to die?" He returned the empty syringe to the table and picked up a beaker full of a substance that looked like purple-tinted water.

Angel forgot to breathe. She'd never considered that she might live through this.

Misinterpreting her reaction, he said, "Your lungs won't be able to expand at all once the plaster solidifies. Right now, the formula is mixing into your cells, converting your body so it becomes compatible with its own unique physiology. It'll take care of your oxygen needs, both in and out of the water."

"How is any of this possible?" she croaked.

"Through a combination of simplicity and genius." He wrung his hands excitedly. "The plaster was originally developed as a shell to hold our observers in the correct position. We could then mold the statues into replicas of the creatures we wanted to study."

"Not statues! People!" The rest of the air left her lungs. She tried desperately to inhale, her mouth opening and closing like a fish pulled from the water.

He waved his hand and continued. "The serum I created to keep my observers alive inside the statues mutated their DNA. I injected you with the serum in the office; it's Phase One.

"Phase Two introduces the plaster to the serum-altered DNA. You received that while you were unconscious. Our original process stopped there.

"We quickly realized the plaster was mixing with the serum in a completely unexpected way. We hadn't just created a shell with a data collector inside, as was our intent. We'd created a shell with a fully conscious and self-aware data collector inside. That's when I began conceptualizing Phase Three. Now, not only are we able to collect sensory data, we can also collect and interpret thoughts, reactions, personal observations and responses. By reading and interpreting your brain activity, we can tell if you're afraid. We can tell if you see something that pleases you. We can collect data with a thoroughness, accuracy, and diversity previously unheard of.

"In a sense, I've created a new form of life."

She no longer felt the need to breathe. The tickling sensation of bugs crawling around inside her faded away. "No, you deranged prick! You've 'created' an abomination!"

"We'll collect data on the Sea Dragon from you," he continued. "Then we'll capture the beast and put it with the others. While it acclimates to its new home, we'll study how it interacts with its peers."

Creepazoid brought the beaker up to her lips. "Time to drink the pheromones. I've mixed an extra potent batch since we no longer have the specialized teeth. I believe the Dragon has an exceptional sense of smell, so its reaction to you should be most exciting to observe."

He put a hand on her chin and poured the liquid into her mouth. She let it fill her cheeks, then spit the pheromone solution back in his face.

"Idiot!" he yelled, frantically wiping it away from his eyes. "You foolish, ignorant idiot!" He stomped over to the metal cupboards and tore open their squeaky doors. After tossing around objects she couldn't see, he grabbed some jars and bottles and moved them to the worktable. Angel supposed he was mixing up another solution.

A moment later, Crofton marched back over to her and pushed a tongue depressor between her tightly pursed lips. She thrashed her head back and forth until he slapped her, hard. She winced, involuntarily opening her mouth as she instinctively tried to breathe. He took a plastic funnel from a pocket in his lab coat, jammed it down her throat, and poured the liquid straight down into it. She gagged and gurgled, but she couldn't stop it.

The plaster reached the base of her neck and continued to climb. She wondered how much time she had left before she lost her mind.

Still fuming over her refusal to cooperate, Crofton yanked the funnel out of her mouth. After once again storming across the room, he tossed the funnel and beaker onto a counter. The beaker landed on its side and rolled off onto the floor, where it shattered. He didn't appear to notice.

From the cupboard he produced a stainless-steel cube. It was about eight inches across on each side, and he grunted as he lifted it. Metal flip switches covered one side, and a bundle of wires with sharp, copper tips hung off the top. Each wire was a different color.

"Consider yourself lucky. I'm using the self-guided electrodes. I seriously considered using the old manual ones, but you're too weak to survive the pain." His scaly fingers parted her hair. She gagged at the revolting feeling, which was somehow worse than when he touched her lips. She remembered how Dr. Meisner had recoiled from his touch.

"Nice," he snorted.

Draping a yellow wire in front of her face, he poked one of the copper spikes into her scalp and held it in place. She bit her tongue so hard it bled.

"OW! What is that for?" The abhorrent violation of her body was tearing at the threads of her sanity. And now, Creepazoid was sticking things in her head.

With his thumb, Crofton flipped a switch on the cube. He let go of the tiny spike on her head as it whirled into motion. The shrill whine of bone turning to dust as the metal penetrated her skull sounded like nails scratching a chalkboard.

Drawing in breath was no longer necessary, nor possible. Her voice was strong anyway. "YOU CAN'T PUT HOLES IN MY SKULL!" she screamed. Crofton grimaced, obviously uncomfortable, so she caterwauled in the shrillest voice she could. She felt something tear in the back of her throat.

"I have a great many of these to install, my dear, and very little time to do it. Shut your mouth, or I'll shut it for you.

"Now, as these tiny sensors form connections with your cerebrum, you're likely to feel ghost pains throughout your body. Try to cope," he added snidely. "The longer you hold out before you go cuckoo, the better our chances of getting accurate data."

The plaster crawled up her chin. She squeezed her lips together, trying to estimate how long she had until her face was completely engulfed. She'd never felt claustrophobia in her life, not until now. Using her only possible defense, she screamed, high-pitched and deafening. Her voice gave out at the end, and the searing pain in her throat spread to her ears.

Crofton jumped backward at the sudden noise. The wire he'd inserted ripped out, and blood flowed freely from her scalp.

"My patience with you has run out," he said softly. "However, your mouth will close permanently in a few seconds, so I won't take the time to sew it shut."

As if in response to his words, the plaster slid over her pursed lips. She could no longer speak.

This can't be happening. This can't be happening. This can't be happening.

Crofton continued inserting the tiny spikes that drilled their way through her skull and into her brain. He flipped switches on the cube after each wire reached its destination. A sensation like water trickling through her brain distracted her from feeling the plaster coat her nostrils.

The door to the lab opened, and Angel's heart skipped a beat. Someone would finally see what was happening and help her. Maybe it was LaDania; she was a badass.

Creepazoid glanced over his shoulder. A man in a gray jumpsuit entered, wheeling in another cart. It was the man who'd serviced the aquarium in the lab.

"Ah, Sampson. Great timing."

Sampson nodded to him but didn't reply. He looked at Angel then quickly looked away.

He's in on it. God, he's in on it.

Crofton studied Angel. "Your body should be fully oxygenating through the plaster by now. If you're feeling faint, don't worry. It'll go away soon. Or maybe it won't. I don't really know, or care." He laughed suddenly while Sampson fidgeted and studied his boots.

"Right now, the machine is calibrating the sensors," Crofton said as he suddenly became serious. "In a moment, the plaster will cover your scalp and the tops of the electrode points. Then I can disconnect the wires.

"Once you're settled in the ocean, your senses will process information that cameras can't. When the Arabian Sea Dragon finds you, you'll detect the nuances of its facial expressions, the smell it emits, the exact sensation of its scales against your plaster skin… With any luck, it'll attempt a mating ritual with you before it realizes you're not a viable mate."

His voice became muffled as the plaster filled her ears, stopping just short of the eardrum. Angel felt like she was buried in cement. Worse, the process was getting faster. The plaster crawled over the bridge of her nose before reaching her eyelids. She tried closing her eyes, but she couldn't blink.

He disconnected the wires and announced, "I do believe we're ready. Bring the cart."

To Angel's surprise, she experienced only a second of darkness as Crofton's magic plaster integrated with her vision. She could see clearly without contact lenses for the first time in almost thirty years. And it wasn't just her eyes: she could hear the swish of Crofton's lab coat as he moved, the tiny squeak of the cart's wheels, and the slight waver of Sampson's breath as he answered, "Yes Doctor." The plaster that was somehow now a part of her was enhancing her senses.

Sampson's shoulders were scrunched together, and his face was locked in a grimace.

"You should prepare yourself for the likelihood that different species of marine life will explore you. Sometimes, they chew off fingers or, occasionally, entire limbs. But don't worry. My research doesn't require you to have limbs, and you won't bleed, because you no longer have blood." He spoke without emotion, like he was talking about using substandard parts to repair a car. "It is most unfortunate that I can't replicate the teeth," he muttered.

He looked at her from all sides. "You're going to pass out again, I think."

With numbing finality, the plaster covered the rest of her scalp with a wet, squishy "plip".

She tried to imagine how it would feel if something chewed off her leg.

With a voice that sounded hundreds of miles away, Crofton said, “You should feel honored by your contribution to human knowledge and understanding.”

Angel wanted to tell him where he could stick his ‘human knowledge and understanding.’ She felt a deep sense of hopelessness, indescribable horror, and loneliness. Then sweet, blissful unconsciousness swept over her, and she stopped feeling anything.

* * *

Frigid waters crushed her from every direction. A beacon directly above her flashed maddening pulses of light on the surface of the water. Its source had to be a boat, likely carrying Crofton and other scientists. It was far, far above her.

Angel realized she could see in the dark. Rocks, coral, fish, plants, and debris surrounded her. More importantly, a shadow was moving toward her, presumably Crofton’s Sea Dragon.

The squishy ground was swallowing her feet, but she couldn’t move. Trapped in her plaster prison, she could do nothing but sink.

With each flash, the creature appeared closer, and closer, and closer. It had the form of a person, except for the addition of a thick, flat tail dragging through the water behind it. Its arms ended in claws, not hands. The front of its face had the same horrible teeth as the statue Dr. Meisner knocked over.

Not a statue. Devin.

In her mind she heard a metallic, grating voice.

"We know what you are," the Arabian Sea Dragon said. "We know you've been hunting us."

It landed in front of her. It thrashed its tail onto the ground, sending sand through the water. She remembered she had a tail now, too, although she hadn't seen it.

"We've survived for millennia. Do you really think you can capture us without repercussions?"

It lunged, slamming into her with the force of a battering ram. She was knocked backward through the water. She drifted until gravity pulled her flat against the ocean floor.

A blood-red crab eagerly crawled over to her. Its giant claw began digging into her plaster stomach like an excavator breaking ground.

"We have plans for you. For all of you," the Sea Dragon continued. "But first, I'm going to hurt you. I'm going to send a message to your species. We are patient beings, but we will not tolerate your abuse any longer."

It swam over her, investigating. Its face came close to her neck, like it was going to nuzzle her. Then it swished its tail, sending tiny bubbles through the water, and swam back and forth above her.

"We know you're not alive, and therefore cannot die. But we also know you are sentient, and more importantly, that you can feel pain while in your human skin."

The crab continued digging, and she could do nothing. Bits of plaster floated up through the water as its claws chipped away at her. The Sea Dragon swam down and bit off her left thumb. It felt like a fake nail breaking away from a fingertip.

Three shapes descended toward them. She wondered if others were coming to dine on her. Creepazoid hadn't mentioned the Sea Dragon having friends. Maybe they'd devour her entirely and save her from this nightmare.

The three new creatures surrounded the raging Sea Dragon, who was so intently chewing her index finger it didn't notice them. Each of them held a dart gun and fired several rounds into the Sea Dragon.

Crofton's people, then, she realized, not more Sea Dragons. They'd caught it unaware, and its body went limp from the drugs in the darts. They wrapped it in a net and dragged it to the surface. A fourth shape knocked the crab away from Angel's stomach and lifted her off the ocean floor.

Now that they'd captured the Sea Dragon, they'd move her to a new location, she supposed. Hopefully, the next creature wouldn't have a taste for thumbs.

* * *

"Angel?" asked a female voice.

How did the creature know her name?

"Angel. Wake up."

She opened her eyes to see the blurry, worried faces of Dr. Meisner and two strangers.

Angel lifted her head and looked around. She was in one of the medical examination chairs in Crofton's lab room. Her body was free of the plaster. She wiggled her fingers. "How?" She cleared her throat. "How am I able to move? How did you get that stuff out of me?"

Dr. Meisner snorted. "No one creates a serum like that without an antidote. Not even a psychotic, sociopathic monster like Crofton." She held up some empty syringes, but Angel couldn't focus well enough to see how many. "How do you feel?"

"Awful. How'd you find me? Why'd Creepazoid let you give me an antidote?" Her tongue felt thick. She pushed it against her teeth to make sure they were still there. Her hand burned where her thumb had been severed and her finger gnawed upon. She ran her intact hand across her stomach and felt a row of wiry stitches.

Dr. Meisner laughed. "Creepazoid. I like it. Personally, I've always called him Dr. Creepifer."

"But—?"

"Creepazoid has been… reassigned."

Angel sat up.

"Easy!" Dr. Meisner said, steadying her with a hand at her back. As Angel got her bearings, she added, "We couldn't save your thumb. I'm sorry."

Angel reached for the top of her head and ran her fingers in her hair. She winced when she touched a tiny bump at the top of her head.

"The electrodes have been removed. There may be some brain damage that affects your sensations of pain and pleasure. We're not sure. We couldn't run tests of that nature while you were unconscious, and we're certainly not the experts here."

"My vision is really blurry. My eyes hurt."

"That's not entirely unexpected," one of the strangers said.

"How long will it last?" Angel rubbed her eyes, trying to clear them.

"We don't know. This is uncharted territory for us. We've only recently learned exactly how far Crofton has taken things and how he's misused my research.

"I'm going to put some medicated drops in your eyes. Hopefully, your vision will improve," Dr. Meisner said. "Here. This will sting."

Hopefully?

Angel had so many questions, but she couldn't find words. Her brain still felt like mashed potatoes. "What happens now?"

"My colleagues and I have wiped Crofton's computers and destroyed his equipment. We've saved the research data, of course, so we can continue where he, ah, left off. But we can do it ethically."

Angel focused her stinging eyes on the woman's face and was able to distinguish bright pink lips and brown hair. Her facial features were still a bit unclear, but Angel's vision was slowly improving.

With a sudden gasp of breath, Angel remembered what Devin had told her the night before he left. "Creepazoid was kidnapping sea creatures! He's got them in some kind of tank. I don't know where it is. You've got to find it and free them!"

Dr. Meisner sighed. "The majority are being stored at a separate location," she admitted reluctantly. "They will be released, if possible, when our research is concluded."

Angel couldn't hold her tears back anymore. "*What?* Are all of you insane?" She tried standing but her legs wobbled, and she fell back to the bed. "I thought scientists were supposed to value life! All life!"

"We do. This work is important, perhaps even vital, to the survival of the human race."

Angel ran a hand over her hair. The sensors truly were gone. The pain and itching were gone.

She wondered if she had brain damage.

"The people in the lab. The statues. Have you saved them? Have you given them the antidote?" Angel looked from person to person. Every still slightly blurry face was devoid of emotion. Angel's voice cracked as she asked, "The others in the ocean?"

Dr. Meisner looked at her colleagues. They shrugged.

With a sigh, she said, "No. Only one dose physically existed, and we gave it to you. Decrypting Crofton's notes about the antidote will take some time. And Angel, even if we managed to restore them after all this time, they'd almost certainly be insane, and their bodies would be irreparably damaged."

"Restore?" Angel exclaimed. "They're not paintings, for God's sake! They're people!"

"We know, Angel. Putting an end to his work was complicated. We stopped him as soon as we could. And your friend… I'm sorry. I'm so sorry."

Angel looked away. "Devin deserves more than 'I'm sorry.'"

Dr. Meisner's free hand reached for Angel's. She didn't pull away. "Let me help you up. Are the drops helping your eyes?"

"They hurt, but I can see a little better."

"Good. I want to show you something."

Dr. Meisner and one of her colleagues helped Angel stand and get her bearings. After a few minutes she was able to walk on her own. Dr. Meisner led her through Crofton's almost empty lab to the office area.

The statues were gone. A set of upholstered chairs and a coffee table occupied the space where they'd stood. The tiled floor was pristine. A painting of a horse running in a field hung on the wall behind them. There was no evidence of the statues ever being there.

Meisner directed her attention to the aquarium. "We've created a one-way opening to the aquarium from the sea. Our subjects will be allowed to stay in there when we're not studying them," she explained. "It's still captivity, but it's less restrictive."

They walked by Devin's desk, and Angel froze when Dr. Meisner pointed at the aquarium. A new statue stood near the castle. The purple disc creature engulfed its head and was chewing on the statue's ear.

"The true genius of what Crofton calls Phase Three is not the increased amount of data it makes available, but the increased life span of the subject. If we understand his lab records correctly, instead of lasting a few weeks, a statue can now stay submerged for years. Decades, maybe. In fact, his stasis research is being studied by upper levels of the government for its potential use in space travel.

"With proper monitoring and upkeep, that statue should be able to stay in the aquarium for say, twenty or thirty years before it begins to deteriorate. We'll only need it for maybe eighteen months, but it looks nice there, don't you think?"

Angel didn't care how it looked. She remembered the Sea Dragon's threat, but she didn't care about that either. All of these people deserved whatever revenge the sea creatures carried out.

The gravity of Dr. Meisner's words hit her with sudden clarity. "Oh my god," Angel whispered. "Is that—"

Dr. Meisner glanced at her, smiling mischievously, and said nothing.

"Twenty or thirty years," Angel repeated. "That… statue will stay in there that long? And not, ah, die?"

"Unless something eats it, but we won't allow that to happen." She glanced at the purple creature. "We won't let any important parts get eaten, anyway."

"The statue is aware of what's happening to it?"

"Oh yes. He – it – is well aware that we must have a living being inside to collect the information we need. The good Dr. Crofton himself frequently reminded us of that. He so desperately wanted to experience sensory interaction with his mythological friends." She shrugged. "We decided it would be fitting to grant his wish."

Made in United States
North Haven, CT
27 December 2022